THE ORANGE MOON AFFAIR

by

AFN CLARKE

A THOMAS GUNN BOOK

CLARKe-BOOKS

First eBook edition published by Clarke-Books LLC in 2013
This print edition published by Clarke-Books LLC in 2014

Book cover design by AFN Clarke.
Cover background image © Steve Lovegrove | Dreamstime.com

ISBN: 978-1-938611-19-3

CLARK*e* - BOOKS
www.afnclarke.com

In Memory of my Brother-in-Arms
Terry Forrestal

ONE

Mojave Desert – October 2012

Flying a helicopter requires a clear mind, concentration, balance and a delicate touch.

Flying a helicopter you are unfamiliar with, in the dark, with two nasty bullet wounds in a body that has not slept in thirty hours, is an exercise in surreal survival. I had ten hours flight time in this model MD 902 Explorer, so it wasn't total guesswork.

I made sure Julie was strapped in tightly and flipped on the switches. There wouldn't be enough time to sit and let the engines warm up completely. We needed to get airborne before the local police showed up. In the distance beyond the factory building, where the car exploded in the arroyo, a pall of smoke billowed into the moon lit night sky.

Once I got the machine off the ground, stabilised and then flying on the heading Danny had given me, I asked Julie to call him and write down the co-ordinates of the destination, then talked her through entering the figures into the GPS navigation system while I concentrated on the instruments. All I had to do was make sure I didn't hit anything flying at an altitude of fifty feet across the desert, following the route on the EFIS from Mojave to Desert Rock airstrip, wherever the hell that was in the vast expanse of the Nevada desert.

As we flew, the rising sun glimmered just below the horizon to our left. Dark sky turning light blue just before the sun appeared as an orange-white ball throwing shadows across the desert. The distant terrain rose in craggy cracked mountains, rising ever higher to nearly five thousand feet, and I had to fly the aircraft through the narrow gorges maintaining the pretence of a special operations training flight at ultra-low level.

"Can you see if there are any sunglasses in the side pocket," I asked Julie, feeling my left arm begin to stiffen.

"Here you go." Her voice sounded strangely distorted in my headphones. Or perhaps it was just my mind beginning to shut down as my body leaked valuable blood onto the seat from the wound in my side.

"Thanks." I tightened the lock on the collective and flexed my left arm, ignoring the pain, just trying to get some feeling back into it. Estimated flight time was just under an hour and a half, and I wasn't confident of being able to last that long.

"I'm sorry I got you into this," I said stupidly, as if what I said would make any difference.

"I could have said no."

"But you didn't."

"Nope. Don't ask me why, but I didn't."

"Did you get the bug into the computer before they ambushed us?"

"I did."

"Well at least one of us accomplished something today. How's your head?"

"Hurts like hell. How's your...?" she paused looking across at me. "Everything?" She laughed. A desperate sound hurled against a bleak outlook.

We hurt more than either of us could describe.

We didn't know what the future held for us, but we laughed anyway as the sun rose across the desert, and I banked the helicopter into the first of the rising mountain ravines.

After an hour throwing the helicopter through the narrow canyons and rocky gorges, I could feel my strength and concentration ebbing slowly away. But that seemed inconsequential in the surreal experience that was the excuse for reality.

Julie massaged her temples, and when she spoke her speech was slow and slurred. I knew she was concussed and slipping into shock.

By 'red-lining' the helicopters engines I could force more speed, but as the sun came up the temperature would rise and everything could go very wrong very quickly.

But there was no choice.

I inched up the collective, dropped the nose and advanced the throttle a touch, watching the gauges creep toward the danger zone.

Waves of nausea blurred my vision, so I used the only tool I had to sharpen my mind.

Pain.

By wriggling in the seat I could press against the wound in my lower abdomen, not too much, but enough pain to sting my sagging consciousness into wakeful concentration. Now was not the time to sink into peaceful, blissful oblivion. I had a precious cargo to deliver, a woman I loved more than my own life.

At any other time, flying low level through the desert canyons as the sun rose above the horizon would have been an extraordinary experience. One of those vivid adventures that stays in the memory forever. But I wanted this experience to be over as soon as possible.

Every part of my body and soul willed the airstrip into view.

Flying is a slow inevitability.

You know you're going to get there, and yet the more desperate you are to arrive, the more time seems to drag.

Another rising ridge after fifteen minutes of undulating desert, and the sweat dripped down my face, arms and back, seeping into the wounds and causing more pain as my body salts stung raw flesh. I glanced quickly at Julie who sagged forward against the seat harness, semi-conscious, head flopping as the helicopter rose, fell, and banked through the ravines. I just wanted to take her in my arms, hold her and tell her everything was going to be fine, but now was not the time to drift into sentimentality, there was still the task of getting this machine on the ground.

The gauges swam in front of my eyes as I struggled to pick out the speed dial. That and the vertical speed indicator were my guides as we crested the ridge and Desert Rock airstrip lay in front of us just beyond a dry lake bed.

Was it a lakebed or a mirage?

I dropped the collective and pulled back slowly on the cyclic, slowing the aircraft down, establishing an approach to the runway. The speed bled off and I nosed down a little to keep the aircraft's forward speed at forty knots, but my eyes refused to focus properly, and darkness appeared at the corners of my vision as if I was looking through a telescope at an image that kept getting smaller. No matter what my mind was telling my body it wasn't responding, running out of blood and slowly shutting down.

But not before I got this machine on the ground.

Only a few more feet.

Maybe twenty-five, maybe thirty-five, maybe....

I didn't know anymore.

Then I saw the FIM-92 Stinger ground-to-air missile spearing up toward us from a far ridge.

My reactions were slow and for a fatal moment I watched the white smoky trail from the rocket motor arc its way through the sky. I pulled on the collective and kicked the anti-torque pedals to port, almost escaping the oncoming death, but the rocket slammed into the tail boom.

The earth spun in a lazy arc as the helicopter arched over backwards at fifty feet above the rocky desert as I lost control, spiralling to the ground, pieces flying in all directions, the only section remaining relatively intact being the forward cockpit, saved because the main rotor head deflected the impact.

There was no pain, just a smashing, grinding, splintering sound. I felt a violent lurch as my head slammed into the side door, then silence. Almost lying on top of me, held by her seat harness, Julie stared into my eyes, blood dripping from her nose and ears, trying to speak.

"Julie," I gasped trying to reach up and touch her face, but my arm wouldn't move.

Car engine noises. Voices.

I was struggling with consciousness. With reality.

Where was I? What had happened? I didn't know.

Images from the past flashed through my mind.

My father's dead face.

Julie naked on the catamaran.

Julie. My Julie.

Then nothing.

TWO

Belfast – Six Weeks Earlier

It was an odd experience to look down on the dead face of the man who had once been my father. Not that I was unfamiliar with seeing dead bodies, I'd seen too many in my previous job, it's just that I never expected I would be staring at *him*.

A single shot to the forehead had killed him instantly. The hole small and dark, not marring the rugged good looks of the man, but I knew that the back of his head would be non-existent. A round fired at close range from a powerful modern 9mm semi-automatic doesn't leave much behind. I felt neither revulsion nor sorrow, somehow those emotions didn't seem to fit with the sterile scrubbed surroundings, and perhaps he would have smiled and approved of my stoicism, or maybe just shaken his head and wondered what had happened to me over the years we hadn't spoken. I knew the lack of emotion I felt meant I had not lost my edge, that I was still a soldier with all the instincts that had been honed in combat. But this wasn't combat. This was murder.

"If you would please sign for these, sir." The white-coated official stood with my father's belongings in an incongruously cheap plastic bag. I duly signed.

The formalities over, it wasn't long before I was loading the body bag into my Cessna Citation Mustang 510 jet at Aldergrove Airport. An undertaker had been instructed to meet me at Norwich airport with an appropriate coffin, and until we landed it was just me and the black rubberised bag lying on the cabin floor. Yet another reminder of my past, and images of dead soldiers insinuated themselves into my thoughts.

As the jet burst through the top of the clouds into bright sunlight, climbing to a cruising altitude of 31,000ft, my mind drifted back to what I thought was an ideal life in paradise.

Lying in the cabin on my catamaran, a lone fifty-seven foot Fountaine Pajot anchored in the crystal clear blue waters off the north western tip of the Mediterranean island of Gozo, waking from a disturbed sleep with one of those unsettling disconnected thoughts that the shit was going to hit the fan in a big way, was not the best way to start the day.

You know the feeling, that odd clawing at the pit of your stomach. A slight headache even though you'd stayed off the booze the night before. I hadn't slept well, but that was nothing new, and it wasn't the reason I felt like crap. What disturbed me was that the odd, undefined, premonition had no logical reason to be in my head.

Cold water and the sight of Julie standing naked on the aft deck washed away the uncomfortable feeling that crowded across my mind. She showered with fresh water from the transom faucet, head back eyes closed, then stood letting the sun dry her bronzed skin as the water ran in rivulets between her perfect breasts.

"I can feel you staring, Thomas," she laughed and squeezed the water from her long blonde hair, her light New England accent drifting gently on the slight breeze.

"Can't think of a better way to wake up," I said, as the last images of the bloodied bodies of my colleagues faded from my on-going nightmare. Eighteen months and it still seemed like yesterday. "Coffee?"

"Juice please. Pineapple and orange."

I took the jug of freshly prepared juice from the fridge, and popped an ice cube into a tall glass as the coffee percolator started bubbling on the stove.

"You had another nightmare last night. Scared the hell out of me," her voice drifted through from the cockpit. "Thrashing about and shouting."

"Really? I don't remember." I did but there was no sense in talking about it. I carried a mug of coffee and the juice into the cockpit.

"Thanks." She took the glass and drank a third quickly, and tossed her head back savouring the morning. "I'd like to go to the festival in the village tonight. Maybe we can eat at Lorenzo's."

"Sounds good."

"And before that I thought we might take the horses out for a trot, have lunch at Godwin's cafe..." she paused and reached her hand to my face, smiling wickedly, "...and then make love in our favourite grotto."

"Got it all worked out, don't you?"

"Of course."

I slid from her grasp before she started something I couldn't stop, and fled to the safety of the galley to prepare breakfast.

"Coward," she shouted happily, wrapped a powder blue sarong around her slim tanned body, stretched out on the starboard cockpit settee, and sipped her juice.

"Want some melon with prosciutto?" I said, preparing two plates in anticipation. I leaned over and turned on the stereo, already tuned into the BBC World Service. It was my morning fix, that and the coffee.

"Yes please."

"….and now at the top of the hour, the news headlines from the BBC World Service read by Jonathan Davis." The familiar music played for a moment or two before the newscaster began talking, and for a few minutes I forgot about my self-imposed, albeit luxurious, exile.

"On his recent trip to the United States, the leader of the new British National Independent Party, Nicholas Hansard, said in an interview with The Wall Street Journal, that the Governments of both countries 'have skewered National Defence' with their failure to increase military spending, and left the door open for increased terrorist activity…."

'Yet another extremist group leaping to the forefront. Left wing, right wing, they're all the same,' I thought cynically wondering why I listened to the news at all, but the BBC World Service was a comforting connection with home.

"Republican Tea Party leader, Wesley Bradford, welcomed his remarks. The recent elections in Israel have seen the Prime Minister and the Likud Party retain control but with a much reduced majority, and the extreme Zionist Ysrael Party led by American born software billionaire Elias Stevens claimed eleven seats in the Knesset…."

"Great. More Middle East problems," I said, aloud this time, thinking of my friends and former colleagues who were still serving in Afghanistan.

"I can hear you muttering, Thomas," Julie called from the aft sun-bed.

"Just bringing your breakfast, milady," I answered in a mock English butler accent, walking through to the cockpit.

"…Sir Ivan Gunn, the billionaire chief of Gunn Group Industries, has

been kidnapped in Belfast. Details are not available and a spokesman for the PSNI (Police Service of Northern Ireland) has stated that no ransom demands have yet been received. Sir Ivan, a leading and-influential industrialist..."

I didn't hear the rest; just felt a numbing sensation between my ears and let the plates crash to the deck.

To me funerals are a morbid display of egoistic emotion, but that's probably my own denial having had to attend too many of them. The experience was uncomfortable, and I was glad to be back in the car headed home. My stepmother Mary had recovered somewhat from the initial shock but tired easily. She lay back in the soft deep leather seat with her eyes closed. Heavily applied make-up did little to hide the lines around her eyes, and when she spoke her voice was thin, brittle.

"You are the head of Gunn Group Industries now Thomas. Control of the company should remain in the family. I know you don't like the idea, but you are just going to have to get used to it."

"This is not the time to discuss it, Mary."

"This is the right time." Her eyes became bright, burning, feverish. "You are going to do it. Tell me you'll do it. Tell me now."

"Let me think about it."

"No. There is no discussion. No debate. You will do it just as your father wanted. What you or I want is immaterial. You'll do it because it is the right thing to do." Her voice rose to a shout, loud enough for Henderson to glance in the rear view mirror.

Julie sat quietly listening to the exchange. "Mary's right. It is the Gunn family company and you are the only one left." Her remark surprised me and I looked angrily at her. I knew they were both right, but I just didn't want the job. I wanted to go back to Gozo and resume my life with Julie. Laze around in the sun, make love, and forget everything. For years I had lived off the family fortune without contributing anything. Now it was time to assume responsibility and I felt the shackles closing around me.

"OK, I'll do it," I said gently, thinking that at least being on the inside I'd have a better chance of discovering why my father had been murdered.

Mary visibly relaxed and closed her eyes again.

The wake that followed the funeral was like a subdued cocktail party. Everyone making meaningless small talk, knocking back as much free booze as possible and pretending all was right with the world. However, it did give me a chance to corner Adrian Newell and tell him the news.

"Don't worry, Thomas, you will pick up the reins in no time." Sarcasm rested easily with Adrian Newell. "If you need to know anything just ask. Your father left a lot of the running of the business in my hands. He didn't like to meddle too much in the mundane day-to-day dealings." I could see what he was angling for. If he could keep me under tight control and out of the running of things, then he would be the man in charge. I must say the idea did have its attractions, a thought he must have known had obviously crossed my mind otherwise he would not have been so open in his suggestion.

"I do plan to find out all there is to know about the way the Group operates, Adrian," I said watching the CEO of my father's company's eyes carefully. I didn't like him and I didn't trust him. "What was my father doing in Northern Ireland?" I was expecting a reaction, but not quite as dramatic as he visibly turned pale and I thought his eyes would pop into his champagne glass. "Is anything wrong, Adrian?" I asked.

He coughed and made little choking noises. "N... n... no. It's OK. I just swallowed a large mouthful of champagne. It went the wrong way." He coughed again and recovered his composure. Adrian seemed to have developed a nervous tick at the corner of his right eye. "It's a new project. A proposed micro-electronics factory to be constructed just outside Belfast. It was your father's own personal project. I'm afraid I don't know much about it." His composure returned and before I could question him further, he excused himself and mingled with the other guests. I let him go as this seemed hardly the time or place to pursue him with the ferocity I felt.

"Adrian seemed to be in a hurry to escape from you." The voice of Hamish McDougall came from behind and I turned to see his friendly face smiling at me. He had been my father's closest friend since before I was born. An MP and Minister of State for Trade and Investment, he seemed to drift through life, tidying up other people's problems quietly and efficiently. He would never be Prime Minister, he just didn't have the flair, but then again he was quite happy looking after his constituents and carrying out a worthwhile job in the Government.

"Yes. I seem to have struck a nerve, though why I don't know." I took a sip of champagne. "Presumably you've heard that I'm taking over as head of the Group?" He nodded and patted me on the arm.

"Yes, I'm glad. It's about time you came out of yourself. You've been ducking and weaving for too long." I tensed ready to let my anger rise again, when I caught his eyes. They were laughing at me. "You have to learn to control that quick temper of yours, too. It just might get you into trouble and there is no room for histrionics in the Board Room." He was right, of course. The shock of grey hair, laughing eyes and relaxed attitude of the man always defused any situation.

"Listen, if you need someone to talk to, just give me a call. Mary has my number." At that moment Julie came over and told me that Mary had gone to rest. Hamish excused himself and we were alone.

"How is she?" I asked.

"Just tired. She's more relaxed than she has been for a long time, probably relived that you've taken the job. Doesn't like Americans much does she?"

"I'm sure she'll make an exception in your case. And she already has in my case."

"How so?"

"I have dual nationality, my mother was American, born in Santa Barbara California."

"I knew that. Well your step mother is relying on you to pull the family together." She hesitated and then, with a touch of mockery, added. "She also wants to see you married and have an heir." She looked at me with a sideways grin, gauging my reaction to the comment.

"No way. Not yet. I like the practice we are getting, but I don't think I'm ready for children."

"That's what I told her. Well, not in so many words, but close enough." We both laughed, awkwardly. Julie had changed over the past few days.

When I first saw her, she was a dream vision floating through the evening twilight and soft streetlights. A sophisticated poised and confident beauty that most men hungered after and very few had the balls to approach. Her grey/green eyes and direct look I knew could freeze any unwanted attention without her having to utter a word, and I was immediately fascinated. I was sure I had seen her on the cover of Vogue, or Elle magazine and continued to watch her easily brush off the young rich 'bar-flies' that frequented Café Carlo.

Perhaps it was the scar that looped across my forehead where the shrapnel had carved my flesh open and cracked my skull that caught her eye, or that I sat quietly watching her, frankly admiring her beauty, amused by the murmur of excitement that ran through the restaurant in Capri.

She turned and saw me, smiled, and walked over, much to the dismay of would-be suitors who were left standing at the bar with their mouths open.

"Carlo tells me that the Fountaine Pajot Sanya 57, is yours." Her New England accent surprised me as I had assumed her to be European.

"It is." I stood and indicated a seat for her to sit down, which she did with the elegance and assurance of a Royal Princess. "My name is...."

"Thomas Gunn," she interrupted easily, smiling. "I do my research, something my father taught me was very important."

"Then I am at a disadvantage, Miss...."

"Sutton. Julie Sutton."

"And your interest in the yacht?"

"Purely selfish. I was looking for a private charter for a week or two and Carlo said you were available."

"Carlo said that did he?"

"He did."

"And how much did you pay Carlo to ensure I was available."

She laughed quickly, a musical sound and mischief in her eyes. "A lot. Too much. Money is not the issue, my privacy is. And I like adventure. You seem to fit the description."

"I wondered why I suddenly had no business this week."

"You are available then? As I said I will cover whatever you lost on your previous charter."

"If you have done your research then you know money has no interest for me. I'm sure Carlo told you that too."

"He did. But I like to pay my way."

"Privacy does have a price."

"I see we think alike."

We fell in love on the second day and sailed to Gozo, where we stayed, anchored in a solitary bay for six months. Julie refused all work, much to her agent's frustration, and I had little to do anyway during my extended convalescence, until the real world crashed our paradise.

Julie squeezed my arm, snapping me back to the present and my duty as host as some of our guests were leaving.

With most of the people gone, I cornered Adrian again and told him that I would be down at Head Office some time during the week to make a start on learning the business.

"I want to know everything about this micro-electronics factory in Belfast before any more decisions are made," I told him firmly.

"But there are still some negotiations to be completed, and other formalities. I really think they ought to be dealt with now, not later," he said in a tone that implied I should let those who know about these things get on with it.

"No. Under the circumstances I'm not rushing us into any decisions." I took vicarious pleasure watching him squirm.

"If you insist," he said stiffly and walked out to his waiting car.

"You seem to have ruffled his feathers a bit," said Julie, standing beside me. "Something tells me you are not going to have an easy time with him."

"I don't trust him."

"Is that why you're goading him? Or do I detect a spark of interest in the Group?" She was laughing at me again.

"I want to know why my father was murdered, and my gut tells me it has something to do with this new project in Northern Ireland."

I knew that the Gunn Group was complicated. It controlled many companies in the fields of electronics, engineering and chemicals. The assets were enormous and profits almost equal to the largest of multi-nationals. No mean feat for a privately owned business. Obviously with the amounts of money involved, there must be very tight controls on security, especially as the areas of micro-electronics and chemicals were high risk and the competition cut throat. I could understand Adrian's reluctance to talk business at the wake, but still there was this nagging doubt in my mind.

"I think I'll have a talk with Mary. Perhaps she can shed some light on the matter."

Julie shook her head. "Don't disturb her just yet. It is the first real rest she's had. How about taking me for a walk around the grounds instead?"

"You're right and they're quite beautiful at this time of year."

We passed the rest of the afternoon wandering the grounds talking. It was the first time since we arrived that we had been alone for any length of time and now that the funeral was over we could look forward to happier times ahead.

I led Julie around to the nondescript barn set aside from the main Hall. The only thing that could give away the fact that the barn was an aircraft hangar was the small round concrete helipad thirty metres from the hangar building.

Julie looked at me askance. "A helicopter?"

"Wealth does have its perks."

"A private jet and a helicopter?"

"Well actually the Gunn Group has two helicopters and two more private jets."

"Of course it does," she said sarcastically.

The electric hangar doors slid open at the touch of the 'app' on my iPhone and revealed the interior of the barn, aside from the helicopter, there was a small yet comprehensively equipped workshop and maintenance area, and outside a five hundred gallon tank of Jet fuel. Julie watched as I wheeled the aircraft out of the hangar onto the pad, disconnected the ground handling wheels, stowed them back in the hangar and checked the fuel. My father always kept the helicopter fully fuelled and ready to go at any time. It made trips to London easy and quick.

It had been a while since I flew the Eurocopter, demanding a different set of skills to the fixed wing Cessna Mustang. This one was equipped with a full EFIS (Electronic Flight Information System) digital 'glass' cockpit, so I could fly 'blind' from Norwich to the London Heliport in Battersea on the river Thames only eight miles from the Gunn Group offices. This particular aircraft had been configured for right seat flying. I liked it better than flying from the left seat, as I could lock off the collective and use my left hand for changing radio frequencies and other instruments.

"When was the last time you flew this?"

"About two years ago. We'll take it tomorrow, I need to make an appearance at the office."

"You'll take it, I have my own business to run and that means mollifying my agent and getting some work."

"Where's your sense of adventure?"

"You get some practice in then we'll talk about my sense of adventure."

Mary reappeared for dinner. The rest had done her good.

Some of the old bounce was back in her walk and conversation. I didn't want to spoil the atmosphere so suppressed my desire to bombard her with questions. There would be plenty of time after the meal.

She had been through a lot in the last eighteen months, having just recovered from a serious car crash the previous year in which two of her closest friends had been killed. After a long period in hospital and private nursing home she had pulled through.

"Mary, there are some things that have been worrying me about Dad," I said, as tactfully as possible. She sipped the brandy delicately. "I keep wondering about this Northern Ireland deal. This afternoon I tried to talk to Adrian about it, but he brushed me off, virtually saying it was none of my business." I paused, waiting for a reply. There was none. "Well, don't you think it is more than just a coincidence?"

She placed her brandy glass carefully on the side table and shook her head. "The police came to the conclusion that it was probably a case of mistaken identity. If there is anything they will find it Thomas." She smiled. "You concentrate on learning the business. Leave the investigating to the experts."

"I need to know what the Northern Ireland deal is all about. Adrian just said it was one of Dad's personal projects. If I'm going to learn about the company then it seems to me to be a good place to start. Did he say anything to you about it?"

"No, of course not. You know what your father was like about business. No work at home. All business was to stay where it belonged, at the office. Perhaps Adrian was just honouring your father's memory by not discussing it here. I'm sure he will tell you all about it when you go in to work." She drew a weary hand across her face. "I must go to bed, Thomas. I'm not really as together as I look."

"Of course." I helped her up and watched as she walked slowly across the room. "Are there any papers that Dad would have left in the house? Presumably, if he was handling the deal on his own he would have something here." I felt I needed to press her on the subject. It was so strange that nobody seemed to know much about it at all. I know that the old man liked to keep business away from his private life as much as possible, but I also know that there were times when he brought very important documents home. Particularly those pertaining to projects in which he was personally involved.

"Please, Thomas. Enough. I never pried into his business affairs at all. Perhaps if I had I could have been a better wife to him. Now please, we can talk again tomorrow, but there is nothing much I can tell you." She stopped at the door, turned and looked at me carefully as if trying to tell me something by telepathy. "I want you to do a good job now that you're in charge," she said, tipped her head on one side as if asking a silent question, then turned and left the room.

Still feeling very much in the dark, I went to my flat in what used to be the old servants quarters. It was private in a separate wing of the Hall and had it's own entrance through the kitchen. Julie poured us two glasses of Pusser's rum, a silent reminder of the catamaran and sunshine, and we sat in front of the large window looking out over the peaceful moonlit countryside.

"I know what you're thinking, Thomas. And I know you want answers. But you're not going to get them tonight." She leaned across and nibbled on my ear, then got up and slowly took off her dress. Beneath it she was naked. She turned and headed for the bedroom.

Well at least in this upside down world there were some things that had not changed. I downed the rum, picked up the discarded dress and followed her.

THREE

London – September 2012

The offices of Gunn Group Industries were not in Central London, as people would expect. They were situated in a tall building in Twickenham. Close enough to the hub of things, but far enough on the outskirts of the City to be easy to get to from the country. The building was called Gunn House and was, appropriately, built by a subsidiary company, Langhorne Construction Limited. It was an eyesore, as are most buildings of this type. I was still contemplating the follies of modern architecture as the lift carried me to the top floor, home of the offices of the Board of Directors.

The collar and tie felt uncomfortable and the suit as if it was four sizes too big. Julie had assured me it wasn't, and Mary also made the correct noises. I was not convinced. The lift bumped to a stop, jerking me out of my daydream and the doors hissed open to reveal the reception area.

Directly opposite the lift was a desk at which sat a beautifully dressed and perfectly made-up young lady who looked up coolly as I walked towards her.

"May I help you, sir?" The standard question used a thousand times a day in a million offices.

"Mr Gunn," I said.

"I'm sorry, sir, but Mr Gunn is not in."

"I am Mr Gunn. Mr Thomas Gunn, the new Chairman."

The girl looked at me blankly until she suddenly grasped what I had said.

"I'm sorry, sir. We aren't expecting you. Mr Newell didn't warn me at all." I held up my hand to stop the flow. A young-looking thirty, with long fair hair, I didn't look the part of a city tycoon.

"Would you just point me in the right direction for my office and tell Mr Newell I'm here. I'll see him in ten minutes." I hoped that sounded as a chairman should and having received her directions, she headed off for the office.

The old man really did believe in the Chairman having an office worthy of the position. It was huge. A thick carpet covered centre of the expanse of wooden floor; mahogany desk in front of the window, and table with settee and easy chairs for entertaining associates. Original modern paintings adorned the walls and the view across Twickenham and the Thames was breath-taking. Beside the desk was a complete console with a computer terminal, closed circuit TV and the usual intercom system. So this is where the Gunn fortune was generated. I could see why Adrian wanted to keep me out of the way. If this was a yardstick with which to judge the power wielded by the Chairman then he must be very upset that it was in my hands.

There was a knock on the door and a very correctly dressed, slightly overweight and rather severe looking woman in her mid thirties entered.

"Mr Gunn, my name is Jennifer Jordan. I am your assistant. I do apologise we weren't expecting you. Would you like some coffee?" She stood in front of the desk, expressionlessly, waiting for a reply.

"Yes please. Milk, two sugars, thank you." I said. She turned and made for the door. I stopped her before she reached it. "Jennifer?" She turned and looked enquiringly. "Please smile, I like happy faces around me." She dropped her chin, smiled shyly, opened the door and left. She returned a few minutes later with a tray of coffee, followed by a tight-lipped, somewhat irritable looking Adrian.

"Thank you, Jennifer. Good morning, Adrian." I knew the use of her first name would annoy him, and that was just what I wanted to do. To make sure that he knew who now sat in the chair. "Please don't say it. I've already heard it twice this morning." He looked a little nonplussed, as if I had just robbed him of a key phrase.

"You could have given me notice that you were coming in."

"Why? What I want from you is a run-down on everything this Group owns, part owns or whatever. I reckon that would be the best place to start." I hoped I sounded as if I knew a little about business. I hadn't a clue and was going to have to do some pretty rapid learning.

"If you had given me some warning then I could have had all the files ready for your inspection. As it is it will take time to get them all together." He spoke stiffly, with his head held up, looking down at me in disgust. Adrian categorised everyone as either a businessman or a layabout. I was one of the latter.

"Adrian, in this day and age all I need is the computer login passwords and I can get all the information I need by just pressing these little buttons." I indicated the terminal by the desk. He had the grace to flush.

He glared at me tight lipped, turned and left the office. I swung the chair around and stared out over the city, watching the slow-moving traffic like a giant worm threading its way through the undergrowth of houses.

I hated cities. Hell I hated offices.

But somehow up here away from the noise, the colours, shapes and shadows had a dream-like quality. I thought through the exchange with Adrian. Why all the blocking manoeuvres?

What was it that he didn't want me to see? Perhaps I wasn't a businessman but eight years as an officer in the Parachute Regiment as part of SFSG (Special Forces Support Group), had given me a suspicious mind and a nose for trouble. Something was afoot, and sure as hell it involved the old man and the kidnapping. There was a knock on the door and Jennifer entered carrying a bulky, blue file.

"Sir Ivan's personal files and computer login passwords, Mr Gunn," she said. "You'll be needing them."

"Thank you. Can you give me a walk through on how the system operates?" In the modern world where access to information was vital, everyone needed reasonable computer skills. As a member of Special Forces I was pretty educated on most systems, but I needed people in the office to think I was a little naïve.

She smiled awkwardly and came around to the side of the desk, laid the file down and opened it at the first page of the text. "You will find all the necessary instructions here. Sir Ivan insisted that the whole system be made as simple as possible. He said he didn't want some computer programmer knowing more about the operation of the

Group than he did."

"That definitely sounds like my father. Was there any information that is *not* on the computer?"

"Not as far as I am aware, except for the design drawings for new projects, building plans, machinery and electronic devices. They are carried on a completely separate set of servers. Only the Chief Designer, the Chief Executive and the Chairman have access to those."

"So the entire Gunn Group, its accounts, day to day running, personnel wages and everything are available from this terminal?"

"Yes. The file you have there has a limited circulation, again only to Board members. Other personnel in other departments have access to information that applies to their department only. Likewise with the Managing Directors and Chairmen of the subsidiaries." She stopped talking and waited for my response. It was certainly a very neat way to keep abreast of all events. And all controlled from this office.

"What about the personnel files of all the Group Board members?"

"They are kept in the wall safe behind the Picasso." She indicated the painting that hung on the wall above the small cocktail bar. I was beginning to get to know why Adrian was so against my appointment. I'm sure he would dearly like to have all the information that was in those files. People are most vulnerable through their personnel files and bank accounts. If you have neither, then as far as the world is concerned you don't exist. Identity is a plastic credit card.

"Thank you, Jennifer. Oh, by the way, who appointed you as my secretary?"

"Sir Ivan. I've been with him for four years. Mr Newell was a little annoyed." She seemed a little embarrassed and dropped her head, not meeting my eyes.

"In that case, Jennifer, I hope you stay on."

She smiled, excused herself and left.

Well, at least, my secretary would not be one of Adrian's pawns, yet another thing that was going to annoy him.

The rest of the morning was spent going through the blue corporate file, trying to make sense out of the meaningless letters and figures. By lunchtime I reckoned to have sorted out enough to be able to make a start removing the information stored in this vast system of circuit, breakers and microchips. Jennifer popped in at about midday to say that if I wanted lunch brought up to the office that could be arranged.

"Please, thank you. Tell me, do you know anything about the project in Northern Ireland?"

"No. I heard some talk, of course. There's always that in an office of this size. Nothing of interest though, just people wondering if they would be promoted and transferred when the factory started up properly."

"Why would anyone be transferred from Head Office? Surely that would be considered a demotion?"

"Oh no. It was common knowledge that the new factory was top secret and under the personal control of Sir Ivan. All the office staff and management would have been selected by him, therefore it must be considered a promotion."

"You say *'would have been'*. Why? Surely the project is still underway? There is no reason to stop it is there?"

"I don't suppose there is. It's just that we all considered it to be Sir Ivan's own baby and nobody else knew any of the details including the Board. He was negotiating direct with the Government." She turned to me frowning. "You do know that the factory is to be built with a Government loan of two and half billion pounds, don't you?"

"I knew there was a loan, but not the amount. I'm intrigued to know how you know so much about it."

"You really don't know much about office life, do you?" she laughed. "The grapevine is as good as jungle drums. All you have to do is interpret the sounds. You should hear what the information is on you. Even the best of bosses thinks that his assistant is a mere typing machine and not capable of rational or logical thought. There is a lot of information passed in the Ladies' Room which should be classified under the Official Secrets Act."

"I shall have to remember that in future. Do you know anything else about the Northern Ireland deal?"

"No, I'm afraid not."

"Let me know if you hear anything." I turned my attention back to my father's personal files and ran through a breakdown of all the companies owned by the Group. I knew the Group was extensive, but had never known just how big it was. Each company had its own unique identity code, and all I had to do to get a detailed look at a specific company, was to enter it along with a confirmation password.

I was so engrossed that I didn't hear the door open and Adrian come into my office.

"I see you're hard at work, Thomas," he said without smiling. "I wondered when you wanted to call a board meeting. The circumstances dictate that we should have one and I'm sure you are anxious to meet the other members. I think we had better clear up the obvious rift between us. I am quite prepared to hand in my resignation if you so wish," he said formally, standing in front of my desk hands clasped behind his back. I looked at him and decided I needed to try another approach if I was to get anything out of him.

"Adrian, this is a private company and I am the majority shareholder, but I do I know my limitations, and I need somebody to teach me. We don't have to like each other just so long as we respect each other's position. If you feel you must leave, then that's up to you." My acting is quite good and I hoped I had just the right amount of sincerity in my voice to catch him off-guard.

"Very well. But I must be allowed to carry out the normal business. With respect, I know this company inside out, and therefore it seems right that I should run it. Your father never interfered with me at all."

"Let's call it a truce, then. Can I count on your support for information and advice?"

He inclined his head. Perhaps his loyalty to the company was stronger than his mistrust and dislike of me. He left without another word, and I sat for a long time thinking about him, wondering just where his loyalties lay. It was my suspicious mind hard at work again. There were so many things I didn't understand, so many things that seemed very strange.

Staring out of the window did little to add to my knowledge so I let my mind drift back to the time I told my father that I wasn't going to enter the family business, but join the Army instead.

There had only been a few times in my life when I had truly seen my father's dark side. I knew it existed, every immensely wealthy man was ruthless to some degree, but he had always been careful to hide it at home.

"Ungrateful little prick," he exploded, throwing down his serviette and knocking over the glass of wine at his right hand. "You'll get nothing."

"I didn't ask for anything," I replied standing, pushing the dining chair back and nearly sending the servant tumbling as she walked behind me. "It's my life and I will live it the way I want."

"There are responsibilities."

"To what?"

"To me. To this house. To the company."

"What about my responsibility to myself?"

"Grow up."

"And be like you? I'd rather not."

He stared at me, his face puce with rage knowing that physically he was no longer a match for me, but I could see that if he had a shotgun in his hand instead of a dinner fork, then my life would quite possibly have ended at that point.

Eight years later, he came to my hospital bed. Sat with me while I lay unconscious hovering between life and death, until I slowly returned to the land of the living. The fury I saw in his eyes was not directed at me, but at the circumstances that nearly killed me. Circumstances that he had been unable to control, and I realised why he had been so angry all those years ago.

Angry because he could not express the fear he felt.

Angry because he loved me and wanted only what he thought was best for me.

Angry because he knew he could not keep me safe forever.

He held my hand and his eyes softened. "Come back to me Thomas. When you are healed, come back to me. I need you now. I need your help. I need your skills."

At the time his words seemed odd, poorly chosen. I didn't feel that he had ever needed me.

His eyes burned into my soul, and I shivered as if a cold wind had blown into the office, then his face faded from my mind, replaced by the grey London skyline, and I had the feeling that whatever had caused his death was already in play on that day nearly eighteen months ago. Eighteen months when I could have been helping him instead of taking my own sweet time with my convalescence and juvenile adventures. That night I flew back to the Hall.

In the following days, Adrian proved to be a good teacher. I returned to the Hall and we communicated via Skype whenever I had a question. With the computer codes in hand, I didn't need to be in the office as there was a desktop computer in the flat.

Besides, it was stifling. A claustrophobic cavern that philosophically I could never understand.

I liked action, not inaction, and wading through the politics and shenanigans of business were proving to be more and more irritating each day. The only reason I stuck at it was because I knew that the riddle of my father's murder lay in the company he built.

Adrian tried his hardest to make the dry, dusty world of figures, balance sheets and contracts come to life, and I wanted to learn because I felt that a knowledge of the financials would help me get at the heart of my father's murder. My mistrust of him remained unchanged and I took great pains to hide my true feelings.

Mary suffered from highs and lows. Some days she was her normal, witty, charming self, others she stayed in her room and shunned all attempts to bring her out of herself.

It was worrying but the doctor said that it was a pretty standard reaction to the situation. Julie travelled for a few modelling jobs much to her agent's great joy, and when not on location occasionally spent a few days in Cambridge visiting her father, a Professor of computer science at the University, whom I'd met four months earlier when Julie flew him out to Gozo. They had different surnames. She reasoned that using her mother's maiden name, Sutton, as a 'stage' name for modelling, sounded better than Oldfield.

I was still ruminating on Julie's father when Jennifer called me on Skype.

"You have something for me?" I asked.

"Yes," she replied. "Not a great deal, just the minutes of a meeting. Seems out-of-place." As my PA she had really settled into the job, taking all the mundane day-to-day problems away from me, allowing me to get on with my learning.

She sent me an instant message. "This is the passcode. OR - 41386/LN2."

I typed in the code and rubbed my eyes waiting for the computer to access the file.

NEW PROJECT OR-41386/LN2
PROPOSED NEW FACTORY IN N.I.

The meeting was declared open by the Chairman, who handed out an outline sheet (see Annex A) to all members of the Board. Having read the details the members were asked to comment on them.

The Chief Executive, Mr Newell, agreed that the plan seemed a sound one, but wondered why the Board had not been consulted at the outset before the land had been purchased.

The Chairman replied that there was little time as the land is in a prime position and there were various tenders for it. He added that the CFO had been informed as had the Company Lawyer. Mr Newell asked if the negotiations for a Government loan had also been completed without his knowledge. The Chairman replied that a tentative approach had been made by himself, but as yet no final details had been decided. Mr Newell started to ask further questions but was interrupted by the Chairman who stated that he was taking full responsibility for the project and had merely approached the Board for their reaction before proceeding. The Chairman stated that because of the Top Secret nature of the company, few Board Members would have access to any information regarding its manufacturing processes.

There being no further business the meeting closed.

The meeting had obviously been very short and very sharp, and the minutes seemed something that a child might write, which struck me as very strange. Attached to the minutes of the meeting was an Annex that laid out the plan that my father had drawn up for the construction of the factory. Reading through it I could see why Adrian had been so upset. It was very detailed not only spelling out the exact nature of the business, the construction of micro-electronic components for the computer industry, but also down to a management and work force organisational breakdown. A footnote to the Annex stated that a complete list of equipment requirements would be available in a week. The minutes and the Annex were dated within a few days of each other. The following pages were the equipment lists, salary and wage structures, dated exactly one week after the first pages.

The last page was headed 'Financial Requirements'. Beneath the heading was a computer code, which I naturally entered to be greeted with an accountant's dream. Lists of numbers, forecasts, cash flow charts, income, expenditure, profitability, loan amortisation charts and so on.

I sat back. There was still no real information. Just an idea on paper and yet it was now well on the way to fruition, judging by the architects drawings and the provisional order for all the equipment that was listed. These last items had been received in the last few days.

Somewhere, there was somebody who knew what it was all about.

Somebody who was controlling the continuation of the project from somewhere other than the Group headquarters in Twickenham.

"Jennifer, can you ask Mr Newell to call me on Skype."

Adrian waited over an hour before he called. The delay was a petty statement of his independence, but I was too tired to let it bother me.

"Presumably you've seen this," I said. He nodded. "And presumably you have seen the drawings and the confirmation of the equipment orders too?" Again he nodded. "Then would you like to tell me who in the hell is running the project?"

"I've been trying to find out. Apparently, your father approached somebody outside the organisation to be Managing Director. As yet, we don't have a name. For some reason, your father was keeping it strictly to himself. An act that, I may say, the Board did not consider to be in the interests of the company," he said little too smugly.

"Not the Board's call to make." I said roughly, continuing before he could reply. "Where was the money coming from to finance it?"

"We have a fund into which each of the subsidiaries contribute. The purpose of it is to provide capital for new development. Venture capital if you like. Sir Ivan insisted that the control of this fund be his alone." By the look on his face, Adrian obviously disagreed with this too.

"How much control of the Northern Ireland business does the Group have?"

"None," he said looking acutely embarrassed.

"You mean, so many hundreds of millions of pounds have been handed over to a company that as yet, nobody knows about and we can do nothing?" I asked incredulously.

"Well, the Group has no control, but you do."

"How so?"

"Both your mother and yourself are named as Directors of the company, which has been registered as Rathborne Micro-Electronics Ltd.," Adrian said reluctantly, looking more and more uncomfortable with each passing moment.

I was dumbstruck. "Why the hell didn't you tell me this before?"

"I had no idea myself until this morning. In fact, I had no idea what the company was called; none of us did," he said and for what seemed an age neither of us spoke. We were too busy trying to absorb all the details and make some sense of it.

"What about the company server, Adrian? Do you think he might have put all the information on that?"

"I've already checked. I can't find anything," he replied.

"Well the files are missing, aren't they?"

He cleared his throat and made himself comfortable before replying. "I think the idea of forming a new company in Northern Ireland was, and is, a sound one. The aid that is available from the Government is enormous and the benefits of cheap land and reasonably low wages make the potential profits very big." He paused, shifted position and continued. "The field of micro-electronics again was a good choice, the market at the moment being on an upward trend. The one oddity is the fact that Sir Ivan chose to go it alone. And yet this can also be considered a shrewd move." I looked up at him and he held up a hand to forestall my question. "Although the potential profits are high, so is the risk of any project in the Province. Your father was a farsighted man and I can only assume that by setting the Company up as a separate organisation he could minimise the risk. As to the unorthodoxy of the methods he used, one can only trust his judgement. If we can find out who the Managing Director is, a lot of the questions will be answered."

I digested what he said and mulled it over in my mind. Was Adrian just telling me what he thought I should know, or was he being straight with me? There was no real way of knowing.

"Wouldn't the Government have demanded a more orthodox approach? After all there is a considerable sum at stake."

"With the contacts your father had in Government I should think that was the last thing on anybody's mind. Just the mention of his name was enough to seal a contract."

"Have there been any noises from Government departments now that he is dead?"

"No. Everyone seems to be satisfied that all was taken care of beforehand. Well, you just have to look at the detail in that report." He indicated the file. "No doubt the Managing Director of Rathborne Micro-Electronics Limited is dealing with the whole thing."

"His name must be on the Register of Companies?"

"No. It just says that the full name would be supplied at a later date." He rose from his seat. "Well, if you don't need me any more then I will be getting back to work."

I nodded absently and sat trying to sort out the puzzle, my brain doing cartwheels. I am a trained Special Forces soldier and I'd better start thinking as if I was sifting through military intelligence reports. All the information was here, somewhere, I knew it, yet it just didn't make sense.

So what was there? A factory still under-construction, no personnel officially appointed except an unknown Managing Director, Mary and myself.

Did Mary know what was going on? The way her mind was right know that was an unknown as well. Right now I wanted to check the computer and the financial requirements of Rathborne Micro-Electronics Limited.

Getting more information was easier than I thought, now that I had the name of the company. I typed in the Rathborne company name and entered *'find'*. The screen did its usual blink and then reeled out some facts and figures relating to the new company. I sat looking at the screen in amazement. I could not really comprehend the amounts that stared me in the face. Rathborne Micro-Electronics Limited had been floated with an initial stake of £225 million from the Gunn Capital Trust Fund. A further £2.5 billion was then allocated to the company from Government sources, totalling £2.75 billion. The thought of that amount of money was staggering enough, but that one man had managed to raise it on his own was even more so. And somewhere there was a person controlling it all.

I quickly Skyped Jennifer. "On your terminal, type in Rathborne Micro-Electronics and then hit the 'find' button. Tell me what happens."

I heard her typing rapidly as I was speaking.

"Nothing. Hasn't found anything."

"Thanks Jennifer."

"Can you tell me what this is about?"

"It's about missing information. I'll fill you in some other time."

Julie was out with one of the horses and Mary was talking to Ron, the farm manager. This gave me time to go through the bag of possessions that I had brought back from Belfast. They had been sitting in a cupboard since my return and I had completely forgotten about them. My memory was only jogged when I tried to find the combination to the safe in the office. The old man had apparently kept it on him at all times and nobody else had any idea as to what it was. Going through his clothes and briefcase was a rather morbid business but I found a bunch of keys.

One of the keys fitted the desk in the study. A quick search revealed a diary and papers regarding the running of the Hall and farm, a few identification sheets of some of the more expensive horses in the stables that it was hoped would be used as breeding stock and other sundry bills and receipts. I flipped through the diary and found a Chubb Safe business card with an eight-digit number written on the back. There was also a box that contained a pile of personal letters. These I left until I'd talked to Mary. Then I booted up his computer and searched for Rathborne Micro-Electronics with no result. Which meant that the computer in the flat was the only one that could access any information. And of course nobody would have thought to look there if they were searching for information, assuming, just as I had done, that all the computers at the Hall were connected. For the first time since the funeral, I could feel a sense of excitement. My father must have thought that if anything happened to him, I'd use the flat and the computer, so that's where he hid the information, at least some of it. And now I was certain he knew he was probably going to die. Rathborne Micro-Electronics was the key.

As my mind tried to ravel together everything I had just learned, I heard Mary's voice asking for tea to be sent into the drawing room. I left the study and joined her. We passed the few minutes until tea was served talking about the farm and the stables. I then broached the subject of Rathborne.

I told her that I had discovered that both of us were Directors of the company and asked her why she hadn't told me.

"I just didn't think it was important. Your father said it was merely a formality and, as usual, I asked no more questions about it." She looked as if she were about to cry so I stopped questioning her.

I found myself walking towards the stables. It was at times like these, when I was confused and angry, that I always sought out Julie. Somehow she managed to calm me down and put me back on the road to rational thought. The stables were at the back of the Hall backing onto a paddock that had been set out as a small jumping course, mainly for schooling young horses and giving good, safe practice for riders. Julie was taking Prince, one of the biggest horses, through his paces. I stopped by the rail and watched.

It wasn't until she had finished that she finally noticed me and waved. She dismounted and handed the horse over to the groom, climbed the fence and took my arm.

"Hey. Done with work for the day?" she said brightly.

"There were some questions that I had to ask Mary. I'm afraid I upset her again."

"You seem to be doing that a lot lately. You know what she's like with these depressions she keeps having."

"I know, I know. But there are some things that I haven't the answers to, and I think she may."

"Can't you drop it, at least until she's over this?"

"No, I don't think there is time. Something is badly wrong and I've got to find out what it is."

"Do you want to tell me about it?" She stopped and stood in front of me, hands on my arms and looked into my eyes. "Perhaps I can help, I'm not so dumb, you know."

We continued on our way and as we walked, I told her everything that I had learned so far, including my suspicions and my fears.

"You think your father was engaged in something dishonest?" she exclaimed. "You can't be serious? He was one of the most respected men in the country."

"I'd like to think he wasn't, but nothing seems to fit. Either he was into something pretty nasty or I didn't know him as well as I thought. I guess a lot of answers may well be locked in that safe at the Head Office."

"Did you say that only your father had the combination?" She said. I nodded. "And you found the combination this afternoon when you were going through his personal effects?" Again I nodded. "Right, then let's go to the office tonight and have a look in that safe. That might solve a lot of mysteries."

"Ready to take that flight then?"

"I guess."

The Eurocopter EC120B is a great little helicopter, fairly quick and agile, with great equipment and, like all helicopters, a panoramic view, and this one was surprisingly quiet. First I had to check in with Norwich ATC for clearance, pressures and traffic information. That done, I lifted the collective, countered the yaw with the anti-torque pedals, pitch and roll with the cyclic, rising about five feet off the

runway before applying more collective and pushing the cyclic forward
to dip the nose and transition to forward flight and climb out from the
Hall helipad. Norwich ATC cleared us to our en-route heading at an
altitude of one thousand feet. As my old skills returned I relaxed and
settled into the flight, following the flight plan on the moving map and
keeping the speed at 120 knots.

I looked across at Julie, who still seemed tense. "Relax. Enjoy the
flight."

"You still have to land this thing. And if I'm not mistaken, very close
to water on a little square barge."

"Not quite, but close."

"Did you fly helicopters in the Army?"

"No. I could already fly before I joined, but it came in handy a couple
of times in Afghanistan."

"And of course you can't tell me, Official Secrets Act and all that
stuff."

I nodded.

"What happens when this is all over?" She looked at me and I stared
straight ahead, not wanting to catch her eye.

"We'll deal with that when the time comes."

"And the company?"

"I don't know. Haven't thought about it." Truth is I didn't want to
think about it. Being bound to a desk for the rest of my life, living in a
mansion in rural England with a wife and family just didn't appeal.

Not right now.

Maybe sometime in the future, but not now.

As we flew closer to London, ATC began to route me past the myriad
airports in the London Terminal Control area, past London City
airport in docklands and up the river toward Battersea. The light was
beginning to fade, but not enough to make this a night landing and
within a few minutes I was being talked down on the approach to the
Heliport jutting out into the Thames on the south bank. The approach
was from the West down to the pad, where I then had to hover, turn
the aircraft ninety degrees and slowly move between the buildings to
where a 'ramper' guided me to landing pad 3. It took all my

concentration to keep the helicopter steady and I breathed a sigh of relief when the skids touched the ground and I shut down. Julie prised her hands off the edge of the seat.

"Safe and sound," I said as cheerfully as I could. I hadn't told her this was the first time I had flown in here without an instructor. She gave me a very 'old-fashioned' look and waited until the rotors stopped before opening the door.

"Well there's never a dull moment that's for sure," she said and gratefully stepped onto the ramp.

George, the night security guard, let us into the lift and immobilised the alarms for the top floor and the safe in my office. There was no other way up to the Group offices except through this lift and at night they were locked and the power switched off. We had caught George just before he armed all the systems, which would then have been under a time lock until six o'clock in the morning when the cleaners went to work.

The lift door opened and we made our way to the office. Julie gave a whistle when I switched the lights on.

"This is your office? Does your personal assistant match the surroundings?" she asked.

"Come on, let's get on with it." I led the way to the wall safe behind the Picasso, which slid aside to reveal the round Chubb Bankers Treasury Safe. I stared at the safe door. There were two combination locks and I only had one number written on the Chubb business card.

Two locks, eight digits 11101213, four for each lock but which number was for which lock? Something niggled me about the numbers and each combination I tried didn't work.

"I hope there's not a lock-out on this safe," Julie said warily.

"Lock-out?"

"Yes. Like when you type in the wrong password three times into a computer, it locks you out and you can't enter anymore passwords."

"Don't say that." I sat back and tried to think why the numbers seemed so familiar. "God I'm such a dumb idiot sometimes," I said in exasperation.

"Meaning what?"

"The numbers. 1110. November 10th, my birthday and 1213, December 13th my mother's death."

"Mary?"

"No my real mother. She died when I was a baby so I never knew her."

I took out the diary and flipped through to the tenth day of November. My father had written *"Thomas' birth. A time to remember"*. And on the thirteenth day of December he had written, *"Ellie's death. Another time to remember"*.

"Curious," Julie said quietly.

"Not really. It's quite clever actually. Now I just have to remember what time I was born and what time my mother died. Two four digit numbers in military time."

"You don't need to remember anything," Julie said excitedly. "Look." She pointed to the page. It was divided into times of the day.

"Nobody is born exactly on the hour, or dies exactly on the half-hour."

"But look at the bottom of the page. Were you born in New York? And did your mother die in Athens?"

"No. But my mother was born in New York. They could be time zones?"

"Why would you think that?"

"I'm a pilot, it makes sense."

"To you maybe."

"Exactly. New York is minus 5 hours and Athens plus two."

Julie shook her head. "But that still whole hours and again who gets born exactly on the hour..." her voice trailed away.

"Unless they are minutes. So my birthday time would be 2205 and my mother's death would be 1602."

Julie's face lit up with excitement. "Okay. Give it a go."

I spun the top dial left to the 2, right to the 2, left to the 0 and right to the 5 and then entered the lower digits, grasped the spokes of the unlock wheel and turned. Almost silently the locks clicked and I pulled open the door.

"How about that," Julie exclaimed.

Inside were some files, a few loose papers and rather oddly, a box containing a small pot of *'Orange Moon Body Butter by Crèma'*. There was nothing else. We took the files and papers over to the desk, made ourselves comfortable, and started to go through them.

The files were the personnel dossiers on every member of the Board. The information was comprehensive and included comments made in my father's handwriting. Fascinating reading though it was, there was nothing to arouse any suspicion. Julie had been going through the odd papers.

"Found anything?" I asked her after about twenty minutes of silence.

"Well, these are just some odd jottings about personnel. One of them is typed, but has been written over. Here look." She passed me the sheet. It was standard company report, but I didn't recognise the name. He certainly was not a Board member.

"What about the others?" I said and Julie passed me the other sheets. They were hand written.

Again I did not recognise any of the names. As with the typed sheets there were no comments except a note attached to one, where my father had written what looked like crossword puzzle clues. The name on the document was Des Ascot.

"Hey, wait a minute, these loose hand written documents could well be a provisional list of possible members of the management team for Rathborne. My guess is that this guy, Mr Des Ascot, maybe the one we're looking for. But then again his name sounds more like a supermarket chain."

"Is there an address?"

"No. Just says he is a *'Top American'*. Presumably the old man was going to import him to run the business. Well, there doesn't seem to be anything else around. Let's pack up and go home." We put the files back in the safe except for the loose hand written sheets, which I kept. I tossed the box containing the small pot of body butter to Julie.

"Here, you might as well have that."

She caught the pack. "I don't use this stuff, but Mary does, I saw a similar jar in her bedroom."

"Julie, I know this might be asking a lot, but do you think your father could help me with the Gunn computer system?"

She took out her iPhone, dialled and then tossed it to me. "Ask him."

"Professor, it's Thomas Gunn."

"Is Julie okay?"

"Of course. Actually I'd like a favour. I need an analysis of the Gunn Group computer system."

"Presumably you are asking me to carry out an appraisal without anyone knowing?"

"Yes."

"Does Julie approve?"

"Yes."

"And I think your father probably would have approved." There was a slight pause. "I was sorry to hear of his death Thomas. Truly," he finished awkwardly.

"Thank you."

"Fill me in on the details."

After I recounted everything I knew and explained how the system seemed to work, he was silent for a moment and then fired questions at me. I was taken aback by the incisiveness of his mind and the speed with which he grasped my dilemma.

"Give me a few hours to do some investigating. I'll call you back."

FOUR

Listening to the mobile phone ringing loudly reminded me that I had to change the annoying musical tone. "I need hands on access to the mainframe," Professor Oldfield said in his usual abrupt manner.

"Okay. How about tonight."

"What time?"

"Twenty one thirty, I don't want the staff here."

"Nine thirty tonight it is," he said brusquely and hung up.

I had warned George, that Julie and I would be working all night, so when I brought Professor Oldfield to the office we were duly let in without any trouble. George promised to keep me informed if anybody else wanted to get in and I showed Professor Oldfield into the main computer room and left him to it.

There was nothing to do whilst he was playing with the machines so I thought I might as well look over the personnel files once more. I don't know how many times I went through the files, but nothing seemed out of place. Finally I gave up and Julie and I went down to the computer room to see how the Professor was getting along. He had been at it for hours and it was past midnight. He didn't look up as we entered, indeed we might as well not have been there at all for all the notice he took. My questions were answered in monosyllables, so I made us some coffee. It looked as if it was going to be a long night. Oldfield was totally engrossed in his work and I thought back to the first time we met.

He was shorter and heavier than I thought he might be considering Julie's tall and slim body. Prematurely bald with sharp inquisitive eyes he appraised me carefully showing neither like nor dislike. It was disconcerting and reminded me of a particular JSIW (Joint Services Interrogation Wing) interrogator who quizzed me for days during Special Forces training. He seemed so anomalous to what I expected.

"I did some work for your father many years ago. Did you know that?"

"Know I didn't," I replied, glancing quickly at Julie to see if she knew.

"You never told me that Dad." She sounded a little irritated.

"It isn't important. Way before he became rich and famous. We met at Cambridge and I was a post grad Rhodes scholar. I used to lecture Business Management students on the business applications of modern computer technology. Of course that was in the analogue days. Well the end of the analogue days really. Digital systems were just starting to come online." He stared into the bottom of his empty whisky glass and I reached across the cockpit table and filled his glass with a passable Glenlivet. "He seemed to like puzzles and that's what computer programming is all about. When he started his first company I designed an encryption for his computer system. Basic stuff and a long time ago."

"I had no idea my father knew anything about computer systems."

"He didn't but he was a fast learner. I remember your father particularly fondly because he was the only one who asked sensible questions."

"How strange life is." Julie stared at her father as if she was seeing him for the first time and appreciating him, differently.

"Did Julie tell you I'm not her real father? Hence the different surname?"

"Yes she did," I lied.

Oldfield smiled, knowing the lie and yet enjoying that I sprang to her defence at the risk of my own integrity. "I like you. Chivalry is alive after all."

Julie stood angrily and went into the saloon. We could hear her crashing about in the galley loading the dishwasher.

"Take care of my little girl. She's all I have." If he thought his whisper couldn't be heard he was wrong.

"I'm not deaf. Dad." She emphasised his family title, still angry. Later, much later, I questioned her about her anger.

"Because he is my father, the only one I've ever known and it angers me that sometimes he doesn't seem to embrace that."

"Personally I appreciate the truth. Family secrets can only haunt and hurt. Besides, he loves you more than you want to accept."

I went down to see George in the security room, leaving Oldfield and

Julie working on the mainframe. He had been in the Army at the same time as me and retired a couple of years ago. As with a lot of retired soldiers, he picked security as the closest thing to his previous way of life. We discussed the old days, the people and places we both knew, into the early hours of the morning. It was good to relax and come down to earth after the events and people of the past months. George proved both witty and perceptive and I thought that if ever the need arose I could rely on him for support, no questions asked.

Oldfield finally finished at a quarter to five in the morning. He looked completely washed out, bloodshot eyes staring out of his pale face.

"That's it," he said. Tired he might be, but he was going to milk our relationship to the last. I resisted the temptation to pump him for information and just let him take his time. When he saw I was not going to bite, he continued. "I've got all the information I need, but it will take a few days to evaluate. I'll have to do it in my spare time."

"Will you need another night here?"

"No, not yet. I'll have to wait until I've had a chance to go through all this." He saw the looked of confusion on my face. "I inserted an access into the base code, a remote 'back-door' into the system. If anything strange is going on I'll know."

"My father had a similar set-up on a computer in my flat at the Hall."

Oldfield looked me sharply. "What do you mean?"

I told him what I had discovered. He smiled gently. "That's the code I showed him how to write back when we were at Cambridge. My own invention. He remembered. Well I'll be damned. It's quite antiquated now, but obviously it still works."

He declined a flight in the helicopter, preferring to keep his feet on the ground and opted to take the train. *'Good meditation time'* was how he put it.

Julie and I flew back to the Hall as dawn broke across a threatening looking sky. A cold front was expected in the early afternoon and I didn't want to be caught out.

As it was, the first spattering of rain began just as we wheeled the aircraft back into the hangar.

It was still raining two days later as we pulled into the parking slot at the University. Big drops splashing down, gathering force until soon it seemed as if we were driving through a waterfall. Oldfield had called and asked us to meet him at the University. Cambridge was only one hour's drive away and with the weather conditions, flying made no sense.

Julie and I dashed to the door and were met by the Professor. He led us through the corridors, greeting students and faculty alike until we finally arrived at his office, a small but immaculately kept room full of reference books on computer theory and computer language. He wasted no time once we were settled into our seats.

"What do you know about the way computers operate?" he said to me.

"Not much. Zeros and ones?" I offered. Julie dug me in the ribs sharply and Oldfield just looked at me as if I was an idiot.

"I know you know more than that. Okay. These days with the Internet and cloud storage, we can keep billions and billions of pieces of information in multiple places, that unless you were specifically looking for, and knew the pathway to, you would never find." He paused and crossed to a filing cabinet, opened it and pulled out a bottle of Talisker Single Malt Scotch Whisky. "Unless you're a very good hacker." He poured two glasses handed one each to Julie and myself, then poured a generous amount into his own glass.

"Now you will appreciate that if a company such as yours takes all its financial, employee records, accounts and other business activities, and stores that information in the 'Cloud', it is particularly susceptible to fraud or sabotage. Indeed a certain gentleman has claimed that he could *steal a company blind in three days and leave its books looking balanced'*. It has been done on numerous occasions and the ones we know about are only the people who have been caught. Now we try to prevent 'hacking' from occurring by employing very sophisticated security encryption programs, but sometimes the base system is so out-dated that it is easy to crawl in through a 'backdoor'. One reason why Governments are always being hacked is that they employ security companies with the lowest bid." He took a long draft of scotch and licked his lips appreciatively before turning his gaze on me. "How do you like the whisky?"

"A little peaty for my taste, but interesting."

He nodded and poured more into his glass. "How did you know that there was something wrong with the system?"

"Well, it's more of a gut feeling. I feel there's something wrong and yet there is no information, which serves to further fuel my feeling that there is something wrong. That and the fact that my father was murdered."

He nodded. "I managed to find out the amount of computer storage that had been used, cross-checked this with the programmes running and the data files. There are seven and a half gigabytes unaccounted for. The computer is simply a machine that relies upon being given information. Very sophisticated and complex information to be sure, but information coded by a human being. In this case you can run through the specific area of Rathborne Micro-Electronics and come up with all the answers to questions relevant to business, but if you then compare the data usage to the function, you come up with a missing seven and a half gigabytes." He looked at me with a smile of satisfaction. "That's the simple explanation."

I sat and thought for a moment. "OK. Now you answer me a question, how did you manage to get that information out of the computer, if there are these encryption security devices for obscuring the data?"

He continued to smile, and I began to feel a fool before he answered. This was his territory and I was an outsider with little understanding.

"It's what I do. Most of the programmers in companies such as yours do not have the time or the expertise to dream up complicated protection devices, so tend to stick to a simple code, or use off-the-shelf systems. Once I unravelled that code, the rest was easy. After all, that is one reason why your father kept the files of the board of directors on paper and in his safe." I was about to ask him how he knew when he held up his hand to silence me. "I know because they are not stored anywhere else."

"So what have we got then? A missing seven gigabytes of data and nothing else?"

"Not quite. I think if you check up on the cash transfers of Rathborne you may find that large sums have been given to contractors. The invoicing seems to be correct but the amounts and method are not in keeping with the rest of the system. That was the only thing I could find that didn't seem quite as it should be."

"Would the IT guys in the Company have noticed this?"

"I would think so, if they had not done it themselves in the first place. Don't forget, the IT guys are rather like computers themselves. They will only react and work to a set of instructions that are given to them."

"So you think there is some fraud going on that emanated from the board room?"

"I think fraud is a little strong, because if someone not involved with the deal was asked to run a programme which he knew to be part of a fraud, then odds are that he would not do it."

"So it was either done by one of the board or a person from elsewhere. That being the case, surely the operators would have noticed something a little strange just as you did?"

"Yes, except that the code used to obscure the Rathborne accounts would probably not have been available to IT."

"Was there anything else strange about the thing?"

"No, just the usual games played by bored operators. Crosswords with cryptic clues and that sort of thing."

"Going back to the missing data. Have you any idea what might be on it? Or where it is?"

"That is virtually impossible to say. My guess would be that it is data that links directly in with the accounting system. It could be the explanation as to why the procedures changed for this particular company. It could be anything. As to where to find the missing seven gigabytes of data, I'd look for a flash drive."

"Couldn't you have told us this over the phone, or on Skype?" Julie asked.

"I need your phones so I can encrypt them." He held out his hand. We handed over our iPhones and watched as he plugged in a cord connected to his computer and busied himself for a few minutes at the keyboard, then handed them back to us along with a small thumb drive and a sheet of hand written notes. "On the drive is a security program you need to install on your computers. Instructions are on the sheet."

The conversation carried on into the realms of speculation. Julie had been very quiet throughout and didn't speak except to say goodbye to Oldfield as we left to drive back to Calder Hall. The rain had ceased leaving the roads shiny under the street lamps, reflecting the safety lights in the shop windows.

"What do you think?" Julie said quietly.

"How do you mean?"

"Are you any closer to understanding what is going on with Rathborne?"

"No. I have some more information now, so I'm going to have another crack at Adrian. I'm sure he knows that the accounting system was strange. And I'm sure he is well aware of the amounts paid to these contractors. Now that your father has given me the code, I will he able to find out who received all the money."

Julie lay back in the seat and closed her eyes. It had been a long day. I drove the remainder of the journey in silence while she dozed.

FIVE

"Mr McDougall is away on a trade mission and will not be back for a few days. Do you want me to make an appointment with one of his assistants? I have his office on hold." Jennifer's face pixelated a little on the monitor as she leaned over to retrieve a document.

"Yes, please. Make it as soon as possible."

"Will do. I'll get back to you in a minute." Our daily Skype routines were proving a good and efficient way to work. She went offline and I accepted Adrian's call. He was seething with anger at the knowledge that I had Oldfield go through the computer without his knowing.

"Do we keep back-up servers in a remote location in addition to the office mainframe?" I asked.

"Of course. But they are in a separate security room in the sub-basement. Not offsite." His voice was tight and barely under control, his dislike of me very apparent. But at this moment I really didn't care what he thought of me. The priority was to get to the bottom of this Rathborne mess.

"Are they secure? By that I mean, who has access to them?"

"Only specific members of the board. The Head of IT of course also has access but only with one of us." I didn't say anything for a while. Just let him wonder what I was going to say next. Whilst we sat and looked at each other in silence, Jennifer confirmed by instant message that I had an appointment with a Mr Jonathan Radley at 1500hrs tomorrow afternoon. I hoped the weather would clear as I didn't fancy the drive from the Hall into central London.

"Do you know how Government business loans are paid to companies, Adrian? Obviously I'm thinking about Rathborne in particular."

"There are various methods. Bank guarantees, letters of credit, immediate cash injections, that sort of thing. How the Rathborne loan was handled I have no idea. I've told you before."

"I don't think you did. There is not a lot that gets past you and I cannot envisage my father making any major decisions without consulting you."

"Are you calling me a liar?" he shouted, his voice rising to a choking screech. "Well, are you?"

"I'm not in the mood for histrionics, Adrian. Sooner or later, with or without your help, I am going to find out what this is all about, and if there is a link to my father's murder."

"Now you listen to me," he snarled, leaning over the desk shaking his finger at me. "I have told you before that if you want my resignation you can have it. Just say the word."

"Tempting Adrian, but you know as well as I do that you won't resign. People like you are too afraid of being unemployed. Besides, who is going to pay you the sort of money you get here?" It was a risky thing to say but I was pretty sure I was right. It was time we had a showdown and it was better now than later.

I wanted to know exactly where he stood. My words seemed to have the desired effect and he slowly crumpled back into the seat.

"I'm sorry, Thomas, but there is nothing I can I tell you about the deal. I tried to get your father to tell me, but he just said that when it was over and settled then I would be put in the picture. Until then the facilities of the Group would be available to the Managing Director of Rathborne. He didn't even tell me the man's name. All the instructions we had were via the encrypted email and the data was fed into the computer. We don't even know who did the programming. Occasionally, your father took away one or both of the external storage drives, presumably for security." He looked tired and defeated.

"You said one or both of the storage drives. Are you sure there were two? There is only one in the computer room."

"Yes, positive. One I know was just general accounting data and movement of money, both in and out of the account, and the other I didn't see too clearly, but it seemed to be a personnel file of some description. Your father switched off the computer before I had a chance to see what it was all about." He leaned forward, about to cut off our Skype link when I interrupted.

49

"Adrian. You are the only one who knows how the Group runs. I'm going to have to rely on you heavily over the next few weeks while I clear up this mess. If, after that, you want to leave just let me know." He looked at me for some long seconds before nodding stiffly in agreement.

Was this just a wild goose chase? Was Adrian telling me the truth about external storage drives? There was something about the way he looked down when he was telling me about the external drives that didn't seem genuine.

There were times when I would cheerfully have walked away from all this, but there was, in the background, the vision of my father lying on the slab in the mortuary with the back of his head blown off, and I had to find out why.

Five minutes to three o'clock the following afternoon, saw me in Victoria at the offices of the Department for Business, Innovation and Skills. All Government buildings have the same effect on me. I want to get out as quickly as possible before getting sucked into the morass of forms and papers. For me there is always a strange feel about these places, as if we, the general public, are a necessary nuisance and that if we didn't exist, it would make the running of government far easier for civil servants. So with a feeling of persecution, I squared my shoulders and prepared to do battle.

Once past the reception and up at the sixth floor to Hamish McDougall's office, I was shown into a side room by Mr Radley's secretary and asked to wait. I got the feeling that if Mr Radley decided he was too busy that I could remain in the room forever and nobody would care. Finally the door opened and the secretary motioned me to follow her. Jonathan Radley rose from his desk, stitched a civil service smile on his face and spoke in a slightly lisping manner. He was medium height, close cropped dark hair, and surprisingly light blue eyes, wearing an expensive Saville Row suit and a distinctive salmon pink Leander Rowing Club tie.

"Good afternoon, Mr Gunn, I hope I haven't kept you waiting long. Such a lot to do these days," he said extending his hand. His grip was firm and brief. I noted that his desk was empty and that the secretary hadn't carried any papers or files out with her.

"Good afternoon," I replied, and sat down before he could offer me a chair. "I really wanted to see Mr McDougall, but I understand he is away for a few days."

"That is correct. However, I'm sure I can be of assistance to you. I handle a lot of his more mundane tasks." I decided I could get to dislike this guy quite easily. It seemed that recently there were not many people whom I had met I didn't take an immediate dislike to. I didn't think his remark worthy of an answer, so I just sat looking at him. His voice and manner belied the look of the man. Beneath the suit jacket was an athlete's body, so the rowing club tie wasn't just for show.

"I believe you are interested in the loan to Rathborne Micro-Electronics Limited. How can I help?"

"Yes, but first how did you know that was the question I was going to ask?"

"Your secretary." His reply was prompt and he didn't bat an eyelid, but I was sure he was lying. Jennifer was very careful about not letting information slip. It didn't seem that important, so I just let it pass.

"The reason I'm curious about the loan is that there seems to be some odd goings on as regards the accounts of the Company, regarding the investments and the Government loan structure. As you may or may not know, the accounts are handled automatically by the Gunn Group computer system, presumably until the factory is completed and they have their own set-up. What puzzles me is that I have not been able to contact the Managing Director, even though both my mother and I are directors of the Company. I was wondering whether or not your department could shed any light on the matter. After all there is a sizeable amount of Government money at stake."

"I'm sorry to sound so negative but there is nothing much I can tell you." Radley put on his civil service smile again, the *this is a Government Department, therefore we don't have to communicate with the general public* smile. "As you probably realise the Company is producing products in a very sensitive area and we have careful who we

51

discuss matters with. So...."

"Are telling me that as the owner of the Gunn Group I am not entitled to know what is happening to my own company?" I interrupted, keeping my voice low and tone civil.

He still didn't bat an eyelid. "....so we keep the information level down to a bare minimum," he continued as if he hadn't heard me. "I'm afraid I'm just as much in the dark as you are, but I shouldn't worry unduly if I were you. The department does keep a strict eye on these things and I'm sure that if anything was amiss, then we would know about it." He paused, waiting for me to interject again and when I didn't he continued. "Because of the nature of the product that is going to be manufactured there, there are certain elements covered under the Official Secrets Act. That being the case only by receiving direct instructions from the Managing Director or the Chairman of Rathborne Micro-Electronics Limited, can we release any information. I'm sorry but that is the way it works." He sat back in his chair watching me. He knew as well as I that short of reverting to physical violence there was no way to get any information at all.

"Interesting. You do know that I have a AAA rating under the Official Secrets Act, don't you, or are there some things even you do not have a high enough rating to know." I wanted to see of there was a reaction. There wasn't. And that told me more about him than if he had answered. Mr Jonathan Radley was not Hamish McDougall's assistant, or anything remotely close. It was just a niggling feeling, an instinct that prickled my Special Forces background. "Assuming you don't know anything about Rathborne because of your low rating, how about giving me the basic outline of how a Government loan is effected. Purely hypothetical, of course."

"I'm sorry, we don't deal in hypothetical cases. Every case is real and different; therefore I cannot discuss this subject with you. Now, if you will excuse me I have a very important meeting to attend." He leaned forward to press the intercom button on his desk. Before he could reach it I slammed his wrist down on the edge of the desk, eliciting a grunt from the arrogant bastard.

"Be careful who you fuck with, Mr Radley. Perhaps Mr McDougall will let you see my file, if you have a high enough clearance."

I released his arm and he slowly, hesitantly reached for the button again.

"Miss Heatherton, would you please show Mr Gunn out. He's just leaving," he said, watching me carefully. Disturbingly he showed no sign of pain as he clasped his hands and placed them on the desk.

Once outside I loosened the collar of my shirt and took a deep breath. That meeting was one of the shortest I had attended in months and left me with the same feeling as before.

Frustration.

Every time I tried to find out about this company there was somebody or something in the way. I was determined that the best thing to do was to approach the Fraud Squad, provide them with as much information as possible and see whether or not they would instigate an investigation. Instinct had kept me alive throughout my Army career and now told me that I needed help.

If only Hamish had been around, it would have been different, but he wasn't and I couldn't wait for him to return from wherever he was.

The taxi dropped me off at the Heliport. The meeting with Radley left me feeling frustrated and impotent. I had two choices and I reckoned I would take both of them. The first was to reveal all my suspicions to the Fraud Squad and see what happened, and the second to visit the factory in Northern Ireland and find out how things were progressing and to see if I could discover anything about Des Ascot.

I find that aeroplanes, baths and toilets are great places for thinking. The flight went by quickly and I was landing at the Hall as the sun slowly dipped below the horizon by which time I had the plan of action all mapped out.

Dinner was oddly strained and tense. Mary was in depths of one of her 'turns' and looked pale and ill. Her hands shook. She just nibbled at her food and consumed glass after glass of wine. She didn't want to talk about the Hall, business or anything, just to wallow in her own grief.

Alone in the flat, Julie paced the floor.

"I'm worried about Mary," she said finally. "It's like she's slipped into some bi-polar disorder. Sometimes up and happy, then way down, depressed and almost suicidal."

"I understand it's got to be hard for you, but you don't have to take on her problems."

Julie stopped pacing and sank onto the bed beside me.

"Can't you see? She is the mother I never had." She lay curled in my arms crying softly. I felt useless. I had been so caught up in my own thoughts and actions that I had not seen what was going on around me. I leaned down and kissed her forehead.

"You've had everything all your life and never had to lift a finger. You just don't appreciate anything," she said quietly.

"That's not true. I hadn't realised it until now, but you mean more to me than I could ever have imagined. But you have to understand. You have to bear with me, Julie. Please." She quietened down and finally drifted off to sleep. I covered her with the down comforter and headed for the local pub in search of some quiet time in a noisy place.

I was sitting thinking about everything when a hand touched my shoulder and the friendly voice of Ron, the Farm Manager, broke in on my thoughts.

"Is this conversation private or can anyone join in?" he said.

"Sit down, Ron. It's nice to see you."

"You look a bit down in the mouth. This high life of business tycoon getting to you, is it?"

I smiled at him. We had known each other since we were small boys, when his father ran the farm, and I felt more at ease in his company than I ever had with my father. We were the same age and were like brothers.

"Yeah, you could say that. How's the farm? I haven't been around much lately."

"Can't complain. Prices all over the place, but we're making ends meet. You're father's happy.... Sorry was.... You know what I mean."

"Is the Mini-Cooper still running?"

"Yes of course," he grinned, and laughed. "You think I wouldn't take care of that little beauty?" He leaned forward conspiratorially. "We had

54

some fun with that when we was kids, didn't we?"

"We did indeed. Okay if I use it if I need to?"

"He reached into his pocket and pulled out a set of keys on a classic Mini-Cooper key fob. "Half yours, half mine. That was our bargain. Still is. Always keep both sets of keys on me, just in case."

"Still in the same place?"

"Still in the same place," he echoed. "I've heard the rumours 'bout you over the years, Thomas, so I figured that someday you'd need the use of our little baby."

The Mini-Cooper was an 'S' with a race tuned 1275cc engine and full rally specifications that Ron and I rebuilt from a wreck when we were teenagers. Both our fathers agreed that it would keep us out of trouble during the school holidays, and we scavenged all the parts from local scrap yards, and what we couldn't find we bought with our pocket money. It took two years and many sleepless nights, but on our eighteenth birthdays we set forth into the world in search of adventure and girls.

We discussed the farm, the Hall, the local cricket team and all the other things that friends talk about over a quiet drink in a country pub in mid-summer. Finally, closing time came and we went our separate ways. Him to his plump, happy wife and children; me to a brooding mansion and uncertain future.

To say that my call to the Fraud Squad was a non-event would be an understatement. At first, I thought that I was going to get somewhere, the officer who answered the call was very pleasant and put me through to someone he described as a *'very senior official'*. I started at the beginning and explained my suspicions and fears and all the things that had happened. He was attentive and interested until he put me on hand while he consulted with another *'very senior official'*. He was away for about ten minutes and when he returned I recognised the closed tone of officialdom. He told me as politely as he could, that there was not enough to go on and anyway, if the Government Department dealing with the loan didn't suspect any fraud, why should I bother myself about it. Knowing I was getting nowhere, I decided I wasn't going to argue and hung up.

Radley was behind this I was sure. But why was I being pushed out?

Or was it that I really had nothing except a gut feeling? I laid out all the facts as I saw them and then put myself into the shoes of Radley and the Fraud Squad.

My father had been kidnapped and killed in Northern Ireland.

There was opposition in the Gunn Group to my appointment.

There was no information regarding Rathborne Micro-Electronics.

It was impossible to get hold of the Managing Director.

And a high level Government official refused to discuss the loan.

There was some funny stuff going on with the account and the missing seven gigabytes of data.

Nobody wanted to talk about any of it at all.

There was nothing substantial, but pieced together, the whole business looked very strange. The question that kept recurring in my mind, was why? Why the blocking?

All the facts, as I knew them, kept pinging around in my brain and I kept coming up with the same conclusion. Rathborne Micro-Electronics had something to do with my father's death. There was only one thing left to do. Visit the factory and find out for myself. Firstly, I figured I'd talk it over with Hamish McDougall and get his opinion, he should have returned from his trip by now and I could get Radley out of my hair at the same time.

Adrian Skyped me before I had time to refocus my mind. By his expression, I realised that he knew where I had been and was obviously not too happy about it. I stopped him before he had the chance to open his mouth and told him that I knew what he was going to say, and to save it because I was going to Northern Ireland as soon as possible to sort this whole mess out once and for all. The argument was, therefore, stillborn, as he had no desire for a repeat of the last one. At least, now I knew that I had him where I wanted.

Before he could reply I cut him off and called Simon the manager of the Gunn Group fleet at Norwich Airport.

"Hi Simon, will you get the guys to prepare the Mustang for Monday next week, I'm flying back to Belfast."

"No problem Boss."

I swivelled the chair so that I could see out over the undulating grounds of the Hall. Julie was not going to like it, nor was Mary. But that was something that they would just have to accept. Then I called Jennifer.

"Would call you Hamish McDougall's office and see if he is available for dinner tomorrow night? I know he will be back by then, so don't let his secretary put you off."

SIX

The taxi swung into park place, a small cul-de-sac off St James' Street, at the end of which was a Georgian building with a simple brass plaque beside the door on which was written Royal Overseas League. Hamish was outside talking to a statuesque woman wearing a chic black raincoat and wide brimmed black hat that partially hid her face, who stepped into a waiting taxi as he held the door open.

"Have you been here before?" Hamish asked as we walked up the steps.

"I have but not in a long time. Dad sponsored me for membership when I was eighteen."

"He was very fond of the club. It is away from all the other more snobby clubs. They've made some very nice changes, I think you'll like it." He was right. The atmosphere was pleasant and reasonably informal, the food and the service good. Our general conversation continued over the meal of smoked salmon, veal Marsala and a fresh fruit dessert, washed down with an ample supply of Pietrantonj Montepulciano D'Abruzzo 2007. One of the things I liked about Hamish was that he went to places he enjoyed and not for the status value and ate and drank what he liked, not what was considered suitable.

When we were finally settled in the lounge with our coffee and brandy, he asked me what he could do.

"I'm assuming Radley told you about our meeting," I said carefully. He nodded. "I'm concerned there is fraud in connection with the loan for Rathborne Micro-Electronics." I went on to relate all the facts including my fruitless interview with a member of the Fraud Squad. Hamish sat listening intently and I warmed to my subject, telling him of Mary's strange behaviour.

When I finished he sat for a while, taking it all in. I had no idea what he was thinking, but I hoped that whatever he had to say would be the result of careful analysis of the facts as I had presented them. He was about to reply when a waiter approached.

"Telephone call for you Mr McDougall."

Hamish thanked him, apologised to me and followed the waiter. I finished the rest of my brandy, poured more coffee and waited. It would be easy to relax in this velvet lined quiet trap, but there was an uneasiness that invaded every part of me. The same instinct that used to warn of bombs, or ambushes, and the same instinct I had ignored to my cost those years ago. In this age of mobile phones, why did Hamish have to answer a telephone call on a landline?

He returned a few minutes smiled briefly and sat down rather stiffly. There was a subtle change in his demeanour, as if he didn't want to be sitting with me, and my uneasiness increased.

He cleared his throat as if he was about to give a speech. "Now to recap. You feel that an investigation is necessary regarding the Government loan procedures to Rathborne Micro-Electronics, right?"

"I think it's a no-brainer."

"Certainly it would be laudable to protect the public purse, but on the minus side, instigating a full scale investigation is both expensive and time consuming." He had lapsed into a condescending, patronising and aloof tone.

"I'm not asking for a full scale investigation, I'm asking for access to the files regarding the loan."

Hamish tilted his head on one side pursing his lips. "That's a bit of a problem. You see there are only a limited number of people allowed that access, and unfortunately you are not one of them."

"Which is absurd as I own the Gunn Group, of which Rathborne Micro-Electronics is a subsidiary."

Hamish placed his fingertips together and touched them to his lips nodding slowly. "I do see your point, but there are procedures and strict rules regarding the distribution of sensitive Government documents, and you don't qualify."

"Really," I said sarcastically. Somebody had reined Hamish in and once again I realised that he had no real authority or power. "I am flying to Belfast on Monday morning to start my own investigation."

"If it helps you find peace-of-mind, by all means go. Perhaps I can dig around and see what I come up with." He smiled, again patronisingly, his eyes narrow and cold. "Listen, if I may give you some advice, Mary has had a very rough time, she needs you, don't do anything that may harm her." He leaned over and patted my forearm. Another patronising gesture as if he was talking to a small boy. "I don't mean to lecture you but it is possible to get so wrapped up in your own thoughts and feelings that others are shut out. That can be very distressing."

"That sounded more like a warning than a lecture, Hamish. You know far more than you are telling me."

"I've been a friend of your family for an awful long time, Thomas, perhaps you do need warning." He stood, and I rose with him. "No, don't get up, finish your coffee. The Porter will get you a taxi when you're ready."

I finished my coffee slowly feeling more like a rat in a trap than a guest in a comfortable club. The very walls seemed to be watching me and I grew very aware that the machinations of Government were not designed to help the citizens of the land.

Feeling the need for some air, I had the taxi driver drop me off at the Embankment, near Cleopatra's Needle. Sometimes I came here just to be able to look out across an expanse of water and just pretend I was back on the catamaran in Gozo with Julie and not a care in the world.

Unless you have experienced a low velocity round passing close by and nicking your cheek, you'd think you'd been stung by a wasp. But I knew the sound and touch all too well, and dropped to the ground as the second shot ricocheted off the base of the obelisk and spun harmlessly away into the Thames.

The pit of my stomach tightened into a knot and my heart seemed about to beat its way out of my chest.

The first miss was not pure chance.

It was a deliberate.

Just a nick on my cheek.

The second, a warning shot.

I ducked behind a low wall scanning the buildings on the other side of the Thames, not that I expected to see anything. The gunman would have gone by now. I straightened and turned to see a Policeman standing staring at me.

"Is there anything the matter, sir?" he said calmly.

"Just turned my ankle," I said as conversationally as I could.

"Have you been drinking by any chance, sir?"

"A couple of glasses of wine and a brandy at lunch. Broke my ankle a few years ago playing rugby and the ligaments are shot."

"I suggest you go home and sleep it off, sir." The brandy on my breath had obviously convinced him that I had just had a liquid lunch. I apologised, he nodded and went on his way. Somewhere in the back of my mind I had a niggling suspicion that whoever missed me, did so on purpose.

"I can't believe it," Julie said when I told her what happened. "Surely there must be some marks where the bullets hit."

"Oh, there are. One on me and a scratch on the pedestal of Cleopatra's Needle, but the spent rounds would have disappeared to the bottom of the Thames. This on my cheek is just the thinnest of touches. The sniper picked the spot so that if he missed, no bullets would be found."

"But that is all just guesswork. How do you know that you were shot at? Perhaps there was some kid throwing stones."

"I do know what a low velocity round sounds like."

"All I'm saying is that you've been under a lot of pressure recently. You could be mistaken."

I crossed to the walk in closet opened the door and went to the far wall, pressed a hidden button and opened the wall safe. Inside were the only tangible pieces of evidence of my service in the British Army. Campaign medals, my Parachute Regiment wings and beret and photographs taken in Afghanistan and Iraq.

"This is my past life," I said laying everything on the bed for Julie to see. "You know I was in the Army, you don't know the full story."

Julie picked up the photographs and slowly looked at them. "I told you when we first met, I do my research. But you're right. I don't know everything about you."

"I joined the Parachute Regiment as a Private soldier, then was commissioned and spent my first tour in Iraq commanding a platoon. Then I was deployed to Afghanistan as part of the Special Forces Support Group." I pointed to the photograph of myself with three other soldiers standing beside a Puma helicopter. "That was taken just prior to our last mission in Lashkar Gah. I was the only survivor," I said trying to keep the bad images out of my mind. "I spent four months in intensive care, have a small plate in my skull that sometimes sets off the metal detectors in airports, and a boat load of bad memories."

Julie stared at the photographs for a long minute, seeing a life full of secrets I had tried to forget, but the past never leaves and now I was going to use that past to discover the present.

"What are you going to do?" Julie said eventually.

"Belfast on Monday, but tonight I need to see an old colleague."

"You're not going to tell me who, are you?"

I shook my head. "Not now."

"I want to come with you to Belfast, it'll make your visit seem more family oriented than investigative." She smiled mischievously. "I like adventure. Remember?"

"You better understand what we could be up against." I went back to safe in the walk-in closet and pulled out my Glock 19 Gen4, two magazines that each held fifteen rounds and a burn phone, one of six I had stashed.

Julie watched carefully. "You're serious about being shot at, aren't you?"

"Very."

I kissed her, tasting her light lip-gloss and feeling the desire and the need to stay, but there were a few things I needed to do tonight.

Tonight I was going back in time.

Tonight I am that bastard killing machine.

Tonight all my old instincts and training were going to be used for my family, and not for a Government who didn't give a crap. I'd been screwing around pretending to be a tycoon long enough, now I had to do what I was most comfortable doing.

Today I had been sent a warning and a calling card and I knew just where to go and who to see.

There was no doubt in my mind that the Hall was under surveillance so I used a route I discovered many years ago when I was rummaging around in the kitchen wine cellar playing feudal ten year old child-games. A passageway which I knew nobody else was aware, the entrance hidden behind one of the cobweb covered dusty wine racks that led two hundred metres to the tower folly near the lake.

It was a lot smaller than I remembered, only a metre and a half tall by a metre wide, dark, dusty and stinking of mould. At the end was an even smaller door, the key to which I had concealed in a brick on the left side over twenty years ago. It was still there and unlocked the door surprisingly easily and quietly. The Tower had no direct view of the house, so there was no way a surveillance team would use it, however caution, silence and speed are the primary elements of any covert operation. The door squeaked a little as I opened it just far enough to slip through and quickly check the tower. A single curving stone staircase led to the upper level gallery, which was empty. I shut the door, locked it and made sure there was no sign anybody had been in the tower before slipping out into the dark moonless night.

It was two miles cross-country in the opposite direction of the village to the small ramshackle looking barn where Ron and I kept the Mini-Cooper. It took two hours to cover the distance, following the tall hedgerows that skirted the sugar beet and maize fields, through small woods and eventually reaching the barn tucked into the corner where the woods bordered a fallow field.

For a further ten minutes I skirted the barn to ensure nobody was watching and then went inside.

Inside, the barn belied its rough exterior. Ron had kept it just as I remembered, a clean workshop that was a joyful trip back to the excitement and adventure of our childhood. The car lay under a dust cover and looked immaculate. It started immediately and I grinned to myself, sitting feeling the small leather bound steering wheel and specially designed gearshift, before getting out and opening the barn door.

On the open road the little car was fun, and after a few minutes throwing it around the country lanes, I settled back to the legal speed limit and drove toward north London. I was headed to Muswell Hill to a place I knew well, and a former colleague who now worked as a stunt co-ordinator for film and television.

The Glock felt a little odd. It had been a while since I wore a shoulder holster but as the miles ticked away I barely noticed it, my mind focused on the meeting ahead and events of the past.

Danny had invited me to join him on a location hunt in Eire (the Republic of Ireland), for a film he was working on as the second unit director and stunt co-ordinator. I was fresh out of hospital and thinking of flying out to the Mediterranean island of Capri to convalesce on my fifty-seven foot catamaran. Danny convinced to me to take the trip; ten days of relaxing and drinking Guinness in the country of his birth, so we decided to make a holiday of it and drove his old BMW 730i to Liverpool, caught the ferry to Dublin and drove across the country to the small village in Sligo.

We had forged a friendship in the cauldron of Afghanistan. He was a Sergeant in 22 SAS and we had worked together on several operations, and he led the team that rescued me before the Taliban could return to finish their bloody task.

For days we drove around Sligo searching for suitable locations during the day and drinking and singing in the local pubs at night.

Then one day everything changed.

The owner of Templar Castle House Hotel, Roland Macafee, was standing in his study staring out across the rolling grounds of Sligo close to the border of Northern Ireland. The house had been in his family for hundreds of years, set in one thousand acres of pristine land, where the air was pure enough to support lichen in the trees. He had renovated the old house, turned most of it into a boutique hotel and employed ten workers from the local village on the farm.

As we entered his study, Roland turned from the window. His face was pale and the hand holding the glass of Jameson was shaking.

"Drink?" He crossed to the open drinks cabinet before we could answer and poured two generous shots of Jameson. "Please sit down." We took the

glasses, sat and looked at each as Roland turned back to stare out across the grounds. "This is very difficult for me," he said slowly. "This afternoon I had a visit from the IRA. They told me that they know who you are and want you gone from here by tomorrow morning."

Roland turned back to us, took a long draught of whiskey and poured more.

"We are no longer in the Army. Don't they know that?" Danny queried, puzzled.

"They mentioned you both by name and especially you, Danny. Called you a traitor and if you're not gone, they'll make sure you both leave in a body bag." He stared down into his glass. "I'm sorry, but I have to ask you to leave."

"They threatened you and your family, didn't they?"

"Yes."

"We understand, Roland. We'll leave tonight."

"Thank you. I'm sorry."

We packed and left just before midnight, driving south to Rosslare to catch the ferry to Pembroke. We drove fast, throwing caution to the wind, knowing that distance and time were our friends. Danny handled the big car easily on the narrow country roads, thankfully empty at this time of night and began to sing softly.

"Over in Killarney, many years ago
My mother sang a song to me
In tones so sweet and low."

I smiled and joined in, singing softly as the car rolled fast through the corners, tyres screeching.

"Just a simple little ditty
In her good old Irish way
And I'd give the world if she could sing
That song to me this day.
Too-ra-loo-ra-loo-ral, Too-ra-loo-ra-li,
Too-ra-loo-ra-loo-ral, hush now don't you cry!
Too-ra-loo-ra-loo-ral, Too-ra-loo-ra-li,
Too-ra-loo-ra-loo-ral, that's an Irish lullaby."

Then burst out laughing, enjoying the adventure and reliving our past lives when life was precarious and exciting.

At two o'clock in the morning, I drove slowly down the street I was looking for and parked about fifty metres from the four storey Victorian house. During some down-time between tours in Afghanistan, I helped renovate the house starting with the basement kitchen that led out into the sheltered back garden and on up to the attic where Danny and I had installed a hidden gun safe. But that was a while ago, and I wasn't going to let friendship get in the way of what I had to do.

Slipping out of the car I quickly made my way to the narrow alley between the houses that led to the back garden, then dialled a number on the 'burn-phone'.

"Thomas?"

"Hi Danny. Nice job yesterday."

"Thank you. You want a meet?"

"That's why I'm calling."

"Usual place, in about say two hours?"

"Suits me."

The phone went dead and I took out the SIM card, smashed the phone and buried it in the neighbour's flowerbed, then waited in the shadows. Five minutes passed before I saw a shadow move quickly down the garden path to where I was waiting. The gate swung open slowly.

"Not a flicker, Danny," I whispered seeing him tense. "Why don't we go inside?"

"I should have known you'd find a way out of the Hall."

"Yes you should."

He turned slowly and I could see the familiar jutting jaw and flattened nose of my friend.

"Still got the Glock I see."

"Always."

He smiled and walked back to the French windows that led into the kitchen and the small sitting room where we used to sit and drink Jameson Irish Whiskey, and listen to old Caruso recordings.

"No need for the gun, Thomas." He crossed to the drinks cabinet and poured two generous measures of Jameson Irish Whiskey, handed me one and sat down in one of the comfortable armchairs and raised his glass.

"Sláinte."

"Cheers," I replied, watching him carefully. "Whose idea was it to take a shot at me."

"That would be me. Only way to get your attention."

"And what were you planning if I *had* met you at the rendezvous?"

"A chat. But here is as good a place as any. I trust you weren't followed."

"Not a chance."

"I wouldn't be too sure about that Thomas. You remember the lads from Section 4 don't you?"

"I thought they called themselves *'The Increment'* or some other such dumb name."

"That's some wannabe's idiot invention, but they are dangerous bastards. They used to be the Government's own personal hit team."

"And now?"

"They've gone deeper undercover. Nobody knows who they're working for." He paused and tossed down the remainder of his whisky before refilling our glasses. "Listen mate, I still keep an ear to the ground, do a little job once in a while, and the word's out that certain people in high places don't want you sticking your nose where they think it doesn't belong."

"Hence the shot."

"They don't know I missed on purpose. And if they did, we wouldn't be talking right now. You'd be attending my funeral."

"Why help me?"

"I don't hurt my friends. Besides, there are other people who want you to figure out why your father was killed."

"Like?"

"You know I can't tell you that." He sighed heavily. "I'm on your side, Thomas. A silent partner if you like. Nobody can know."

I nodded slowly. Danny and I had been through a few tough times, a few rowdy times and had a bond that was based on trust. If it hadn't been, I probably would have shot him in the kneecap before asking questions.

"I'm off to Belfast on Monday."

"You may be needing that," he said pointing to the Glock resting on the side table. "Remember what happened last time. The IRA have long memories. I'll make sure security looks the other way."

"You can still do that?"

He shrugged and the grin was back. "As I said, I do a few little jobs every now and then. With a name like Danny Sullivan, the boys in Whitehall like to keep me on the payroll."

"From what I see you don't need the money. Bond films must pay well."

"True, I'm building myself a little house and stables out in Oxfordshire. For my retirement you understand. Films are just play acting, this is real, so be careful."

"I got the message. And nothing you do is *'little'*."

He laughed and raised his glass. "You're right, but what's life for except for living." He sighed and stared into the glass for a moment and became sombre. "You got a girl?"

"I do."

"Know much about her?"

"Enough."

"Really?"

"Off limits, Danny."

He shrugged. "It's your life." He stared into his glass, tossed off the last mouthful and looked at me his eyes dark and full of emotion. "We're family, Thomas, remember that. I have your back, just as you have mine."

I picked up the bottle, filled our glasses and looked at my friend.

"Always. But you know I'll kill you if you betray our trust."

Danny touched his glass to mine. "Likewise." He grinned, his eyes alive with mischief. "Just like old times."

"Indeed. I need a resupply of burn phones."

"No problem."

SEVEN

The approach to Belfast city airport is straightforward. There is only one runway. Surprisingly the weather was clear, but unsurprisingly rain was expected in the late afternoon.

As we crossed the Irish Sea, Julie dozed and I sat listening to Air Traffic Control until they gave me instructions to join the ILS (Instrument Landing System) approach for runway 22. The runway was long enough for big commercial jets, so no problem for the agile Mustang.

Julie stirred, yawned and rubbed her eyes. "We there yet?"

"Nearly. About fifteen minutes."

"Your buddy going to be here?"

"Probably not." I told her about my meeting with Danny, but left out the details of our past dealings as they were covered under the Official Secrets Act.

"Bet he's not happy to have me tagging along."

"Not his call."

Air Traffic Control interrupted. "Victor Bravo tower you're clear to land Runway Two Two. Wind Two Five Zero at Five."

I selected full flap, nudged the speed brake a little and lowered the landing gear as we angled down to the runway on the edge of city. The early morning sun glistened off the waters of Belfast Lough, and on the port side of the aircraft, Stormont Castle stood out an impressive landmark south of the city. The little jet touched down just beyond the threshold.

"Victor Bravo turn left taxiway 'A' and proceed to the ramp."

I let the jet roll fast down to the end of the runway then braked, turning left onto the taxiway that led to the General Aviation parking ramp, where a 'ramper' holding orange-coloured paddles directed me to a parking spot. Behind him and to the left I saw a figure, dressed in the uniform of Airport Security, who I knew wasn't who he seemed to be.

Danny must have flown him in last night, true to his word of watching my back. I wondered if Whitehall knew, and what they had planned. He was all business, checking the aircraft before leading us to the security checkpoint in the small General Aviation building and swiftly searching our bags, without once giving any sign of knowing me. At this moment I really began to fully realise this wasn't a game I was playing.

"Thank you sir, ma'am," the man said in a broad Belfast accent. "Enjoy your stay." He looked at me and then glanced casually at a man standing next to a cab just outside the door. Just a slight upward nod of the head that no one else would notice, told me what I needed to know. The hairs stood up on the back of my neck and it was all I could do to act like a normal businessman preoccupied with his own world.

It was a ten-minute drive to the Stormont Hotel near the main gates to Stormont Castle. I paid the 'taxi-driver' and followed the porter who carried our suitcases into the hotel lobby. Within minutes we were inside breathing a sigh of relief.

Julie flopped onto the belt. "I was sure that security man was going to find the gun," she whispered.

I pulled it out of the waistband of my pants where I had it tucked into the small of my back beneath my dark blue blazer, and slid it under the pillow.

Julie reached up and pulled me down onto the bed, her nostrils flared and mouth slightly open. "You need to relax and I need sex," she said huskily.

"Anything for the lady."

"I'm no lady right now."

We made love urgently, passionately, the tension of the weeks and days vanishing in the moment. It was the first time we had been alone since returning to England and Julie was going to make the most of it.

The rental car was waiting at the front entrance at exactly nine in the morning, as I had ordered and we drove to Dundonald to visit the factory site of Rathborne Micro-Electronics.

As we approached the site I was surprised to see that the construction

70

was not as big as I expected, considering the amount of invested capital. It should, by my reckoning, have been a hell of a sight bigger.

Again the inconsistency.

The old man would never willingly have gone along with this. The main manufacturing building was already complete save the internal fixtures and fittings, with what seemed an odd square annex on one side with no windows and a large roller door. I parked the car and walked over to what I took to be the construction office. As usual with most building sites, the office was empty.

I sat down at the desk and looked through the drawers.

"Should you be doing that?" Julie asked nervously.

"I am a director of this company."

"Good point."

"Who the hell are you and what the hell are you doing," came an angry American accented voice from the doorway.

"Thomas Gunn, owner of the Gunn Group and a Director of Rathborne Micro-Electronics," I said, staring at the slightly paunchy but well built man. "Who the hell are you."

"I run this site. Whaddaya want?" he said, his stubble-covered chin pushed forward aggressively.

"You may have heard that my father, who started this project, was murdered recently. I'm here to find out what the hell is going on."

The mention of murder and the implied accusation that it may have something to do with the project, caused a slight change in the man's attitude, and a nervous flicker of his eyes from me to Julie and back to me.

"Listen. I was told that I only discuss business with the Boss."

"I just told you my father was murdered and I *am* the Boss."

"I don't know nuthin' about that. I do what Mr Ascot tells me."

"What's your name?"

"Boyd," he grinned unpleasantly. "You can call me Mister."

I ignored him, and continued to search through the drawers, throwing papers across the desk. "Where can I find Mr Ascot?"

"You say you own this outfit, if you don't know, how do you expect me to know? He just calls me on the cell every now and again. Tells me what to do." He stood looking at me and I knew he was lying.

"I don't see a computer in the office. Where is it?"

"I use a laptop."

"Where is it?"

"None of your business."

I picked up a receipt from the desk and held it up for him to see. "I think it is, especially as this is a receipt for a Unisys mainframe computer system, four laptops, four smartphones and four iPads, all paid for by Gunn Group money."

"Listen, that ain't me, that's Mr Ascot."

"Then where are the computers?"

"Dunno. Better ask him. I do as I'm told," he said sulkily.

"How did you get this job? A mainframe computer is a hard piece of equipment to miss." I pointed to the odd looking square building. "Is it in there?"

He didn't answer, looked down and shuffled his feet nervously.

"You're American, what are you doing here?"

"Mr Ascot wanted me personal. He pays me to make sure all the work is done good. OK?"

"So you run the whole thing here? Pay the bills for materials, wages, all that stuff."

"No, Mr Ascot does that. Just sends me cash to pay incidentals. Now like I said, you wanna know, you ask him."

"Isn't it odd that a well-known Irish contractor isn't employed on this job?"

"As I said, ask Mr Ascot."

"Fine. We'll take a look around, but first I want Mr Ascot's mobile number."

He didn't say a word, just turned and walked out of the office.

"Not the finest example of a fellow countryman," Julie said wryly. "You are right, something about this whole business smells very stinky."

We followed him out of the office and saw him disappear around the corner of the main manufacturing building, and a moment later heard the sound of a car starting up and being driven away at speed.

We wandered through the buildings that seemed a complete shambles, and any discussions with the small Irish labour force were none existent as if they had been warned against talking to strangers.

At the side of the factory was a large area under excavation, as if it was to be a huge underground parking area and another area beyond that looked more like a racetrack than anything else.

This didn't seem like a factory for the manufacturing of micro-electronics, more like heavy industry.

We went back to the office and rummaged around in the desk but couldn't find anything, so drove back to the hotel for lunch before driving into Belfast for an appointment with an official of the Northern Ireland Department of Enterprise Trade and Investment.

"Mr Gunn, Miss....?" the short, overweight amiable man in the Department stuttered.

"Sutton."

"Right, Miss Sutton. My name is Johnson, I had a call from Whitehall, Mr McDougall's office, what can I do for you?"

"As you know I have taken over the Gunn Group of companies and there are some questions about one of our subsidiaries, Rathborne Micro-Electronics, that is being built in Dundonald."

"Yes I am aware of the company, a very large investment and superb for the economy here. Hopefully it will help keep the City Airport open with all the business it will generate," he said enthusiastically. "We really need the jobs."

"I think there maybe something untoward happening. Fraud perhaps," I said as casually as I could. "There is a lot of money unaccounted for."

"Really. I'm not aware of anything untoward. But there was something I saw a day or so ago that I thought was odd." He typed with surprising dexterity with his fat fingers on the computer keyboard. "Here it is. A few days ago we received letter from the President of an American company requesting information about buying the stock of Rathborne Micro-Electronics. We of course referred the matter to your Head Office. I'm surprised you are not aware of the offer. He apparently heard that the company was in financial trouble after the death of Sir Ivan."

"I am certainly not aware," I said, trying to sound as astonished as I thought I should be. The truth is nothing astonished me anymore, it just fed into the growing conviction that Julie and I had been thrown into something far bigger than we thought. "Just to whom at Head Office was this information to be passed?"

"Well, actually, according to my records, a Des Ascot who apparently denied that there was such a financial problem and said that the company was certainly not for sale."

"May I enquire as to the name of this American who wants to buy Rathborne?" I asked.

"Well that would be most irregular. You see, matters such as this are most confidential and are not supposed to be released without sanction from Whitehall," he said uncomfortably.

"From Mr McDougall's office no doubt? The very office that set up this meeting we are having." I was careful to keep my tone friendly, if insistent. Julie shot me a warning glance.

"Well, I don't know. It's most irregular." He scratched his chin and slowly, typed quickly and nodded his head. "I... well... excuse me if I pop out for a moment, if you understand." He looked at me, nodded to the screen, got up and left the office, closing the door behind him. I heard him talking to his secretary, walked around the desk and stared at the screen. Julie leaned over my shoulder. It was a letter from a company called De Costas Automotive with an address in California. It was indeed an introduction letter with an offer to buy Rathborne Micro-Electronics, just as Johnson said, and it was signed, Samuel De Costas.

"We need this. Move," Julie said, pushing me aside typing quickly. The printer on the other side of the office clicked and rapidly spat out two copies of the letter. Then Julie typed quickly, accessing an email account that didn't seem to have anything to do with a Government Department, and sent a copy to her father's email address.

"How do you know all the stuff?"

She smiled. "My father's a computer whizz remember. I did pick some things up as a child. Get the copies from the printer before Johnson gets back."

I folded the copies, slipped them into my pocket then we returned to our seats just as the door opened and our helpful friend returned. He sat down, saw that his screen was just as he left it, and smiled briefly.

"I had dealings with Sir Ivan, Mr Gunn, I was very shocked and saddened to hear of his murder. If there is anything I can do." He slid a business card across the desk, which I picked up and slipped into my inside pocket.

"What are you thinking?" Julie asked as we drove back to the hotel.

"That I'm missing something that's right under my nose."

"Like what?"

"Like something so obvious nobody would notice."

Julie looked across at me as if the same thought occurred to her. "I know what you mean. At least I think I know what you mean."

"No way it can be that simple," I said as I pulled the car into a parking lot and sat gripping the steering wheel before taking out a pen and Johnson's business card. He had written his private cell phone number on the back and below it I wrote DES ASCOT in capital letter and then DE COSTAS. There it was. Des Ascot was a stupidly simple anagram of De Costas. It seemed a long shot but I knew I was right. Now the missing computer information fitted. It would contain information about the mysterious Ascot/De Costas.

"So if Ascot is De Costas, why write a letter about the company being in financial trouble?" Julie asked echoing my thoughts. "Unless your investigation has triggered unwanted interest. If that was the case then by alerting the authorities and letting the fraud, or whatever it is, be uncovered, that would leave De Costas free to buy out Rathborne for a song."

"Well it's a theory. But we have no proof." I pulled out of the parking lot and we drove back to the hotel. There were so many unanswered questions.

We ate an early dinner in our suite having called Mary to check on her, and then I swapped to the burn phone and called Danny.

"My boys looking after you?" he said cheerfully.

"Indeed they are, but their tailing technique could use a little re-training."

"I'll let them know. I had them put an extra weapon in your bag. Untraceable. Just in case."

"You are thorough."

"I try to be."

"Can you run a check on two names? Des Ascot and Samuel De Costas. Americans."

"Already ran the first one, didn't come up with anything. And before you ask, his is the name on Rathborne Micro-Electronics."

"I wasn't asking, I figured you'd unravel that one. It's the second one that interests me."

"Why?" he asked and I could picture him leaning forward in anticipation.

"I think they are one and the same."

"Interesting. I'll see what I can do."

"We'll be back in Norfolk tomorrow midday."

Julie watched me carefully, thinking. "I've heard of De Costas before. About a year ago I was doing a commercial for a new exotic super-car and his name came up. I thought I knew it from somewhere." She paused deep in thought.

"And?" I asked impatiently.

"Bit of a recluse. Mega bucks." She glanced at me sheepishly. "Well let's say probably not as rich as your father, and now I guess you. Don't know anything else but I'm sure a little research online will help." She pulled out her iPad mini and was soon searching through the web for anything she could find.

The hotel phone rang softly and I picked it up watching Julie scrolling through web pages. There was only the sound of breathing on the other end of the line.

"Who is this?"

"Boyd, we met this morning. I got information that will interest you." I recognised the voice of the man in charge of the Rathborne construction.

"What information."

"It's gonna cost you. I'll meet you at the office in two hours." The receiver clicked and then reverted to the dial tone as he rang off. I replaced the receiver slowly.

"Who was that?" Julie asked without taken her eyes off the iPad.

"Boyd, from the site. He wants to meet in two hours."

Julie looked up sharply. "It's a set-up."

"I know. But I have to go."

"Not without me you don't."

"Do you know how to use a gun?" I asked pointedly.

She held her hand out and I passed her the Glock. Quickly she slipped out the magazine, checked the chamber and dismantled the gun. Then just as quickly re-assembled it and handed it back to me.

"Self-defence training. It included a handgun course." She shrugged. "A girl alone in New York, once mugged twice shy, third time the bastard's dead."

"Okay. You can come." I unzipped my suitcase and found the hidden handgun, a Beretta BU9 Nano nine millimetre with two magazines each holding six rounds and a box of spare rounds. "Here." I tossed the gun over to her, then a magazine.

"Ladies gun," she snorted unappreciatively.

"It'll still do the job and it's small enough for you to conceal." There was still much I didn't know about Julie, and I was beginning to wonder what she wasn't telling me.

A dull glow of light shone from the grimy office windows. I parked the car, switched off the engine and lights, and waited. Somewhere behind I knew Danny's boys were watching, covering our backs. A slight movement in the office caught my eye.

"He's there," I said to Julie. "Stay behind me and a little to my right."

I headed over towards the office, Julie following behind. The door was open and I could see Boyd sitting at the desk looking at a sheaf of papers.

I stopped short of the door.

"I'm here Boyd, what's this information you have?" I asked just loud enough for him to hear. He stopped what he was doing and looked up.

"Come in."

I signalled Julie to stay in the shadow and stepped towards the door just as Boyd brought a big Colt Magnum up from behind the desk.

The first round slammed into the wooden doorframe where my head would have been had I stayed still. The second whined harmlessly across the site and buried itself into a heap of sand. I fired hitting him in the upper chest, spinning him around and throwing him back against the wall. My next shot put a neat hole in his forehead and took the back of his head clean off, spraying a red mist of blood and brain against the wall. He slid slowly to the floor.

This wasn't the way I wanted it to go. I needed him alive so I could pump him for information, but I wasn't going to argue with a Magnum.

There was the sharp crack of the Beretta, and I leapt outside to see Julie taking aim at one of Danny's boys, who had the good sense to take cover.

"Julie, stop," I shouted and she turned, pale with fear, the gun pointed directly at me. "Okay. Take a deep breath and hand me the gun." She gave it to me slowly, shaking. Danny's man approached us.

"I'm Paul. We have to leave, now. The police will be here in no time. Follow me keep your lights off. You know the drill."

We followed him back to my rental car and he made us follow him out through a back gate onto a dirt road without using our lights and slowly we made our way in a circuitous route back to the main road. Then stopped at the side of the road.

Paul walked back to us and leaned in through the window. "I need the guns, both of them." I handed them over including the magazines and my shoulder holster. "Nobody followed you to the site, I made sure of that, and we'll scrub the phone logs both here and at the hotel."

"Thanks Paul."

"Thank Danny, I owe him. Next time you see me, you may not be thanking me. Gypsy's warning mate." He walked back to his car and drove away.

"What did he mean?" Julie said hesitantly, still shaking.

"Let's just say it's a fluid situation. Nothing is what it seems. And you're lucky he didn't shoot you."

"Can we go home now?" She managed a weak smile.

EIGHT

While Julie slept I lay awake trying to figure out this puzzle that just seemed to dive off in another direction every time I thought I had it figured.

We checked out at eight in the morning and were airborne by nine.

Such a lot had happened that I needed the time to relax and think of the next move. To wonder whether I should tell Hamish anything of what had happened. Somebody was obviously logging my every move and just as obviously, wanted me out of the way permanently. I was on the right track and either had, or very nearly had, the information to blow this whole mystery. I was sure that Samuel De Costas or Ascot or whatever his true name was, would be able to supply the answer.

I didn't know whom I could trust, so decided that the best tactic would be to keep quiet and just do some gentle probing.

By the time I thought all this through about a dozen times, it was time to call up Norwich airport for landing instructions. As this was the aircraft's home base the controller recognised the identifying letters and cleared me straight in on runway 09.

There was very little traffic, just a few Piper Warriors on the circuit and a helicopter making practice approaches.

Once on the ground, I handed the Mustang over to Simon and the ground crew, and with my arm around Julie, walked over to the car.

"Would you call your father and ask him if he would drive up to the Hall this afternoon."

She looked at me a little taken aback. "Why on earth would he do that? He doesn't even like driving to the airport. You know that."

"He can take the train then. Henderson can meet him at the station. I need to talk to him face-to-face, not on the phone or Skype."

At first I thought she was going to refuse, but instead she said. "If you tell me what's on your mind?"

"Remember those loose papers we found in the safe? The one with

Des Ascot's name on it?"

"Yes."

"Attached to it was a note with what I thought were clues to a crossword puzzle. I didn't think about it because my father was always doing crosswords and even created his own which he submitted to the local paper. I think he called himself *The Question Meister* or some ridiculous thing."

"What's that got to do with anything?"

"When your dad was going through the mainframe, he said he found some stuff that he said were bored IT guys playing games on company time."

Julie sat up in her seat, iPhone already in her hand. "So you think that was your Dad's way of pointing to where the missing data is."

"Yeah. Not missing. Hidden."

"Dad, it's Julie. Thomas needs to talk to you." She handed me the phone and after a brief conversation, he agreed to be at the Hall by two in the afternoon.

I was glad and surprised that she had recovered from the horror of seeing somebody shot. She had managed to sleep on the flight and looked pale, but in control.

Back at the Hall we checked on Mary who seemed to be in one of her positive and happy moods, then went to the flat. The papers where I'd left them and as Julie turned on the desktop computer, I found the sheet with the attached note.

"See what I mean. Above Ascot's name he wrote *'Top American'*, and on the note these phrases; *'is yet kindlier to our taxi drivers'*, then *'obnoxiously evil road'* and lastly *'the reverse is a true'*.

We both looked at the phrases and then Julie typed them in upper case into a Word document. On their own, they did not make sense and looked just like cryptic crossword puzzle clues. At the bottom of Des Ascot's main personnel sheet, a list of his previous work record, was a scrawled a reference code: OR 443 121/TQ followed by another cryptic crossword puzzle clue, *'Olympic swimmer's key stroke'* scrawled in pencil as if my father was thinking about crossword puzzle clues.

"Let's start with these companies Ascot worked for," Julie offered, typing the names into Google. They were all public shell companies. "That's interesting. Ascot's like his résumé. Fake. What the hell is he up to."

"There are a lot of ways to use shell companies, some of them legal, some of them not. Some are also used by Governments to hide large transfers of money into covert operations and all sorts of other shady dealings. In the interests of national security, of course."

"Of course. You would know something about that."

"We used shell companies to pump money to informants in Iraq, Iran and Afghanistan, not to mention some of our allies we wanted to keep a close eye on."

"We're still no closer to finding out who he is. He's not listed on any of these shell companies; in fact they are as mysterious as he is. The only difference is that they exist, and he doesn't."

Professor Oldfield arrived at the Hall in the early afternoon, and was shown to the flat.

"I'm glad to see you Dad," Julie said hugging him briefly.

"Me too," he said crisply, giving her a perfunctory kiss on the cheek. He shook my hand briefly. "Show me what you have."

I showed him the page where I had written out the phrases my father attached to the bogus personnel sheet. "We've been trying to work out the code, but nothing seems to fit." He sat looking at the page for a long time.

"Did you say your father was a crossword puzzle creator?" he asked quickly. I nodded. "Then I think I may know where some of the answers lie." He sat down at the desk and began to type quickly. "I'm accessing the mainframe. Now, watch this," he said.

He typed rapidly and the screen went blank.

He typed more code and again nothing happened, then on the third try an unfilled crossword puzzle grid filled the screen.

"When I first went through it, I thought that maybe one of the IT guys was in the process of creating a game hadn't finished what he set out to do. As you can see, there are only seven horizontal rows, but there are ten vertical columns."

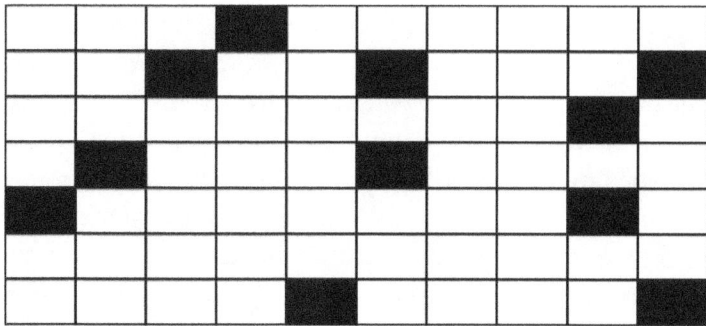

"Okay." I said cautiously, glancing at Julie who looked just as baffled.

"How many clues are there on that note? Four. Now, it may be a long shot but I think there is a relationship. Let's see. Julie open an excel document in that laptop and create a grid exactly like this one."

She did as he asked, and when she finished sat back looked at her father, who gazed at her questioningly at her and then at the note. Her face cleared. "Oh. I see." Quickly she typed the phrases starting at the top left until she reached the end of the third phrase. "That's it. The last clue doesn't fit."

T	O	P	■	A	M	E	R	I	C
A	N	■	I	S	■	Y	E	T	■
K	I	N	D	L	I	E	R	■	T
O	■	O	U	R	■	T	A	X	I
■	D	R	I	V	E	R	S	■	O
B	N	O	X	I	O	U	S	L	Y
E	V	I	L	■	R	O	A	D	■

I stared at the puzzle. "They're not clues they're answers. It's not an encryption, the answer is right in front of us. If the reverse is true, then if we read it backwards starting at the bottom right to top left, then we get..." I read the letters backwards. "Total gibberish."

"Assume the crossword is the method of blocking out letters." Oldfield said cautiously. "Your father would have left another clue as to which letters are blocked, which would then reveal the answer."

"There is one comment he scrawled on the bottom of Ascot's personnel sheet," Julie said laying the note in front of her father. "*'Olympic swimmer's key stroke'* whatever that means."

Oldfield looked at it for a moment and then burst out laughing, thumping the table. "Clever bastard and really bloody obvious."

Both Julie and I stared at each other as Oldfield started typing code rapidly. "He remembered me because he checked up on you, Julie. Somebody in his position would want to know everything about the girl in his son's life. This last phrase is for me. Years ago I wrote a program that identified and remembered specific *keystrokes*, even if the original document had been erased." He filled in the squares of the letters that are unusable. "Watch." He pressed the return key and sat back. Almost immediately, the letters began to be blocked out until the last square on the bottom right was filled. "See."

Oldfield beamed at us. "Now read it backwards."

"Drive in box at ROL key in crema pot," Julie read aloud. "Okay, but I've no idea what that means."

"I do," I said, my mind finally clicking into gear. "Do you remember that small box of body butter that was in the safe?"

"That Orange Moon stuff?"

"Yes, but the full name on the box reads *'Orange Moon Body Butter by Crèma'*. Do you still have it?"

"I do. I've been meaning to give it to Mary, I know she uses it," she said crossing to the bathroom and retrieving the box. I followed her. She opened it and handed me the small pot.

I unscrewed the lid and dug my finger into the thick cream, located the key and pulled it out, then washed it and my hands. It was a standard looking key that any number of places use for safety deposit style boxes, or lockers.

Julie echoed my thoughts. "Safety deposit box?"

"Maybe."

"Which bank?"

"Not a bank," I said going back to where Oldfield sat basking in satisfaction at his work. I looked at the sentence again, at the letters R.O.L. "It's a key to a box at the Royal Overseas League. The message reads, *'Drive in box at Royal Overseas League, key in Crèma pot'.* The hard drive, or flash drive or whatever, is in my Dad's mail box at the club."

"I guess that's another helicopter flight to London," Julie said resignedly.

"Indeed."

"No helicopters for me," Oldfield said briskly. "You don't need me there anyway, just hook up the drive or flash stick to a laptop and call me when you're ready."

I had Milly show him to the guest room, then rang the Royal Overseas League, quoted my membership number and booked Julie and I into the suite my father kept reserved. Before we left I took the second Glock with two magazines from my hidden closet, and two burn phones with attachments, then I called Danny's burn number, told him where we were going, and asked for a two man cover group.

On arriving at Battersea heliport, I went to the office, paid my landing and parking fee, and told them we'd be staying overnight at the Royal Overseas League if I needed to be contacted.

"Your car is waiting for you outside sir," the receptionist said efficiently and within a few minutes we were being driven through early evening London traffic across the river to Saint James's. Twenty minutes later the car stopped outside the club at the end of Park Place, and the chauffeur opened the doors as a porter took our bags inside.

"Mr Gunn how delighted we are to see you sir. Your father's suite is ready," the male receptionist said politely, handing me the key. "Edwards will show you the way."

The porter looked as if he had been at the Club since its inception in 1910. Thin, short and stooped with thick lens glasses and wisps of grey hair on his *'liver'* spotted scalp. He moved slowly, wheeling our bags to the elevator, standing silently without looking at us as we rose to the sixth floor.

Edwards opened the door and led us in.

The suite was comfortably simple, clean, with king size bed, a settee, two armchairs, desk, and looked out over Green Park. Edwards placed the bags in the corner of the room next to the walk-in closet, then turned and walked over to me. He waved his hand as if beckoning me to bend so he could whisper in my ear.

"I believe you have a key, sir," he said, so quietly that I could barely hear. I nodded. "Meet me in the bar of the Golden Lion on King Street. Ten o'clock tonight." With that he slowly walked out of the room and closed the door softly.

"What a funny little man," Julie laughed, then caught my expression. "What?"

"I'll tell you later, right now I could do with a shower, a drink, and food. And you can join me for all three."

We made love in the shower, after which I told her what Edwards had said, before we dressed and went to the Buttery for a large vodka tonic each and a simple meal of herb crumbed veal escalope, with asparagus and sautéed potatoes.

Julie looked stunning in a black trouser suit, simple pearl necklace offset by her golden tan and blonde hair, the atmosphere of the club relaxing her; it was as if nothing bad had happened, or was going to happen. We were in a tiny bubble of contentment.

At least for an hour.

King Street was a block away from Park Place, a two-minute walk to the bustling, colourful Golden Lion Inn sandwiched between office buildings. I spotted Danny dressed incongruously in a very expensive suit staring into the window of an art gallery, and I knew one of his trusted men would be close by.

Young tourists and middle age professionals stood side-by-side sipping martinis, white wine and draught bitter amid a hubbub of voices clamouring to be heard. Edwards was at the back of the bar, sitting on his own with an almost empty glass of stout in front of him. When he saw us, he quickly finished his drink, stood, made a slight motion of his hand showing five fingers, then walked to a stairway behind him and disappeared down out of view. I took this to mean we should follow in five minutes. Julie and I casually ordered two vodka tonics, sat in the booth just vacated by Edwards and tried to look like a couple of young love struck tourists. Nobody paid us any attention.

"This is all a little elaborate isn't it?" Julie said under her breath.

"It does seem so."

Five minutes later we slipped away down the stairs to where Edwards stood waiting. He turned and, surprisingly quickly, made his way through the basement to a seemingly empty room, took an iPad mini from his coat pocket and typed onto the screen. A section of wall clicked open revealing a concealed doorway and another set of stairs leading downwards. We stepped through and the door closed silently behind us.

"That's a neat trick," I muttered.

"It's a security app," Edwards said matter-of-factly. "You can download it from the Internet."

Julie stifled a laugh and followed Edwards down the steps. It smelled musty, and somewhere in the dimly lit passageway, water dripped. I guessed it was an access to the hundreds of miles of London's Victorian sewer tunnels. We followed Edwards to another tunnel that went straight for about sixty feet to another set of stairs, this time leading upward.

"Where are we?" I asked.

"This leads to a room beneath Christie's basement."

The Christie's auction house was almost directly across the street from the Golden Lion. Anyone who might have seen us enter the Inn and was waiting outside would never have thought we had just walked beneath them to the building opposite.

"I started work here about sixty-five years ago, just after World War Two. That's when I discovered the passageways. I was just a lad, did odd jobs, cleaning, stuff like that, moved up the ladder, so to speak, became Head of Porters before I retired. I got the job at the Overseas League when the missus died about ten years ago, just to keep myself busy," Edwards said conversationally as we reached a dead end, with a blank brick wall. "Your father was very good to me over the years. A sad, sad loss." He again typed into his iPad mini. Large blocks of stone slid out from the wall, forming steps leading diagonally up the wall to a small door that we had failed to notice.

Edwards turned and grinned at us. "Whoever built this was either a thief, or a philanderer and wanted a way to leave the building without anyone noticing. We just modernised the mechanics with this." He held up the iPad mini. "Your father liked electronics." He led the way up the steps and opened the door to a brightly lit room. Wooden crates lined one wall and an office chair incongruously stood in the middle of the floor facing the crates.

"The key if you will," Edwards asked, holding out his hand. I gave it to him and watched as he bent down and inserted it into the gap between what had seemed to be two wooden crates. The false front of the crates slid apart to reveal a desk and computer monitor.

"Not the box I was expecting," I said as the computer automatically booted up.

"I feel like I landed in a Doctor Who episode," Julie exclaimed.

"Just a little something I cooked up. Sir Ivan wanted a safe quiet place so I had a few friends knock this up."

"You are a surprising man, Edwards."

His eyes twinkled mischievously. "Nobody pays attention to little old men. We're invisible."

"Well I will from now on," I told him sitting down and staring at the screen, which consisted of a little box asking for the password. "Give me a break."

"Wait a minute," Julie stood with her hands on her hips thinking, then took out her iPhone. "I know where the password is."

"Women are so much smarter than men," Edwards said with a smile.

"Better to look at too."

"You've been taking your Viagra then, Edwards."

"No need young man, you should see me with the fillies down the old people's home," he said laughing and shuffled his feet in a mock dance.

Julie ignored us and called the Professor. "Dad? Have you got the notes we were looking at?"

"I do."

"The one that says *'Olympic swimmer's key stroke'* it has a code on it starting O.R."

"Yup. Letters in uppercase reads OR 443 121/TQ," he said as I typed. "Do you have the box?"

"Just a minute."

The computer whirred for what seemed a lifetime but was probably less than a second and the face of my father appeared on the screen, sitting in this very room.

"We have it Dad, switch to video, so you can see this." Julie held her iPhone so the camera could see the screen.

"I hope this is Thomas watching this recording. If it is then it means I am dead. If it isn't then whoever it is won't be able access the rest of the clip." The screen went blank and an in-screen box appeared with my father's voice-over.

"When we sat on the dock, by the old mill clock, and sang to the moon a nonsense tune. How many fish did we catch?"

"Dear God, I was five years old," I exclaimed as if talking to him.

"Take your time and remember."

"How paranoid can you get?"

"Think Thomas," Julie said urgently.

I thought back to a time when life was easy, carefree, before my real mother died, when everything was fun, when my father laughed at every stupid, silly, child thing I said.

The light bulb went off in my memory.

"No fish. Just six eels," I blurted out, typing as I said it and feeling more than a little silly.

My father's face appeared again seemingly heaving a sigh of relief. "I hope that worked and you remembered. A childish but effective encryption I'm sure the Professor will agree."

When I looked at his face on the monitor, I noticed how old he seemed. Worn down, weathered and sick. The intensity that used to be in his eyes no longer there, as if he knew his life was about to end.

"Much has happened, much that I have had to keep to myself while I am still alive, but with my death, Thomas, you will have to get to the bottom of this mess." He paused and smiled grimly. "Your military training will come in handy now, and by now you will have realised that I know Julie's father. A long time ago, but I always remembered him. Make sure he knows that. You'll need him. The truth is that I have allowed myself to be blackmailed. It was only way to get to the bottom of this conspiracy. Yes I use the word deliberately because I believe that's what it is. A conspiracy."

There was utter silence in the room as my father paused, steadying himself.

"At first I thought this was something I could deal with, but there is something more sinister than just a scheme to extort money from me and the company. It stems from Mary's car accident years ago. As you may remember she was in acute pain as a result of her injuries. What I didn't know is that she became addicted to prescription pain medication. Over the years she has been receiving drugs from a London supplier, who I think is linked to Samuel De Costas, the man who is threatening to take over the Northern Ireland project." He paused again and sighed heavily. "I went to the authorities immediately, of course, but the inquiries have gone nowhere. Tomorrow I fly to Belfast to find out for myself, and then on to San Francisco to meet Samuel de Costas. Something bigger than a drug deal is afoot, Thomas, and if I don't come back alive, you need to continue the investigation. I should have come to you in the first place, but what is done is done. You were in no shape to help. I hope now you have fully recovered and that you now can. I believe that money is being siphoned from the Gunn Group accounts into some offshore banks. The trail is complex, hidden beneath layers of blind companies, which is why you will need Professor Oldfield's help to unravel it all. I believe there are some Government officials who may well be involved in this, but you and your associates would know more about Government funds being used through fake companies to fund operations around the world, than I do. Samuel de Costas is the key. Find him. The next screen will give you everything I know about him, which is not much I'm afraid. Find out who is doing this Thomas. Find out and stop them. I have the greatest faith in you Thomas, I always have. Edwards has a letter for you. I love you son."

That last bit must have been difficult for him to say, which really added to the gravity of the situation. It was the final testament of a man who knew he was going to die. I looked at Edwards who handed me an envelope with a heavy wax seal over the back flap. I looked at it, opened it and read the contents then handed it back to him.

"Would you keep it for safety, until this is done?"

"Of course sir."

My father's face faded from the screen, replaced by a dossier on Samuel De Costas. It was a complete run down of his life. A self made millionaire, he started his business career selling war surplus materials. Everything from thermal underwear to tanks and aeroplanes. Then branched out into many different fields from consumer electronics, to adult entertainment. There were accusations of fraud and tax evasion and more serious charges of murder on two counts but nothing was ever proved. It was after the acquittal on the murder charges, that his life seemed to change. For the past fifteen years he had been a model citizen, and recently re-emerged as a leader in the automotive industry, having funded a new super-car project using the latest engine, micro-computer and robotic fabrication technologies.

I wondered how the old man had got hold of all this information. It was interesting reading but nothing that gave any indication that Ascot was De Costas, or the link to Rathborne Micro-Electronics, except for the micro-computer that ran the engine and transmission system for the car.

"What do you make of it?" I said to Oldfield as we finished reading.

"I would say Mr De Costas is not the sort of fellow I would invite for dinner. However, there is nothing here that links him with anything that has gone on. To prove that this man is Des Ascot would be very difficult."

"What about bank accounts?"

"There are thousands of ways to obscure the exact source and destination of the money."

"I guess that's why my father wanted you involved. I get the information, you figure out the code. And we know two sources of money, the Gunn Group and the British Government and we know one destination, Rathborne Micro-Electronics."

"I need to link to the computer," Oldfield said quickly.

Edwards shook his head. "No direct phone line connection. Sir Ivan was very adamant. This has to remain secure."

"I'm sure he would have given me a way in," Oldfield said, pursing his lips and frowning. "Julie activate the AirLink app on your iPhone, I'll connect through that, and clone the hard drive."

"Not such a good idea," I said before Julie had a chance to take out the tether. "We don't know who might be trying to hack into your phone."

"I put an encrypted scrambler on it remember?" Oldfield said smugly. "If anyone is trying to hack into my system I'll know immediately and so will they when their system goes down."

Julie grinned and connected her phone to the computer. "It's done."

"Good. It'll take a moment."

"Would you both like a wee dram while we wait?" Edwards asked producing two bottles of The Macallan Fine and Rare 1948 from a cabinet beside the computer. "Sir Ivan always kept a few bottles down here."

I smiled and accepted the glass from the old man. "The year of my father's birth."

Julie myself and Edwards silently raised our glasses to what was the only real and meaningful tribute to my father's life, as Oldfield silently worked on the hard drive.

"I have it," the Professor said. "And if there is a spare bottle I would surely be thankful."

"Indeed there is, Sir Ivan was most insistent that one be kept for yourself, Professor." Edwards held up a bottle for Oldfield to see.

"Can we go now," Julie asked, shivering, "this place is a little creepy."

Edwards shut down the computer and led us back the way we had come, but instead of returning to the bar, showed us a door.

"This leads to the alleyway beside the building. Good luck to you both. Here is my private telephone number. Sir Ivan was kind enough to set me up with a phone as well as the iPad mini. Very kind of him. Call me anytime."

"Thank you Edwards," Julie said leaning forward and kissing his cheek. He blushed slightly, then shuffled back to the bar, just another insignificant old man in a crowd. If only they knew.

The door opened out onto the darkened alley, just as Edwards said, and although there was a full moon in the cloudless sky, dark shadows covered any number of hiding places an assassin may choose to hide. There was no point in trying to avoid detection, so I strode into the middle of the alley and waited for Julie as she dutifully closed the door behind her.

It was over before it really began.

I saw a fleeting shadow and the silhouette of a handgun followed by a soft 'plopping' noise. The shadow slid to the ground and Danny appeared by my side.

"Glad you're on time Danny."

"You're welcome."

Julie stood rooted to the spot.

"Danny, Julie. Julie, Danny. Now let's get out of here."

Back in the suite at the Overseas League, Julie sat shaking, comforted by a glass of The Macallan as Danny and I went over the evening's events.

"They're not mucking about," he said seriously. "You recognised him, didn't you?"

"Joe Stannings. Didn't like the son-of-bitch back in Afghanistan. Never trusted the psycho."

"Well that's what these clowns are like, Thomas. Fucking psychos all of them. You know that. Most of Section 4's like that. You can't train people to be assassins and expect them to be normal once their service is up. Killing's a disease. You and me, we did it because we had to.

Fuckers like Stannings do it because they like it. He didn't give a fuck that you saved his life out there. That's why they're in the Increment. MI5 doesn't care so long as the job gets done. And you, my son, are top of the list of targets."

"Then I must be doing something right. Do you have your man watching the helicopter?"

"I do." He paused and looked at me earnestly. "You're getting too close to whatever's going on."

"And I'm going to get closer." I looked across at Julie who had recovered and was watching and listening.

"At least we have one ally. Thank you Danny," she said gratefully.

"Anything for a beautiful girl," Danny countered, his broad face splitting into a wide smile, eyes sparkling with mischief.

"Thomas is lucky I met him first," she teased.

"There's still time, love. When you've figured out he's just all mouth and money."

"Thank you friends." The banter broke the tension and we laughed and drank the £12,000 bottle of The Macallan Fine & Rare 1948. Before he left I asked Danny for one last favour. "Do you have any friends on the other side of the pond?"

"California?"

"Oregon."

"A couple of former SEALS we worked with in Afghanistan. They owe me a favour. What do you want?"

"Easy clearance through customs and immigration in Portland, Oregon. Some hardware positioned at The Pines Country Club, near Crescent City California, two cars, two stand-ins, a change of clothes for Julie and myself, what's on this list and a place to stay near San Francisco that is not a hotel. I'll have the pilots reposition the jet to Los Angeles when we're ready to come home." I handed him the list. He read it quickly.

"Bit elaborate isn't it?"

"Not for what I have in mind." I quickly ran through the plan I had formed.

"Anybody else know about trip?"

"Nope, just you me and Julie. I'll file a flight plan for Chicago, we have a Gunn Group office there, then we'll re-route to Oregon, as if for a holiday."

"It's done. I'll have somebody meet you in Portland. When do you leave?"

"Tomorrow night from Norwich."

"Which passport are you using?"

"American to enter the US and British to get back here."

"You have the numbers on you?"

I took out my passports and handed them to him. He quickly wrote down the numbers and handed them back to me.

Julie watched. "You carry your passports with you?"

"Always." Danny and I replied in unison, and then laughed.

The flight back to the Hall in the morning was uneventful. After the initial fear of the take off from Battersea Heliport - she was still wary of my *'rusty helicopter skills'* - Julie slept, the monotonous sound of the jet engine and rotor blades sending her into a land I could only fathom. She was an enigma to me. After all we had been through so far, she was still determined to stay the course and travel with me to San Francisco in search of the elusive Samuel De Costas.

Mary was sitting in the conservatory when we arrived, vacantly staring out across the grounds, and Julie and I now knew why. We weren't going to tell her that we knew, that would have been cruel. What did surprise me, though, was that Hamish McDougall was standing next to Mary. He turned and by the look on his face, was astonished to see Julie and I.

"Thomas. What a surprise."

"Indeed. What brings you here Hamish, I thought you were tied up in some critical economic meeting at Checkers."

"Postponed. I knew you were away, so I thought I'd check on Mary."

"This is my home, Hamish, and I've a company to run. Can't stay away for too long."

Mary turned to me, and I could see had been crying. Julie walked across and sat down beside her.

Hamish looked uncomfortable under my enquiring scrutiny, smiled quickly and clapped his hands together. "Well, I'll be off then. Meeting's tomorrow at Checkers and it's quite a drive." He smiled again and walked past me out of the conservatory. It was strange behaviour and I had one of those 'not-so-good' feelings stirring in the pit of my stomach. I followed Hamish and caught up with him by the front door, just as his bodyguard opened it for him.

"What were you really doing here, Hamish?"

He turned slowly and looked at me his eyes cold. "Personal matter. Between Mary and myself. Not for discussion."

"Anything that affects Mary *is* up for discussion, Hamish. This is *our* house and what happens here is my concern."

"You abandoned your right to this house when you abandoned your family," he said venomously, and turned to leave.

I grasped his arm and spun him around to face me. The bodyguard was across the space within seconds, but halted when I drew the Glock and pointed it at his head.

"This is my house. What goes on here is my concern. Who visits this house does so at my request. Tell me Hamish, did you know that a man I once knew, who was tied to the Increment or E Squadron or Section 4 or whatever you want to call it, tried to kill Julie and me last night?" I said looking straight at the bodyguard.

Hamish paled and the bodyguard stiffened noticeably. "Put that gun away," Hamish whispered, fear in his eyes and voice.

"You did know, didn't you?" I whispered watching them both carefully. "Was that before or after the attack?"

"After. I learned afterwards. You don't know what game you're playing Thomas and it's going to hurt all of us. You, Julie, Mary and me. I tried to warn you in London as tactfully as I could to let us handle this, but you just don't listen do you? Now let go of my arm."

I let go and watched as he turned and walked quickly out of the door. I still had my gun pointed at the bodyguard, who turned and hurried after Hamish.

"I will find out what you're hiding Hamish," I shouted, but he ignored me, got into his limousine and drove away.

NINE

Oregon USA - October 2012

Flying to the west coast of America is a long haul. Even with the comforts of luxury travel on the Gunn Group Gulfstream G550, it becomes monotonous. Filtered air and the constant sound of jet engines finally get to you, even though we could stretch out and sleep on full size beds. Not that I slept, there was just too much going through my mind, particularly Hamish McDougall. His behaviour was strange and he wasn't the man I thought I knew.

Just how much was he hiding?

The question kept hammering in my mind.

Just before we began our approach to Chicago O'Hare, I gave the pilots the new flight plan, redirecting us to Portland, Oregon. They didn't question the order, simply re-filed with ATC and reset the Flight Computer for the new High Airways route. Three hours later it was a relief to see the mountains and winding Columbia River as we descended into an unusual autumn heat wave with correspondingly high humidity that enveloped Portland International.

True to his word Danny had one of his contacts, a pretty woman in her early fifties, meet us at the Terminal and whisk us through Customs and Immigration as if it didn't exist. It helped that we were perceived as returning US citizens with our US passports. Outside, our contact handed over the keys to a purposefully high profile and expensive brand new *Bentley New Continental GT Speed* in Sequin Blue, befitting a wealthy couple that had just stepped from a Gulfstream G550. And, predictably, all eyes turned to stare as we stepped into the leather luxury and drove away from the terminal.

"I always wanted one of these," Julie sighed happily as she snuggled into the soft leather seat. "It's just so comfortable."

"Good because we have a long drive ahead of us."

"Lovely. Almost feels like a vacation. And strange too. It's the first time I've been back to the States in seven years."

"A long time."

"Maybe. Europe has become my home, so I feel a bit like a tourist."

"I know the feeling. Sometimes I feel I don't really have a home. Except the catamaran in Gozo."

"Where are we going?"

"Danny and I talked it over while you were sleeping off the whisky," I teased. Julie stuck her tongue out at me, and I was glad she was relaxed after the adventures of the last few weeks. "Interstate 5 south towards Eugene, before turning off at exit 228 toward Corvallis and then Newport, where we turn south on US 101 to Crescent City, just inside the California border. We're staying the night at a Private Country Club ten miles south of there. My family have been members for years. Then the fun begins."

"Fun? What fun?"

"Wait and see, and enjoy this car while you can."

"That sounds ominous."

As we drove out of Portland, I kept my eye on the rear view to see if we had picked up a tail, but with the traffic on the Interstate, that would be difficult to spot, so I just enjoyed driving the Bentley until the GPS navigation system told me to turn off at exit 228 to the coastal town of Newport. I checked the rear view mirror and saw a grey sedan several hundred yards behind us turn off the Interstate as well and follow us. It didn't mean anything, but I kept an eye on the mirror.

Many years ago before I joined the Army, I sailed a thirty-four foot sloop from Portland on a delivery to Ventura in California, and was blasted by a huge low pressure that built forty-foot waves, which battered the little sloop and dismasted us one hundred miles out at sea, and fifty miles south of Newport. Luckily the engine held out and I managed to bring myself, my crew of two and the yacht safely into Newport Harbour.

That was well before the events that changed my life, and I felt a soft spot for the town and the people who lined the dock as we brought the yacht into port at six in the morning; people who had stayed awake for three days and nights listening to the Coastguard radio as we struggled through the freezing storm, fighting to reach the port. They brought us flasks of hot coffee, warm fresh bread, scrambled eggs and bacon, hot oatmeal, many bottles of bourbon and, strangely, crates of ice-cold beer.

Julie listened as I rambled on about the adventure and the little city on Oregon's coast, as we drove slowly through and pulled into the parking lot of the incongruously named *Mario's Seafood Grill.*

"It doesn't look much, but this is the best seafood on the Oregon Coast," I told Julie as we stepped out the car and walked to the door. "At least I hope it still is."

Just before we stepped inside I quickly scanned the street and spotted the grey sedan I saw earlier pull into a parking space just down the road. The occupants stayed in the car.

We were shown to our table in the funky restaurant that was full of happy customers and given the menu, which Julie eyed with surprised delight.

"I hope the food's as good as the menu promises."

"It was the last time I was here."

"You are full of surprises, Thomas Gunn."

"Money doesn't buy everything and great food doesn't have to be expensive."

A homely waitress, with bright eyes and winning smile approached the table. "Hi, my name is Amy and I'll be your server today. Are you ready to order?" she asked welcomingly.

"I'm having the fresh Dungeness crab steamed in sake with aioli and avocado, red onion, apple and endive salad," Julie replied decisively. "And a glass of ice cold Chablis."

"The lady knows what she wants. And I'll have the Spicy Alaskan Salmon cakes, with hot and sour sauce and the same salad. But being a simple soul I'll have an ice cold Sam Adams draught Boston Lager."

"Great choices, I'll be right back with your drinks," Amy said approvingly and walked busily away to the back of the restaurant.

"You said I should enjoy this car while it lasts. What did you mean?" Julie said quietly.

"We change when we get to the Country Club. The Bentley goes back to Portland with a couple who look surprisingly like us and we carry on to San Francisco."

"I thought as much. And I did see the grey sedan."

"You're getting way to good at this."

"Nobody pays any attention to a woman looking in a mirror, and I'm just trying to stay alive," she said gravely as Amy approached the table with our drinks.

"Here you go, I'll have your meals here in ten minutes. Anything else I can get you?"

"This is great, thanks," I said giving her the biggest smile I could muster.

"Who are the people in the sedan?" Julie asked as soon as Amy walked away.

"Rogue British Special Forces, now working for some group within the UK Government. Or De Costas' men."

"I have a funny feeling about this Thomas."

"We're just on a fishing expedition."

"Sure, but you didn't say how big the sharks were."

We were back on the road within the hour, feeling as if we had dined at the most expensive restaurant in the world. Julie gushed about the crab for ten minutes, before settling down in the comfortable seat and falling asleep. Her ability to do that amazed me. If there is something on my mind, I can't sleep. It bothers me; worries me; nags at me until I find a solution. And if I don't find a solution, I stay awake until I do.

Not Julie.

It was one of the things that attracted me to her. Apart from the obvious stunning body and intelligence that flowed from her like some sort of ghostly plasma. No wonder men just stared, and women looked as if they could kill her and happily serve time.

She was an enigma.

The free soul I so desperately wanted to be.

She slept, and I drove on alone with my thoughts about the 'mission' at hand. But I was flying blind as usual. I thought I had a plan. I thought I knew what I was doing, but being here in the US with fond memories of a life in a country that seemed so easy and carefree, with a beautiful woman that I loved, I wondered if Hamish was right. Why didn't I just leave it alone and let Hamish and the Government investigate?

But there was this part of me that couldn't let go. That needed to know everything. That didn't trust the Government. That didn't trust anybody.

Coos Bay went by as a blur and before I knew it, we were entering California just south of Brookings. Julie woke from her nap and looked around as the sun began to dip to the ocean, an orange light bulb shaped illusion that kissed the horizon for a brief moment before disappearing from view.

"Beautiful," she breathed.

"Sleep well?"

"Just a little nap. We there yet?"

"Close. Another hour."

"Grey sedan still with us?"

"Yup. Lay back about a mile, but closed up in the last five minutes. He's hoping he won't lose us through Crescent City."

"But you won't let him."

"Nope. I want him on our tail all the way to the country club." And that is precisely what happened, and as we turned into the driveway of the Club stopping to clear through security before entering the grounds, I watched as the grey sedan slowed and then accelerated past the entrance as it became obvious they would not get past security. Wealth has its advantages and expensive, exclusive Country Clubs with serious security is one of them. Of course any well-trained professional can breach any security, but it takes time, and by then we would be long gone and our 'stand-ins' on their way back to Portland in the Bentley.

Timing is everything.

Julie had warmed to her role as the girl friend of a wealthy businessman, striding into reception as if she owned the place, smiling winningly at the young man behind the counter as I handed over my membership card.

"Thank you Mr Gunn, we have been expecting you and your suite is ready. Alicia will show you the way."

Alicia, a pretty nineteen year-old, was well trained, pleasant and efficient. Once in our suite, Julie heaved a sigh of relief and headed for the bathroom, discarding her clothes as she went.

"I want to lie in hot soapy water for an hour with a tall glass of ice cold vodka tonic, one ice cube and two olives."

"Yes ma'am," I replied. "I'll follow you on both counts, just hope the bath tub is big enough."

"Oh it certainly is," came Julie's muffled reply followed by the sound of running water. I checked the drawer in the side table beside the bed and found credit cards and driver's licenses in the name of Tommy and Martha Blacket, my mother's maiden name, and the keys to a three year-old Volvo XC70. Then I poured two strong vodka tonics, with one cube of ice and two pimento stuffed olives, stripped naked and walked to the bathroom.

"There you are," Julie said quietly. "After I soak for a while, finish my drink and ravish your body, what do you have planned?" She snaked a long leg out of the bubble filled bath and rubbed it up my thigh.

"I've forgotten already," I said, staring at her beauty and wishing this was another time.

"Come on in, the water's lovely," she said taking her drink. "I'll help you remember."

The light knock on the door was barely discernible, but I was awake and expecting it. Julie finished dressing and watched as I crossed the room, Glock in hand and, standing to the side, tapped twice, paused and then tapped once more. There was a responding two taps. I opened the door carefully and let the man and woman into the suite. They looked exact twins of Julie and me. The prosthetics were unbelievable and nobody would be any the wiser when they checked out of the Club in the early morning.

"Down the hall to your right, there is a staff door, this electronic key opens it. Take the stairs to the first floor. One of our men is waiting for you. He'll get you out of the grounds," the woman said quickly, sounding disturbingly like Julie. "Good luck."

As she left the room, Julie smiled at them. "Enjoy the Bentley," she said mischievously and followed me down the corridor to the '*Staff Only*' door.

Between three and four o'clock in the morning is always the best time to start a battle or leave a building unnoticed. Most people are deep into REM sleep and those that aren't are either insomniacs or up-to-no-good. I doubted our friends with the grey sedan would have had time to fully reconnoitre the clubs grounds and form a plan, so I wasn't concerned about them.

At the bottom of the stairs, the Security Guard who had checked us as we arrived stood waiting.

"The electronic key please." He asked crisply. I handed it over. "Follow me."

It took nearly forty-five minutes meandering through the woods that skirted the golf course at the back of the Club, before our guide pointed to a small group of houses on the edge of the golf course.

"The house on the right is the one you want. Car's in the garage and the hardware you requested is in the back under the floor. Go in through the gate on the right hand side. Back door's open. Make yourselves some breakfast. Wait until six before you leave, that's when the neighbours get up and they won't be surprised to hear you go."

"Thanks. We appreciate your help."

"Any friend of Danny's..." he smiled and let the sentence hang, shook my hand and disappeared. Within a few minutes we were in the house, making breakfast, and at six o'clock, went through into the garage. I checked the false floor in the back of the Volvo and was happy with the weapons and spare clips that were secreted there. The Volvo was full of fuel, the electric garage door slid open at the touch of a switch and we were on our way, following the route pre-programmed into the GPS navigation system.

"What do we call ourselves?" Julie asked.

"Tommy for me, and this is for you." I handed her the driver's license and credit cards.

"Martha Blacket? Dear God, do I look like a Martha?"

I glanced at her and grinned. "Oh I don't know, kinda suits you hon, and we are husband and wife," I laughed trying my American accent.

"You're gonna have to work on that, hon. Try just doing a New England accent, it's lazy British with a bit of West Country. Then you'll get away with it."

"These are just so nobody can track us from here to San Francisco. Once we confront De Costas, all bets are off."

The drive was uneventful. For the first hour Julie slept, and then took over while I tried to rest, unsuccessfully. There was too much going on in my mind and I still kept a look out behind, just to make sure our cover hadn't been blown. Hopefully by now the grey sedan was following the Bentley back to Portland.

Julie turned off Highway 101 at Novato and headed across country to Stinson Beach just as the female voice on the Navigation system instructed.

"God that voice is so sleazy," she said seeing I was awake. "Makes my skin crawl."

I reached over and changed the settings. "There, no more voice."

"You could have done that a few hours ago, you know."

"Thought it would keep you company."

She snorted and turned right onto the road that led to Stinson Beach, rounding the lagoon and turning down Calle del Arroyo towards the gated community where a beach house awaited us.

Julie pulled up at the security gate. "Mr and Mrs Blacket. We're renting a property." She handed over her driver's license.

"Yes Mrs Dawson is expecting you at the house. Take a left here and follow the road," he said handing back her license.

"Thank you," Julie flashed her toothy smile, and watched as the security guard blushed beneath his California tan.

The split level beach house, with the lounge, dining room and kitchen on beach level; bedrooms, bathrooms, den on the top, drive level. The living room opened out onto a large deck with steps leading down to the beach. I stood and looked out to where the surf ran up the sand,

and thought once again how easy it would be to forget the reason we were here. Julie came quietly up behind me and took my arm, snuggling into my shoulder.

"Well, when do we start work? " She didn't look at me, just stared at the waves breaking on the shore.

"Not today, that's for sure," I said. She turned, smiled and handed me a pair of swimming shorts.

"That's exactly what I hoped you would say. There's plenty of time, let's just enjoy a few days, without any hassles."

So we did.

Free of any pressures or worries. We forgot everything and swam, enjoyed beach barbecues and pretended we really were Tommy and Martha Blacket from Rhode Island on vacation at the beach. We regained our Mediterranean tans and made love in the king size bed as if nothing else in the world mattered.

But of course we couldn't forget, and Julie brought it up over dinner as we sat on the deck watching the last glows of the sun eating a delicious clambake.

"I see you brooding, Thomas," she said and took a sip of chilled Pinot Grigio. "You're anxious, antsy. I feel it too."

"It's time to rattle Mr Samuel De Costas' cage."

I got up, went into the house and came back with a manila envelope, handing it to Julie. "I found this in the mail box this afternoon."

She pulled the sheets of paper from the envelope and read through them quickly. "Wow. These from Danny?"

"Yes."

"So that guy you shot in Belfast, Boyd, his real name is Charlie Mullen, with a rap sheet that goes back decades, mostly for drugs and smuggling illegal immigrants into the country. It says here that he worked for Coltrane Engineering and Construction Company outside Mojave. Near Edwards Air Base, or spaceport or whatever it's called now."

"But there doesn't seem to be any connection to De Costas, at least nothing Danny could find. But we do know that De Costas has a new office building downtown and there is an opening gala tomorrow

105

evening."

Julie put the papers back into the envelope and tossed it onto the table. "So what's your plan?"

"Crash the party and see what Samuel De Costas has to say for himself. I want to know what this guy looks and sounds like."

"And just how do you propose to get invited?"

I paused for a moment smiling before answering. "Your father. Get him on the phone, I know it's early but he can add us to the computer's guest list as Mr and Mrs Thomas Gunn. We don't want our aliases compromised."

"Is that a proposal, Thomas? I thought you weren't into the whole marriage thing."

I leaned over and kissed her. "Maybe. Guess you have to wait to find out."

"Yeah, right I won't hold my breath. Anyway I'm not sure he's going to want to hack into somebody's system," Julie said doubtfully.

"Don't be too sure. And I want a recording of my father's video as well as schematics of the building."

We waited another hour so it wasn't too early and then Julie called. I was right, Professor Oldfield was more than happy to oblige, even providing Julie with an algorithm to install in De Costas' computer system if we could get to the mainframe, which would enable us to track all De Costas' online transactions, past present and future. Julie downloaded it to a small flash drive.

The new headquarters of De Costas Global Enterprises was impressive. A tall, thin, glass and steel skyscraper with transparent lift shafts running up the outside of the building.

As we walked towards the entrance I thought that this structure made the Gunn Group office look like a shabby back street walk-up. Once inside the foyer, we discovered a sign on one of the elevators for the *'De Costas Automotive Gala'*. The ride up to the twentieth floor was spectacular as San Francisco unfolded below us. It was a shame when the elevator stopped and the doors opened to reveal the reception area. A girl with a bright smile greeted us and asked us for our names which she checked off against the computer list. Beyond her, in the ballroom sized conference room, the sound of light jazz and murmur of voices, drifted sinuously through the sterile air dampened by the plush carpet and insulated walls.

"That's wonderful, enjoy the party Mr and Mrs Gunn," the receptionist breathed showing off her extremely white teeth.

"Actually I have a meeting with Mr De Costas. Please tell him we are here."

The girl frowned. "He asked not to be disturbed for the next thirty minutes. If you don't mind waiting until he returns to the party."

I turned and looked at Julie. "A bit rude to leave your own party, isn't?" I said turning back to the girl, who was now flustered.

"He hasn't actually arrived yet."

"Then perhaps we should wait in his office until he does, he did give a specific time for the meeting." There was no way we were going to be allowed to wait in De Costas office, but that's not what I was looking for, it was the involuntary movement of her eyes which pointed the way to De Costas' office.

"Please if you will join the party I will let him know you are here just as soon as he arrives," she said nervously, and again flickered her eyes down the corridor to the right.

Julie smiled and took my arm. "I want a glass of champagne and a plate of caviar please darling. Business can wait."

I put my best *I'm pissed off but I'll do what my wife says'* face on, glowered at the receptionist and allowed Julie to steer me into the party.

Galas are the same the world over. Expensive food, expensive drink, beautiful women hanging onto the arms of mostly balding rich old men, and young *wannabes* eying the room for any opportunities to enter the elite circle of the city's wealthiest and most powerful people.

But I wasn't thinking about any of that, I was looking for a door at the end of the conference room that would lead back into the corridor and so to De Costas' office. I saw what I was looking for and steered Julie slowly across the room, stood with my back to the door and tried the handle. It opened and we slipped out into the corridor unnoticed.

The receptionist was busy with more guests and did not see us walk away down the corridor and turn the corner. In front of us was the outer office to De Costas' suite, with a well-built young man sitting at a desk facing us. He looked up as we walked toward him.

"May I help you?" he asked politely, his eyes cold and a slight bump beneath the left breast of his immaculately tailored suit, indicating a small automatic, I guessed a Beretta rather like the one I had given Julie.

"Thomas Gunn to see Mr Samuel De Costas."

"I'm afraid Mr De Costas is...." the young man began.

"Please. Just tell him I'm here," I said quietly but firmly.

"Really...." the young man started to say, then rose quickly to his feet as I crossed to the closed door and flung it open before he could stop me.

There were three men and one woman in the office. One man I took to be Samuel De Costas sat behind a large oak desk with his back to the window overlooking San Francisco Bay. The woman seated in an armchair to the side and two well built young men, obviously bodyguards, standing on either side of the room. They moved quickly toward me as I walked toward the desk. The man behind the desk waved the young bodyguards away and stared at me.

"Mr Thomas Gunn. What may I do for you?" he said. Samuel De Costas looked more like a benign accountant. He was short, slim with a slightly egg shaped balding head with amber eyes that flickered and glittered like a cobra. I turned to the woman who was probably in her mid thirties, expensively dressed, tall with long dark hair and striking green eyes. She looked at me with air of a Countess, as if I were something unpleasant stuck to the bottom of her shoe. I thought I had seen her somewhere before, but just couldn't think where, perhaps because I was more concerned about De Costas.

The woman looked at De Costas disdainfully; rose, collected a file from the desk, and paused. "I'll be expecting that consignment in ten days." It sounded like a command.

She swept past Julie and glanced at me with a slight smile, and I caught the faint smell of vanilla and another odour I was not familiar with, in her perfume.

I turned back to De Costas. "Rathborne Micro-Electronics Ltd."

De Costas sat back gently in his oversized chair, watching me without smiling. He seemed uneasy and little irritated. "What about it?"

"It seems you are trying to buy it, or should I say steal it from my company. I would like to know why." There's nothing like getting straight to the point.

"I heard you was, how shall I say, a little hot-headed Mr Gunn and I will try to not take offence, even if, where I come from, your accusations could get you hurt," he said in a bad Brooklyn accent.

"Sounds like everything I read about you is true, then, including the phoney Brooklyn *I-belong-to-the-mob* accent."

If his eyes could get any colder and more malevolent they just did.

"Whose the girl?" he said, his eyes flickering over to Julie.

"None of your business. Now Rathborne Micro-Electronics Ltd. What do you want with the company?"

"I make global investments. This seems like a good investment. I talked it over with your father and he agreed with me." He paused and leaned forward his mouth curving into a slight smile that did not touch his eyes. "My condolences."

"Really. That's interesting, because I talked it over with my father, and he doesn't agree with you. In fact he sent me here to find out just what kind of game you're playing."

If any more blood could have drained from his face it just did.

"Your father was killed. I saw it on the news...." De Costas blurted out before stopping himself. "You're not quite as stupid as they say you are, Mr Gunn."

"True." I reached into my pocket and took out my cell phone as the bodyguards lunged for their guns. I turned on the audio playback feature and held it up so everyone could hear.

"Over the years Mary has been receiving drugs from a London supplier, who I think is linked to Samuel De Costas, the man who is threatening to take over the Northern Ireland project. I went to the authorities of course but the inquiries have gone nowhere. I want you to fly to Belfast. Find out and then go to San Francisco. Find Samuel de Costas. Something bigger

than a drug deal is afoot, Thomas." Earlier in the day I edited the transcript, taking out some words to make it sound as if my father was briefing me, and I was sure De Costas wouldn't notice the slight hesitations in the audio.

"You have nothing, just some words of a failed businessman who can't keep up with the new world," De Costas said, but I detected uncertainty and a tinge of fear in his voice.

"I don't know what you are up to, De Costas, but I will find out and I will come for you. You can bet on that." I turned, took Julie's arm, crossed the office, and walked down the corridor to the elevator.

"Holy crap, when you said rattle his cage you really meant it, didn't you?" Julie whispered. "Are we going to get out of here alive?"

"Oh yes. He's not that stupid, but when we get outside that's a whole different ball game. Did you catch the name on the file that woman took with her?"

"Coltrane Engineering."

"Guess that's our next stop."

"And she was wearing Clive Christian No.1."

"Oh yeah? And what's that?"

"Just the most expensive perfume in the world. That woman is loaded," she said tartly. "Personally I don't care for the smell of Ylang-Ylang."

We stepped into the elevator and the doors closed just before two of De Costas' bodyguards could reach us. They would not be far behind, so I had better think of a plan quickly. We had parked the car two blocks away, so I had to deal with the two bodyguards before we could make our way back to it. I pressed the button for Parking Level One, ignoring Julie's questioning look.

The second elevator, the only one the bodyguards could use, was still ascending as we began to drop, and only began to descend when we were over half way down.

"De Costas won't want a scene here, so he'll have a reception committee at street level. That's why we're going to Parking Level One. Buy us a little more time."

"I brought a little insurance," Julie said pulling up her dress and extricating the Beretta.

"You're lucky they didn't have a metal detector."

"It was a party, not airport security."

As we passed the ground floor, I could see two more bodyguards waiting for us in the lobby, caught off-guard as the elevator sped underground. According to the building schematics, there was a loading and unloading bay for the kitchens and laundry adjacent to Parking Level one, which could be accessed by a security door from the garage.

"Text your father to unlock the security door in thirty seconds."

Julie rapidly sent the text as the elevator glided to a halt and the doors hissed open. We were out and running toward the security door as the sound of footsteps clattered on the metal emergency exit staircase, signifying that the bodyguards would be here in moments. I just hoped my timing was right and Oldfield managed to trip the lock. As my hand closed on the handle I heard the electronic lock trip, gently opened the door and followed Julie through as the emergency exit door banged open on the other side of the parking garage.

So far so good.

The door locked comfortingly behind us as we walked quickly up the ramp and out of the loading bay into the cool San Francisco night.

"Quite some trick from halfway around the world," Julie said breathlessly as we kept to the shadows and put as much distance between us and the De Costas building as possible before circling back to the Volvo.

"Mainframe computers are instantaneous. Doesn't matter where you are, if the connection is fast enough."

"Now what?"

"We can't go back to the beach house, the bridges have surveillance cameras so I guess it's Mojave and have a look at what De Costas is hiding out in the desert."

"Back to being Mr and Mrs Blacket then?"

"Indeed."

Driving out of the city was a matter of keeping to side streets and avoiding the main highways. I'd taken the precaution of filling up with gas before leaving Stinson Beach, at a small local gas station where I knew they didn't have cameras, so we snaked our way down the peninsula to San Jose, then cut across to Sonora where a winding highway took us across the mountains to the Nevada border. From there it was a straight run down the west side of Death Valley to the Mojave Desert. Well not straight exactly, but if anyone decided to follow Mr and Mrs Blacket, it would be a long hot drive.

"There's a motel I know near Panamint Springs on the edge of Death Valley. We'll stay there tomorrow night."

"Sounds wonderful. Just as long as they have air conditioning."

"They do. What's more important is that it's quiet, private and is exactly where Mr and Mrs Blacket would stay."

"Well OK. Hon" Julie drawled. "I juz caint wait to snuggle up with you in a nice little 'itsy-bitsy' motel."

TEN

We arrived in Panamint Springs at seven in the morning having driven all night, tired, dusty, and ready for a shower and breakfast. The motel was pretty much as I remembered. Quaint, simple, and clean, perched on the edge of nowhere in Death Valley National Park. It was already hot, dry and dusty, and it wasn't going to get any cooler, so once we checked in and cleaned up, Julie and I went over to the restaurant, sat on the porch, ordered ice cold orange juice, scrambled eggs and bacon.

"How did you find this place?" Julie asked stroking the head of an old Australian sheepdog that wandered up, hoping for a scrap or two. "Hey fella, nothing here for you I'm afraid." The dog licked her hand and gazed at her adoringly.

"When I was travelling after I left school, I wanted to see Death Valley, ended up here and liked it. So far away from my own cloistered life."

"You can say that again."

After breakfast I called the pilot of the G550 on one of my burn phones, and asked him to reposition the aircraft to Henderson Executive Airport near Las Vegas. Then Julie and I drove to the trailhead of Darwin Falls. It is perhaps the unlikeliest place in Death Valley, a year round waterfall at the head of a narrow gorge about three and a half miles in from the main road. The hike was flat most of the way, but required a little scrambling over rocks. As we went deeper into the gorge, we escaped the direct heat from the sun and finally reached the small twenty-foot tall waterfall. Surrounded by ferns and other flora, it just shouldn't be in a desert at all.

"My God, who would have thought," Julie marvelled, sitting on a rock in the cool of the gorge.

"Runs year round from a spring which feeds the Motel."

"I'm glad we came. It's a tiny jewel in a moonscape."

"Death Valley's full of weird things."

"And it's taken an Englishman who is half American to show me parts of my country I've never seen."

"We get around. It's in the blood."

For several hours we sat, talked and wandered back to the car, a gentle break before the reality of our purpose brought back the tension and uncertainty of the future. But not before I showed her some of the other attractions of Death Valley and we lunched in Furnace Creek, drove through Artist's Drive and then to Dante's View just as typical tourists would do, cementing our identities as Mr and Mrs Blacket.

We arrived back late in the afternoon, tired, dusty and hot despite the car's air-conditioning, ready for an early dinner and bed.

The Australian sheepdog joined us for dinner on the porch and received some of Julie's fresh Angus beef burger for his amber eyed imploring, eating with relish. After dinner we lay on the grass with the dog, which had taken a fancy to Julie, and watched shooting stars light up the clear night sky.

"It's so quiet and yet so loud with the cicadas. There's such a sense of infinity here." Julie whispered, as if afraid to wake the sleeping gods and spoil the magic of the night.

All too soon the night of gentle lovemaking was over and we were back on the road, following the GPS to the co-ordinates Professor Oldfield had supplied for Coltrane Engineering, ten miles North East of Mojave Airport. It seemed an odd out-of-the-way place to establish a company supposedly dealing in the manufacture of oil and gas pumps, but nothing about my life at this moment was normal, everything absurdly surreal. Such a short time ago, Julie and I were naïve boat bums, sunning ourselves in the Mediterranean without a care in the world, now we were hiding from would-be killers and searching for answers to the murder of my father.

Mojave is a small dusty town hiding a spaceport where wealthy civilian potential astronauts lined up to take a Virgin Galactic flight into space. The desert is a perfect flat empty space for experimental aircraft; the test pilot flight school at Edwards Air Force Base and returning space shuttle flights. I followed the road out of town past the spaceport, following the GPS navigator, then turn left onto a small potholed road five miles out of town that petered out into a dusty track.

"Stranger and stranger," Julie muttered. "Who the hell would build an engineering plant that has no access for big trucks?"

"We're coming in the back way," I grinned. "I figured De Costas might have a reception committee lined up if we came in the front door."

"Good thinking."

A good two miles from Coltrane Engineering, I pulled the car into a shallow arroyo, hidden from view to anyone but the most earnest hunters. I collected a couple of handguns, two sleeping bags, two small cans of compressed liquid nitrogen, heavy duty rubberised industrial gloves and a pair of high powered binoculars from the back of the car, while Julie packed sandwiches, energy bars, glucose tablets and water into two back packs. Once we had everything we needed, I wired an explosive charge to a cell phone and tucked it under the fuel tank.

"What's that for?"

"A nasty surprise for De Costas' men, just in case they find the car."

"If that happens, how the hell do we get out of here? Walk?"

"There's always a way."

We hiked along the arroyo for half an hour following the directions on a handheld GPS, until we were confronted by a ten-foot electrified wire fence that looked new.

"Whatever's going on here is recent, that's for sure," Julie remarked. "And they don't want visitors."

"But as yet no remote CCTV cameras. Looks like they are ready to install them but haven't got around to it yet." There was a scuffling noise to our right and a gopher shot from a hole, ran to the fence, struggled through and dove into another hole on the other side. "And no electricity to the fence yet either."

"That'll make life easier."

To our right the edge of the arroyo rose sharply to a ridge about fifty feet high. The only access via a narrow cleft that wound through the rock and disappeared around a sharp corner. Julie followed as I explored the opening, reaching a dead end about one hundred metres in, but with a simple climb up to the back of the ridge that edged the arroyo. From there we had a good view across the open land to the Coltrane Engineering buildings a good eight hundred metres from where we lay. Between the buildings and us two graders flattened the ground, pushing the dirt to one side but apart from that there seemed little movement in and around the buildings. An MD-902 Explorer helicopter sat on a helipad at the East side of the property, with three SUVs parked nearby beside a low structure, which I took to be the offices attached to the main square, windowless, concrete construction facility. Whatever was happening here had a direct connection to De Costas and Rathborne Micro-Electronics in Belfast. The door to the office block opened and the woman we had seen at De Costas office walked across to the helicopter, followed by a man. Through the binoculars I could see them very clearly. The pilot was obviously already on board, because I heard the engines start just as the passengers boarded, and within a minute the aircraft was airborne and headed away from us toward Mojave.

"I told you she was loaded," Julie murmured.

"She looks familiar, but I can't place her."

"She was in De Costas office."

"No, before then. I've seen her, but I just can't remember where. If I could just get the context I'd know."

"It's going to bug you isn't it?"

"Yes it is. I hate loose ends."

"Well let's get in there and find out what's going on."

"We will, but not until tomorrow."

"What," Julie exclaimed. "Where the hell are we going to sleep?"

"Right here. Until about two thirty in the morning."

"Wonderful."

"Well I'll have a sandwich and imagine it's that delicious crab we had in Newport."

Covert observation posts are perhaps one of the most boring and yet stressful tasks anyone can undertake, even if it's only for a half a day and half a night. There is absolutely nothing to do, except keep still, watch and stay out-of-sight. The cover and shadows provided by the large boulders scattered across the rocky ridgeline above the arroyo provided us a measure of shelter from the intense heat and hid us from view. Comfortable it was not, but Julie managed to find a sandy soft spot tucked up beneath an overhang where the desert sand had blown in and was able to scrape herself a 'bed' that was at least softer than solid rock. And, as was her uncanny ability, fell fast asleep while the sun dipped toward the horizon, the only sound now that the graders had stopped, was the helicopter returning from wherever it flew. The pilot shut down, walked toward the office and five minutes later several men and two women exited, climbed into the SUVs and drove away, presumably to their homes in Mojave.

As darkness fell, the quiet of the evening was broken only by the sounds of nocturnal creatures venturing out from their burrows to hunt and feast in the cool desert night, until the sun forced them back underground to sleep away the heat of the day.

At two o'clock in the morning, as the half moon descended toward the horizon several hours before the pale light of dawn would begin to filter across the desert-scape, I started packing up our little camp site. Julie lay sleeping, wrapped up against the cold, mouth slightly open and eyelids twitching in REM sleep, stirring as I gently shook her shoulder.

"Time to go," I whispered. She nodded eyes still closed, and promptly turned and fell asleep again. This time I pinched her ear lobe. Her eyes snapped open, unfocused for a moment, hand reaching up to rub her ear.

"What was that?" she said groggily.

"Me. Time to go."

As I finished clearing up, Julie struggled out of her sleeping bag, rolled it up and took the bottle of energy drink from me, sipping slowly in the cool night air.

"Did you sleep?" she asked, taking a chocolate covered muesli bar from her backpack.

"No."

"You should have woken me earlier."

"I wasn't sleepy."

"That's not true."

I shrugged. She was right, but I was too edgy to sleep, watching hour after hour for any signs of movement from the Coltrane Buildings and seeing nothing. But that's what observation posts are all about.

We finished stowing everything away, slung the packs over our shoulders and headed for the wire fence. Taking the compressed liquid nitrogen can from my backpack and the gardening gloves, I set to work on the fence. After spraying a horizontal line along the chain links, about three inches up from the ground, I pulled hard on the fence and the links broke at the spray line. All I had to do to create a hole big enough to crawl through, was to spray another two vertical lines two feet high from either end of the broken fence, then bend the fence up. It was quiet and once through, I bent the fence back and used a couple of the broken links to 'tie' together the hole I'd made. From six feet away it would be difficult to spot by a casual observer.

Within ten minutes, Julie and I crossed the rough ground where the graders had been hard at work, and knelt against the concrete wall of the main factory building.

Apart from foraging night animals, there seemed to be no signs of life.

We waited for two minutes, just listening before we moved. Better to take time and be sure. I glanced up at the lightening sky and as I did so I caught sight of a small window open, high up on the wall near the roof.

"An open window but no way to get to it," I whispered. Just above the window was the edge of the flat roof. "There must be some way to get to the roof. If I could do that then it would be a relatively simple process to swing down to the window ledge and in."

"Okay," Julie replied doubtfully.

We carried on cautiously round the building.

Access onto the roof came in the form of one of the trucks that had been parked close up against the wall. The top of the cab was about seven feet below the overhanging edge of the roof. I hadn't exerted myself so much since the Army, and despite the cool desert night, dripped with sweat. Once on the flat roof I lay still for a minute catching my breath, listening again for sounds of any movement.

"Stay there, I'll open the office block door as soon as I've cleared the building." I whispered down to Julie, who walked around the corner of the building toward the office block. I moved over to where I estimated the window was, flipped myself over the edge of the roof and through the open window. There was a stack of crates against the wall. They were stacked in steps so it was easy to get down to ground level.

It seemed as if I was in the despatch area to judge from the markings on the crates. The address on each crate was to Venus Automotive, Dundonald Northern Ireland, which I knew did not exist. The only company in Dundonald to which De Costas had any affiliation, was Rathborne Micro-Electronics. All the crates were firmly sealed except for one at the end of the row. The lid came off easily and beneath a layer of packing material were rows of hollow rectangular aluminium beams about seven feet long by nine inches high and five inches wide. There was no time to examine these any closer, so I moved on and came to a door that led to a small machine room. All the equipment was new and looked as if it had never been used. I carried on through the door at the end and found myself in what looked like the fabrication area for the aluminium beams. Empty crates were stacked against one wall, a jig for the fabrication of the beams and two other jigs for fabricating what looked like pressure pipes, valves and small odd-looking pressure vessels.

Access to the offices was through unlocked double glass swing doors, into an open plan office with partitioned cubicles. There were new carpets on the floor, new typewriters on the desks; indeed the furniture was brand new, clean and shiny. The door I was looking for was off to the right, an exit that led out to the helipad and parking lot where Julie should be waiting for me.

Just as I passed a venetian blind covered window, I saw the shadow of a man backlit by the moon. My heart stopped as I pictured Julie lying cold and broken outside the door.

"That's just your imagination. Slow down," I thought rapidly, steadying myself against the worst possible thought I could have. The shadow was moving toward the door just as I was, the door that opened outwards as

every exit door should for fire safety reasons.

The cool military part of me waited until I estimated that the man was just up to the door, and then twisted the handle and slammed my shoulder against it at the same time.

The door flew open and caught the surprised figure with the force of a two hundred pound sledgehammer. I heard his wrist break, then his nose and jaw as the solid steel fire door met soft tissue and bone. He was flung backwards and I heard, with satisfaction, the crunch as the back of his head hit the edge of the unyielding concrete of the helipad walkway. It was all over in a second or two, and I stood listening for the sound of a partner. There must be one, but the only sounds I could hear was the cicadas and the bubbling sound of the man's blood filling his lungs.

Slowly I slipped out of the building, looking for Julie.

And then I saw her, lying crumpled at the corner. By the time I crossed the ten yards to her, she stirred and pushed herself up into a sitting position.

"Slowly. Let me see," I said taking her in my arms, lifting and carrying her into the office; laying her down on one the settees in the reception area. There was blood on the back of her head and a nasty looking four-inch wound that would need stitches.

"Dear God, what hit me?"

"One of De Costas' goons. There's bound to be another somewhere."

"We have to put the bug in the mainframe, just like Dad said." She held up the flash drive.

"We have to get out of here."

"The computer," Julie said defiantly. "I'm not having my head cracked open for nothing."

"Okay. You deal with the computer stuff, I'll check to see if our friend has other friends," I said quietly, pulling the Glock from my backpack and walking slowly back to the main manufacturing building. I turned to see Julie searching for the office server. Then I heard the sound of footsteps and melted into the shadow of a doorway. There was laboured breathing and I saw another man appear in the outer office. He could have been a brother of the giants, and in his massive hand he clutched a very mean looking revolver. He was headed straight for the office.

There was no time for heroics, so my plan was just to shoot the son-of-bitch, but there was a third gunman I hadn't noticed, who fired from about five feet away. The round caught me in the right side before I could spin out of the way. It tore straight through front to back, tearing a chunk of muscle out just above my hipbone, and knocking me over as the second round clipped my upper left bicep, again going straight through. He wasn't so lucky. I fired as I was falling, hitting him in the throat sending him over backwards, crashing in a heap on the floor.

I looked for the other gunman, and instead stared straight into the barrel of his revolver, watching as the chamber rotated as he began to pull the trigger, and then saw his face explode as Julie shot him in the back of the head. She staggered over to me, helped me into a sitting position and looked at the wounds just as a radio crackled to life.

"Unit one this is two we found the car."

"Jesus, there's an army out there," Julie cried, tears of pain and fear coursing down her cheeks. She roughly brushed them aside. "We have to get you to a hospital."

"Get the radio, it's on his belt."

She unclipped it and handed it to me. "Unit Two, standby," I said as indistinctly as I could.

"Roger that. Standing by."

"Okay so now what?"

"Phone. In my backpack." I grunted in pain as she helped me off with the pack, found the phone and handed it to me. I dialled Danny's burn number. It was a minute before he answered.

"This better be good, Thomas."

"I need you to ask your pals to clear me a special operations helicopter flight plan, very low level from Mojave to somewhere in Nevada. Tell them it's a secret training flight, I don't want the guys from China Lake air base lighting me up with Mavericks."

"What happened?"

"I'm shot, Julie's got a crack on the head and there's a bunch of guys out to bury our arses in the desert."

"Give me five minutes."

"Unit one this is two, what's going on?" This time the voice on the radio was a woman's.

"Wait unit two," I whispered sounding pissed that somebody might have compromised my position.

Julie had found a first aid kit, with snakebite anti serum amongst other things, hydrogen peroxide and sterile gauze pads with adhesive tape. She quickly staunched the bleeding and taped the gauze in place. Now that the initial shock had worn off, I was feeling the pain, which was good, because in five minutes I had to fly us out of this place.

"Let me have a look at your head."

Julie turned around and I dabbed the wound with hydrogen peroxide, making her wince, but it at least would keep any infection at bay until she could get proper medical aid. Then I grabbed the radio again.

"Unit two, this one, check out the car, we have the packages secured."

"Unit two roger that."

I took Julie's hands and looked into her eyes. For two reasons: the first to make sure she wasn't concussed and the second because I wanted her to see that what I was about to do didn't please me one bit.

"I have to do this," I said, lifting the phone and dialling a pre-programmed number.

"I know," she said simply.

I pressed the talk button and a split second later, there was a distant explosion. Then my phone rang.

"Danny?"

"You have your clearance from Mojave to Desert Rock. Call me when you're airborne. Fly 033° and I'll give you the GPS coordinates in a minute, now get the hell out of there before the people in uniforms show up."

ELEVEN

Baja Sud - Mexico - January 2013

Head injuries are unpredictable, especially when the patient is unconscious or even in a coma. And the guessing game as to the seriousness of the injury is further exacerbated by a lack of high-tech equipment. Why? Because the patient needs to be kept 'out-of-sight' in a secure remote location.

Struggling back to consciousness seemed like running a marathon in mud. I was aware of something, but not enough to break through into full consciousness. I wanted to, but those ghostly images and muted sounds seemed so far away.

Then it was as if the curtain fell away and immediately I knew I was alive, lying in bed in the semi-dark with only the faint light of a new moon shining in through the window. I felt rested, my mind surprisingly clear, as if I had enjoyed the best sleep of my life. It was so pleasant lying here with the soft sound of waves and the smell of the ocean. And it didn't matter that I had no idea where I was or what had happened, everything just seemed right. And that feeling was perhaps because short-term amnesia wipes away all the stress I would have felt if I remembered what happened.

Perhaps I was still at the country club, but the room seemed different and Julie wasn't beside me in bed. Maybe she was preparing breakfast or swimming, and we were back in Gozo. Random thoughts drifting across my sterilised mind, as if my body was trying to paint colour back into my soul. Turning from the window, I saw the outline of somebody sitting in a chair across the room.

"Julie?" I asked in what I thought was my normal voice, but it came out as a hoarse whisper.

I felt fine, why was my voice so weak?

Then I tried to lift myself up to a sitting position and found that difficult, as if I was trying to bench press five hundred pounds, and fell back exhausted with the effort.

"Julie?" I said again, and again the voice sounded like the whisper of an old man on his deathbed. Perhaps that's where I was, but maybe I had transitioned from my earthly life to a halfway house between Heaven and Hell. Images burst into my consciousness.

An explosion.

A fire.

Voices shouting, and Julie's face turned to me, eyes closed, blood dripping from her nose and ears.

"No," I screamed and struggled once again to get out of bed. This time I managed to swing my legs off the bed and onto the cool, smooth tiled floor. My head span and I felt nauseous. It would pass, I knew that from past experience, and slowly struggled to my feet. Pain seared through my leg and I crumpled to the floor. I couldn't reach the figure sleeping in the chair unless I crawled. I ignored the pain. I only had one purpose in mind.

Julie. My Julie.

As I touched the figure in the chair, it stirred and the head turned. In the moonlight I saw a face, blond, beautiful, young, eyes trying to focus as sleep fell away.

"Julie?"

The figure moved quickly catching me as I slid onto the floor.

"Not Julie," I heard a voice say but I couldn't place the accent. The voice sounded foreign, and I wondered if it was my brain playing tricks on me. "Let's get you back to bed."

I didn't struggle, just let the woman help me into bed, and then the room was bathed in soft light as she turned on the bedside lamp.

"Julie," I said again not seemingly able to say anything else.

"My name is Morgan Alvarez," the woman said, again in that strange accent, a mixture of English and Spanish maybe.

"Where am I? How long have I been here?"

"My house near La Paz, Baja. I'm a friend of Danny's," the voice said. "You've been here nearly two months. Lie back and sleep now."

"Okay," I said unnecessarily. "Bah what?" I asked, my brain trying to keep up.

"Baja Sud. Mexico."

"Oh. Right. *'The Log of the Sea of Cortez'*. Steinbeck. Read it once. Long time ago." I muttered inanely. "Where's Julie?"

"Lie back and sleep."

"Where is she?" I looked at the woman who was a stranger to me. And her face betrayed what subconsciously I already knew. "No," I screamed. "She can't be. She's not dead. Tell me she's not dead."

"I'm sorry...."

I collapsed back onto the bed, tears streaming down my face, pain wracking every part of my body, but it was not as much as the pain in my soul enveloping me with the knowledge that I'd never see the love of my life ever again. Darkness closed over my mind and once more I slipped into comforting unconsciousness.

Nightmares crowded my sleep and I woke in a sweat, some twelve hours later, gasping for air and thought that Julie's death was just a nightmare, a figment of my imagination.

But I knew it wasn't.

I needed air and crawled to the door leading out onto the patio that overlooked the beach and the Sea of Cortez. It felt similar to Gozo but it was subtly different; the smell of dry sage tinged the slight breeze and somewhere close by, lingering smoke from a mesquite barbecue blew lazily across the beach.

Bile rose in my mouth and I dry retched onto the sand as the image of Julie, bloodied and broken in the helicopter, blasted into my mind.

The moment passed and I sat at the water's edge as small wavelets ran up the beach and sank into the sand.

Julie's death killed something in me. Something I thought I had recovered from after my last tour in Afghanistan. She gave my life a soul that had been destroyed, and now with her death, my soul was as dark as it had ever been.

De Costas would pay for her death.

All that was left in me was the instinct for survival and revenge; the only emotion, pure hatred for the man that had caused all this. It was this that had kept me alive when I should have been dead. It was this that created the desire to fight back to full health.

An hour later I hobbled slowly back to the bedroom, lay down and fell into a dreamless sleep.

I stood in front of the mirror in the bedroom and looked at the stranger who stared back. Shaved head, broken nose, and cold blue, strangely expressionless eyes sunk in deep hollows. What I didn't have was the scar from my wound in Afghanistan. Instead there was redness where a very skilled plastic surgeon had all but erased the evidence with careful skin grafts. My right leg was encased in a cast up to the knee, the pain still excruciating every time I put weight on it. I barely recognised the skeletal creature, turned away from the sight and hobbled out of the house onto the rear veranda that overlooked the yard bordering the beach.

"Good to see you up and about."

I turned to see Morgan walking across from the paddock where two Arabian horses whinnied softly, wearing jeans and a tee shirt, cowboy boots and battered Stetson. "How are you feeling today," she continued in her comfortingly soft accent.

"I've been better." My voice surprised me. I knew it was me that had spoken, but the harshness of my tone startled me.

"I can't say your temper has improved," she said sitting down in one of the wicker chairs. I shrugged and gazed out over the desert. Images of Julie and Gozo flickered through my mind, replaced by the sight of the burning helicopter and her face. I felt myself tense and break out in a sweat.

"Are you OK? Here sit down." I sat down on the offered chair and let out a long slow sigh.

"Its OK. Sometimes the pain is a little strong."

"Of course, your leg was smashed pretty badly. The Doc says the cast will come off next week." She paused looking at me carefully.

"Julie's dead," I said quietly.

She nodded and her eyes softened as she leaned over to touch my hand. "Yes she is. I've been there too. I lost my husband in Iraq. I know what you must be feeling. Don't be ashamed of it."

I couldn't hold her eyes and turned back to the view of the desert.

"We were shot down. I was set up. Danny has a lot to answer for."

"It wasn't Danny. Somebody else knew your destination." Morgan leaned over and laid her hand on mine. "We arrived when it was all over, so I can't tell you who it was. You're lucky to be alive."

"Lucky? Julie's dead and I survived. It should have been the other way around."

"She wouldn't have wanted it that way."

I shook her hand loose and stared at her, angrier than I had been for a long time. "How would you know?"

"I didn't mean...."

The anger fell away quickly. I knew Julie wouldn't have wanted me taking it out on someone else. Besides, I knew who was responsible. De Costas already had his men waiting for us at the factory. They didn't get us there so he must have been able to track the helicopter, or listen in on the communications between Danny and myself. The truth was, I was responsible for Julie's death, no one else.

"Tell me about yourself. You know about me, tell me about yourself," I asked, as gently as I could, trying to take the rough edge off my tone.

"There's not a lot to tell. I'm one of thousands of war widows trying to pick up the pieces of my life. I guess I'm lucky because of the ranch. I have good friends, like the Doc. Now I'm just a country girl doing her thing and not worrying about how the rest of the world is getting on. I've done that bit," she said wistfully.

"Tell me about the Doc."

"He's an old friend from my days in the Agency."

"You were CIA?" I blurted out in surprise.

"Liaison in Kabul. That's how I met Danny."

"Why did you leave?"

"Got too close to an IED. Blast injuries, PTSD the usual thing. The Doc helped me rehabilitate and we've been friends ever since." She stopped, observing my unspoken question, and cut it off before I asked. "We were never lovers. Just friends. Anyway I bought this ranch with some money I had saved up and the pension from the Agency." She sat with a slight smile on her face seemingly content. There was nothing I could say. My own wounds, both physical and mental were too fresh, the images too vivid.

"What do you do now?"

"I am an investigative journalist."

"Investigating anything in particular?"

"Banks and financial institutions mostly. The sub-prime mortgage scam, offshore money laundering, that sort of thing."

"Why here?"

"It's my retreat from work. An escape. This was my grandfather's house. I decided to keep it after my parents passed away. I'm part Mexican, part American."

"Julie liked horses," I said watching Morgan's Arabians canter across the paddock, my voice a whisper as I remembered her taking Prince over the jumps at the Hall. How long ago that seemed. "Who did the plastic surgery?"

"A specialist the Doc knows."

"Danny's idea?"

"Yes." She paused searching my face with her quiet eyes. "He knows you well."

"Meaning?"

"He knows what you're going to do next. He told me a little about Julie."

I talked about Julie then. Told Morgan everything of our life together. Told it in a matter of fact way, as if it was a dream that had no substance in reality. She listened quietly and by the time I had finished, I felt a sense of relief, as if I had just explained to Julie herself the depth of my feeling. Something had died in me that day and been replaced by a steel hardness, a consuming sense of revenge. A cold, cruel sense of purpose, and I knew that I was going to kill De Costas but not until I had destroyed his empire.

But first I had to talk to Julie's father. The thought of explaining to him that I had survived and his only daughter hadn't, filled me with dread. It was a conversation I had to have, and the sooner I did the better.

"Thomas, you're alive," he said his voice cracking.

"I'm sorry Professor. I should have saved Julie. I couldn't I'm sorry," I stuttered knowing exactly how he felt.

"I don't know how to feel about you, Thomas. She was your responsibility. You should never have put her in that position."

"You are right, Professor. I cared more about my own agenda than I did for her safety. That is something I have to live with."

"I know you didn't kill her, Thomas, but I want you to promise me you'll get the bastard who did. Promise me, otherwise she will have died for nothing. It won't bring her back but her death should mean something. Her life should mean something. Do it for me. Do it for Julie. You owe us both."

"I promise."

"If you need my help tracking down the bastard who did this, call me."

Oldfield hung up before I had the chance to say anymore, which was perhaps just as well because there was little I could add. He was right. Julie's life was my responsibility and had I failed her and her father. If my own father's death wasn't enough incentive to uncover the truth, Julie's had directed my focus. Nothing else existed. Every waking moment was concentrated on healing and preparing myself for war. I was going to start with De Costas and see where the trail of breadcrumbs led.

The next few weeks after the cast came off my leg were spent getting back into shape. I followed a strict routine of exercise, each day doing a little more, each night collapsing exhausted on my bed. Morgan tried to get me to slow down, the Doc threatened all sorts of relapses, but something inside drove me. My will combated the pain and forced my reluctant body to become fit and strong.

During this time, I tried to forget about De Costas and let Danny and his friends do the digging for me. To take my mind off everything I concentrated on the leg that had been badly broken.

The Doc told me that I would find walking difficult and would probably not run again. I was going to prove him wrong. The bone had been smashed and a chunk of muscle was missing but gradually, through many hours of pain, I began to take control of it once more. The rest of me healed rapidly, the sun quickly tanned my pale skin and from all the weight lifting, my arms and chest strengthened. I had just finished a bout of training when Morgan came with the first piece of news.

"One of our friends tells me that Coltrane Engineering and Construction Company has really ramped up their production of high pressure pumps and valves." She waited to see the effect the news had on me. "They are the main supplier for a company in the UK."

She sat down at the computer and typed rapidly, then turned the screen for me to see. It was the front page of a San Francisco newspaper devoted to De Costas. A large photograph of him stared at me underneath the headline:

SAMUEL De COSTAS OPENS NEW FACTORY IN NORTHERN IRELAND

Samuel De Costas, well-known San Francisco businessman, today announced the completion of his new factory, Venus Automotive, in Northern Ireland. The factory, which has been partly subsidised by the British Government, will manufacture the new De Costas Venus GT, a revolutionary sports car. Plans are under way to build the car in the province for export to the USA, thereby helping the already dire unemployment problem in Northern Ireland. Mr De Costas says that the new car has advanced on-board computer technology, details of which are still under wraps.

"He's using the factory that was built for Rathborne. I can see now why the place is so big. It was designed especially for the car business."

"Doesn't that mean that your father had something to do with it right from the very beginning?" she said slowly. It was a fact that I had refused to acknowledge. Now it was staring me in the face.

"No. In his last message he was insistent that there is something else going on."

"So what can you do?"

"I'm going to Northern Ireland. The answer is there and I'll find it," I said. "I need to get in touch with Danny."

Morgan didn't say anything straight away. Just stared out of the window. Finally she spoke. "Shouldn't you think it through a little more? I mean, it's a big step and a dangerous one. It needs some planning."

"I'm going back," I said again, my mind already made up. "The answer is there."

Morgan walked out onto the veranda, watching a Jeep drive toward the house trailing a loud of dust. "The Doc's here to check your leg." The Jeep slid to a halt and the Doc climbed out dragging his medical bag with him.

"He's leaving us. Going to Northern Ireland," Morgan said as he walked up the steps onto the veranda.

"Really?"

"Yes."

"Are you sure you're up to it?" He studied me carefully. Sizing me up like an Army doctor being asked to approve a wounded soldier for combat duty.

"Yes."

"Then I'd better make sure." He followed me in. "A man can be a pretty dumb animal at times," he said as I lay on the bed whilst he checked my leg.

"What do you mean?"

"Well, he gets ideas into his head and fails to see what's going on around him."

"I still don't see what you're trying to tell me," I said irritably.

He stopped his examination and peered into my face. "You have to be one of the dumbest people I know. You have an idea for revenge and it clouds your judgement."

"Listen doc. I've just had all that from Morgan. What I do is my own affair."

"Is it? Don't you think she has a stake in it too? I mean, she gave up all her time to nurse you back to health. Isn't that worth something?" He packed up his bag and glanced at me. "The leg still isn't completely healed. It'll hold up, but you still need to be careful. No jumping out of airplanes." Then he left.

"You've upset the doc."

"Can't think why."

"No, I guess you can't," she said and studied me for a moment. "I guess you can't," she said again, turned and left the room. I got off the bed and followed her into the living room.

"Just what is all this stuff about? First I get you going on at me, then the doc, then you again. All cryptic remarks, and still I don't know what the hell is happening."

"It doesn't matter, Thomas. It really doesn't matter. When are you leaving?"

"As soon as possible," I replied.

She shook her head slowly. "OK."

"Listen, if I've upset you, then tell me why?"

"If you don't know, then there is no point discussing it any more." She walked out and left me. I still didn't know why, and what was worse, I really didn't give a crap. Julie's death had uncovered the miserable bastard killer and De Costas was my target.

Alone in my room that night, I started to plan my return.

The only way to destroy the man was to get close to him and that would be difficult. It was no good trying to beat him on his own ground in America. Besides, I wouldn't be able to find out what was really behind my father's death. I was convinced the answer lay in Belfast. That being the case, I had to get out of this country into Northern Ireland with a new identity.

To the rest of the world, Thomas Gunn was dead, just another victim of a road traffic accident.

"Danny, it's Thomas."

"Who else would be calling in the middle of the night?"

"I need cross border access from the Republic. I'll be flying into Dublin on Friday."

"Okay. I'll arrange it, but not Dublin, fly to Shannon. Morgan has a new passport for you and will arrange the flights."

"She didn't tell me."

"She doesn't want you to leave."

"I know, but I don't know why?"

"Maybe she thinks all her hard work will go to waste when you get killed."

"That's not going to happen."

"I'll have a contact meet you at Shannon airport."

"I have an American passport. I can travel on that."

"Keep it clean. It maybe your 'get-out-of-jail-free' card."

"Thanks."

"Don't thank me yet," he said brusquely. "What do you plan to do when you get to Belfast?"

"Get employed by the Venus Automotive Company."

"I have a better idea. I'll tell you when you get to Shannon. And Thomas…. I'm sorry I didn't have your back. Somebody talked."

"Morgan told me. Any idea who?"

"No, but when I find out you'll be the first to know."

"Good enough."

I hung up and lay back on the bed. I had no idea what Danny was thinking, but I knew him, and it would a way for me to get into the factory without arousing suspicion. I got off the bed, switched on the light and looked at myself in the mirror. The face that coolly stared back at me from the glass confirmed my thoughts. Only someone who was very close to me would ever recognise me now. The shaved head and broken nose, all helped to change my physical appearance, but it was the eyes that completed the transformation. There was no softness there. No humour, just a dangerous directness that seemed to belong to somebody else.

There was unfinished business before I left Baja, so I went in search of Morgan. I found her sitting on the beach, reading an eBook on her Kindle with a small briefcase and a tray that held a cocktail shaker and two glasses, one of which was full. She reached down picked up the glass and sipped.

"May I join you?" I asked awkwardly.

"Of course. Gibson?"

"Thanks, I will."

She poured the ice cold vodka from the cocktail shaker, skewered two cocktail onions and dropped them into the glass.

"Your passport is in the briefcase and some papers Danny wanted you to have. Your flight leaves in three days," she said matter-of-factly and continued reading.

"Why didn't you tell me you had talked to Danny?"

"The time wasn't right." She put down the Kindle and looked at me. "And I still don't know if you are ready. Revenge is not a good motive."

"It's all I have."

"You don't have to carry the weight alone, Thomas. You have friends."

"It's dangerous to be a friend of mine. I don't want that responsibility."

"Danny is your friend."

"Danny knows the risks."

"You are a hard man to know Thomas."

"I don't know who I am, so how can anyone else." I didn't mean to sound so harsh, it just came out that way, so I raised my glass and smiled quickly at Morgan. "I appreciate everything you have done for me. I just don't seem to be able to show it. Not yet anyway. Maybe never."

"I understand."

"Thank you."

TWELVE

Eire - February 2013

My first view of Eire in nearly three years, was through the intermittent breaks in the cloud on final approach, and naturally it was raining. The trip from Baja was long, and had taken days. Driving to San Diego, flying to Newark New Jersey, and then the flight to Shannon.

It wasn't until I stepped out of the aircraft that I remembered it was winter. Cold Atlantic wind blew stinging rain like tiny icicles, and reminded me why I liked warm climates, sandy beaches and late night barbecues. The first thing I had to do was get myself a good anorak or freeze to death. Despite the discomfort, it was refreshing to smell the rain, see the green grass and listen to the growling wind blowing in from the cold grey ocean.

True to his word, Danny's contact was waiting for me at the airport. A young woman dressed as a working nun carrying a white sign with my alias printed carefully on it. She spotted me immediately and waved as I walked toward her.

"Father Grissom, welcome, I'm Sister Angelica. We are thrilled you agreed to help us with the renovations," she gushed, taking my suitcase and wheeling it toward the exit, talking non-stop until we were outside and away from prying eyes and inquisitive ears. She led me to a white mini-van in which another nun waited in the driver's seat. Within moments we were driving away from the airport and on the road toward the small town of Shannon.

Sister Angelica turned to me, the smile gone and her gushing excitement turned to business. "We'll stay the night at Saint Theresa's House and travel to the border crossing, tomorrow."

"Saint Theresa's House?" I asked, feeling that I should say something.

"We look after homeless teenagers. Mostly run-a-ways from bad homes who end up on the streets of Dublin. We try to reintegrate them into society."

"Oh," I muttered, surprised that the cover was a working institution.

"Danny's idea. He said it is a way to give back."

I smiled. There were so many things I didn't know about my friend, and yet this didn't surprise me. Behind the killer's mask was a humanitarian who cried over Jameson Irish Whiskey and Caruso, and I hoped that when this was all over I too could do something similar. Julie would have liked that.

"Good for him," I said.

"He remembered what it was like when he was a child in the same situation," Sister Angelica said holding my eyes, searching for a glimmer of humanity. But I didn't feel any humanity, surprise, but not humanity. Not yet and maybe never. Julie's death was my death too.

"Good for him," I said again and turned to stare at the passing cars and small houses on the outskirts of Shannon.

"Danny's my brother, Mr Gunn."

If anyone had hit me over the head with a brick I wouldn't have been more surprised. When I looked at her, Sister Angelica's eyes held no animosity, just curiosity.

"I didn't know he had a sister."

"And I didn't know he had any friends, so I think that perhaps we are equally ignorant on some matters."

"I guess we are," I answered feeling like a child who felt guilty that he had not been punished for being a selfish little bugger.

"You will be asking yourself what we are doing helping a former British soldier. Will you not?"

"Not the first thing that sprang to mind."

"Oh," she said, a slight smile creasing the corner of her mouth. "Then you'll be wondering why Danny's sister is a nun."

"I confess that did cross my mind," I replied wondering where this conversation was going.

"We are both warriors, just in a different way. Danny assures me that you are a good man. That is the only reason we are helping you, Mr Gunn."

"Please, call me Thomas."

"Perhaps you can do something for the children when this is all over, Thomas. If you are of a mind," she said quietly, holding on tightly as the van braked suddenly and turned into a driveway that led up to a modest size Georgian house surrounded by a stand of alder and aspen trees a short distance from the house. To the side was a garage and stable complex.

"You'll stay in the stable flat tonight, we'll be leaving early," Sister Angelica said as she led me to the small apartment above the stable. "I'll have dinner brought to you later. Rest now, Danny will call at seven this evening."

Left alone with my thoughts and a splitting headache, I lay down on the bed listening to the wind in the trees and distant murmur of voices from the house, thinking of how I was going to get myself employed at the Venus Automotive factory. But any amount of worrying the problem was not going to solve it. I had to be on the ground and integrated into the local population before I would find the way.

One of the Sisters brought me dinner at six o'clock, a simple but delicious meal of Atlantic salmon served with a slice of lemon, boiled new potatoes tossed in butter and Italian parsley, a savoury carrot layer, and a generous glass of smooth red wine that went surprisingly well with the fish.

At precisely seven o'clock my burn phone rang.

"I trust you dined well, Thomas," Danny's voice quietly mocked me.

"Your sister? Really?"

"Some things are private, you should appreciate that."

"Touché. What have you got for me?"

"You'll be dropped off in Crossmaglen. There's a car at the church with a passport, driver's licence, chequebook and credit cards, another burn phone, a normal iPhone and a MacBook Pro laptop. The access code is our last mission together in Afghanistan. Do you remember?"

"I do," I answered grimly.

"Just don't spend all the money, it's my personal alter ego you are using, and my money. I'm not rich like you so I'd appreciate a refund. I've arranged a job for you at the factory. Your name is Tom Nelson and you're a central control systems analyst from Orion Electronics in

San Francisco, the company that supplies the central computer that controls all the car's functions. They asked for him to sort out a bug in the software."

"He's a real person?"

"Yup. On a brief sabbatical until you're done. I have a man in the factory, Billy O'Brien, who'll take care of the software problem, so just act nerdy. Nelson is known to be a bit strange, likes to be on his own and not mix with the crowd, so find yourself a B&B in Dundonald."

"And then?"

"You're on your own. Billy's a good man, but you're on your own until you're out of there."

"Okay. I appreciate the help."

"You'll pay eventually."

"Saint Theresa's House? I'll be happy to."

"Good," he said with feeling.

At the height of 'The Troubles' in Northern Ireland in the 1970s, Crossmaglen in South Armagh was probably the most dangerous place in Northern Ireland for a British Soldier. The countryside littered with roadside bombs and booby traps, and a porous border with Eire that the Provisional IRA could cross at will and ambush patrols. Now it seemed a sleepy country town, the old Army Base near the town centre was gone, as was the heavily fortified Sanger that once looked out across the town square.

The car was exactly where Danny said it would be, and after a few minutes checking it out, and a quick goodbye to the Sisters I was on my way north towards Dundonald, hoping I would be able to find a B&B fairly close to the Venus Automotive factory.

There were no vehicle checkpoints on the road, which surprised me, as three days previously a car bomb had been discovered just north of Newry. I had no detailed plan, and was just taking each moment as it came.

Once I reached the outskirts of Dundonald, I headed for the factory and was amazed at the transformation. All the builder's rubble was gone, and where Julie and I had killed Boyd, De Costas' less than savoury henchman, was a smooth new parking lot in front of a modern glass and concrete structure, with the offices along the front hiding the main manufacturing facility at the rear. As far as major car manufacturers were concerned this was a small operation. Small it may be, but I knew what it had cost in money and blood.

I drove on and stopped at the nearest service station. The attendant filled the car and gave me directions to a B&B. It didn't take me long to find the cul-de-sac that he had mentioned. The lady who answered the door was about fifty-five with a cheery face and homely figure.

"Good afternoon, my name is Tom Nelson," I said holding out my hand. Her grasp was firm and dry. "The guy at the gas station told me you may have a room for rent," I said in my best American accent.

"That's right I do. I'm Katie Dillon. Kevin called ahead and said you'd be by. Come on in." She stepped aside and let me pass. "How long would you be wanting it for?"

"Oh, it's difficult to say really. I have been brought over for a temporary job at Venus Automotive."

"Well it's a small world, my daughter works there."

"Really. What a co-incidence."

"Indeed. Here we are." She showed me into a reasonably good size room, well furnished and clean. "Will this be what you're looking for?"

"Perfect."

"Meals are served in the dining-room. Breakfast at seven, dinner at seven-thirty in the evening if you've a mind. That's extra. The bathroom is just over to the right." She gestured down the corridor. "You are the only one in at the moment. Winter is usually a very slack time. Once you're settled in I'll have a cup of tea waiting for you in the kitchen."

"Thank you." We discussed the cost and payment, and then I collected my small suitcase and backpack from the car, returned to the room, unpacked and went down to the kitchen.

Katie Dillon placed a mug of steaming tea on the kitchen table and a plate with several slices of fruitcake in front of me and sat down with her cup. "You fellers from the factory usually stay at the Hotel," she said watching me carefully. After all the years of violence in Northern

Ireland, a strong sense of wariness ran through the community when strangers visited their doorstep.

"Yes they do," I replied smoothly picking up a slice of cake and taking a bite. "This is delicious and also one of the reasons I like to stay in B&B's. Hotel's are too soulless and it's good to get away from work for a few hours."

She smiled quietly, seemingly satisfied with my reasons. "Where do you come from in America?"

"California. I was born in Santa Barbara, just north of Los Angeles."

"Really, I have a sister who lives in Mendocino," she said excitedly. "Has done for the past twenty years. Married a lawyer."

"Which is why they can afford to live in Mendocino," I said laughing. She picked up on the joke and her face cracked into a broad grin.

"She keeps asking us to visit, but I really can't just now. Too many bills to pay."

I heard the front door open and close and footsteps in the hall. A young, attractive black-haired girl came into the kitchen.

"Hello, I'm Eileen. My mother told me we had a guest. It's unusual at this time of year." She held out her hand and I shook it. Her disturbingly blue-grey eyes surveyed me frankly, as women do in this country. It was unnerving. Evidently she liked what she saw, as she smiled warmly and sat down in the chair opposite.

"Tom Nelson," I said.

She smiled. "Yes I know, from Orion Electronics to sort out the software problem on the central control system."

"Word gets around quickly," I said easily. If only she knew the truth.

"We can't release the cars until that's done, the glitch is shutting down the engine fuel control."

"You work with Billy O'Brien?"

"That's right. Not that I'm technical at all, that's your department, I just manage the paperwork."

I could feel the sweat prickle on the back of my neck and wondered just how much she knew about the real Tom Nelson.

"Eileen love, I'm sure Tom would rather just relax and not think about work tonight."

Eileen poured herself a mug of tea and sat down at the table, looking at me over the top of her mug ignoring her mother and chatting about the factory and her job. As she sat and talked, it was my turn to study her. She was of medium height with a good figure. Her mouth perhaps just a little over-generous but her eyes held a hidden warning. My guess was that if she decided to she could be a physical and passionate lover, or a violent and passionate enemy. Just like the country itself.

Eileen talked all through dinner, asking questions about America and California in particular, and then invited me to the local pub to round off the evening, where he introduced me to a couple of her friends who also worked at the Venus Automotive. For an hour they flooded me with questions about California and I thanked God I knew the State well and could talk as if I had lived there all my life. Eileen basked in the glow my presence seemed to excite, and if I had not been so focused on my mission, I would have enjoyed the attention, but instead I thought that when I turned up at the factory in the morning, I would have unsuspecting allies that would cement my identity.

The four martinis Eileen had tucked away made it a little awkward as I tried to slip into my room once we had returned to the B&B. For a moment she blocked the way, her mouth slightly open, eyes staring at me dreamily.

"Goodnight and thank you for a lovely evening," I said and gently slipped away from her intended embrace, closed and locked the door behind me and heaved a sigh of relief.

I didn't need complications.

At breakfast the following morning, Eileen showed no hint of the near encounter the night before.

"Bright and early I see Tom," she said as she joined her mother and I at the table. "Billy O'Brien does like his staff to be punctual."

The drive to the factory took ten minutes and Eileen showed me where to park then walked me to the office at the side of the main factory building. Billy O'Brien was nothing like I expected. Tall, barrel-chested with grizzled grey hair and a ruddy complexion. He looked more like a farmer than a software computer programmer.

"Tom, good to meet you, I hear you're staying at Eileen's Mum's B&B," his voice boomed across the office as he strode over to shake my hand.

"Happy to be here Mr O'Brien."

Billy looked at me a mischievous sparkle in his eye and I knew Danny had filled him in on my background.

"It's Billy. Follow me, I'll give you the ten cent tour." He turned and strode off. I looked at Eileen who squeezed my arm and winked before walking to her desk.

The factory was an eye-opener. The first place he showed me was the main assembly line. We entered what I almost mistook for the central control at Houston. There was an array of panels, switches, lights, dials and television monitors. The room itself was three-sided glass, looking out over the production line. It was like something from outer space. It was the first fully automated assembly line I had ever seen and I was staggered. Through the glass I saw car shells being moved about, welded, turned, sprayed, dipped, all without any help from a single human being. I had to close my eyes and look again.

"The monocoque chassis are made from pre-formed aluminium beams that are assembled and welded automatically. Once the main monocoque gets to the end, the engines, wheels, suspension and interior are all carried out by our own work force. By using robots for the body construction we can cut manpower by a third and speed up production. It also allows us to pay the workers more than if we had to pay a team of specialist aluminium welders. Come. Follow me."

I still had my mouth open. So this is where the money had gone. I was still going to kill De Costas but now I had a grudging respect for his ability to get things done. Billy behaved like a boy with a new toy as he showed me around the factory. It was the best equipped and most modern of its type in the world, full of the latest inventions in computer controlled assembly. But I didn't see it costing anywhere near £2.75 billion.

It was housed in a building close to the factory's own private test track. The last time I was here I had wondered why so large an area was being excavated. Now I could see why. It had everything. Rough road conditions, high-speed circuit, crash testing facilities, the lot. The building we were headed towards was about the size of one of those light industrial units you see on small town industrial estates. Billy opened the door and I followed him inside.

There, sitting in front of me, was the most beautiful looking car I'd ever seen in my life. The De Costas Venus GT.

It was metallic light blue with tinted glass, wide wheels and tyres, and the general appearance of having stepped straight out of a science fiction film.

"Go on. Get in," Billy said. I went up to the car.

There were no door handles.

"And just where is the biometrics pad?" I said. Billy chuckled again, leaned past me and pressed his thumb on the door pillar. The gull wing door hissed open to reveal the sumptuous interior. All leather and wood.

"The whole pillar or just a section?"

"A three inch section, the exact position is different on each car. It's the owner's choice. When we get back to the office, I'll code your thumb print into the system so you can get into the car." He waved his hand toward the cockpit. I climbed in and lowered myself into the incredibly comfortable and snug seat. The steering wheel fell easily to hand, the paddle shifters just where they should be. The dashboard was a series of LCD digital displays that were linked to the central computer. There was everything. A display for fuel consumption, ignition function, oil pressure and consistency, water temperature, electrical discharge and alternator function and a diagrammatic fault tracing chart for the engine, plus full communications console with Smartphone connection, GPS navigation display and rear video camera. It was a 2+2, but still with ample room in the rear for two adults.

"Jesus." I said and let out a low whistle. "This is some machine."

"V6 3 litre engine just behind the rear seats, capable of 545 bhp and a fuel consumption of 60 mpg or in new parlance, 21 kilometres per litre. It's assembled here too. It's just the fuel-metering problem that needs to be sorted. Here have a look." I climbed out of the car and went around to the back. The engine was neatly housed and surprisingly accessible, mainly because the whole of the back end of the car lifted up. After we'd discussed the engine, Billy showed me the rest of the test and development area. It took up half the building and contained all the necessary monitoring equipment, ramps, and a special booth for simulating hot and cold conditions. There was a suspension testing device and a machine that tested bearings to destruction. The other half of the building was secret and only the top designers and De Costas himself were allowed inside. Although I was enthralled by all this high technology and the superb workmanship of the car, I was also aware of everything around me. I took mental notes of my surroundings.

"I'd invite you to take a drive, but as you know we have a fuel metering problem." He winked and moved his head as if to say '*follow me*', then strode away to the rear of the building.

"They have cameras on the car, but not over here," Billy whispered. "You'll be interested in 'The Lab', as they call it. Only a handful of people are allowed in and they don't mix with the other employees. I don't know just how you are going to get in, but Danny says to give you everything you need."

"Right now I need a quick lesson in computer software so my cover doesn't get blown."

"Don't worry I've got that under control, I'll show you when we get back to the office. I'll take you past 'The Lab' on the way."

From the outside, 'The Lab' was built on the excavated area I had seen when I visited last year. It looked like an afterthought thrust against the side of the main manufacturing plant, with almost unnoticeable CCTV cameras on the corners under the flat roof overhang, that covered every approach angle, so there would be no access from outside. Just as we were passing by the door, a stocky, well-muscled man appeared from the main building and walked toward us. I could tell from the lump in his ill-fitting jacket that he was carrying a large automatic, and from his expression I knew he had been tracking us on the CCTV monitor inside.

"Who's your friend Billy?" the man said with no hint of friendship.

"Tom Nelson from Orion Electronics here to fix the computer problem, Sean."

"This area's off limits, you know that."

"Just taking a short cut back to the office. Been giving Tom the ten cent tour."

"Take the five cent tour and the long route next time," Sean said rudely and waited until we were well on our way before returning to his lair.

"Sean Flynn. Definitely not an average worker," Billy said quietly as we walked back to the office. As we walked I was thinking that I'd have to call Professor Oldfield. It had been a while since I talked to him about Julie's death, but he wanted to help and I needed a way of accessing the De Costas factory's building plans. There still had to be an entrance into 'The Lab' from inside the main manufacturing floor, as witnessed by the fact that Sean Flynn had come from there as we walked past 'The Lab's' main door.

"I've programmed your computer as a clone of mine. Anything I do to the software will show up as your work no matter what buttons you press," Billy was saying. "Anyone casually glancing at your screen will think you're the real genius."

Billy and I stayed long after everyone had left the office for the day, under the pretence of the urgent need to fix the software problem, which mysteriously seemed to resist all our attempts to solve it. It provided the excuse to have access to the prototype Venus GT so that we could use a laptop to run diagnostics and various 'fixes'. None of which worked of course. The night security made their rounds and gave us a cursory inspection before leaving us to our 'work'.

Retreating to the far corner of the workshop out of sight of the cameras, I dialled Oldfield.

"What do you need," he said without preamble, knowing that I was calling for help.

"The building plans for the Venus Automotive factory in Dundonald. It used to be Rathborne Micro-Electronics and may still be listed as that with the planning department."

"I'll send you a code access for a secure website when I've tracked the plans down. What mobile can I text you on?" I could hear him already typing furiously on his keyboard. I gave him the burn number. "I'll get back to you," he said crisply.

Billy and I continued on for another two hours, acting out our 'frustration' at not being to 'solve' the problem, and eventually shut everything down at midnight.

Eileen was waiting for me in the drawing room dressed in a thick white floor length Terry towelling dressing gown, when I arrived back at the B&B. Beside her on the coffee table were two shot glasses and an unlabelled bottle of clear liquor.

"Come on in, I thought you might like a nightcap." She leaned forward and lifted the bottle. "My mother's supply of very old Poteen. My uncle makes it," she whispered.

"It's a bit late," I said dubiously eying the bottle, knowing what 'old' Poteen could do to your mind.

"Go on. Try it," she said, poured me a shot glass full and handed it to me. I took a sip of the clear liquid. It was smooth to taste, and then the 90 proof alcohol caught up as it burned all the way down my throat. It was good and reminded me of sitting with Danny, listening to Caruso and drinking until we could barely see straight.

It was comfortable in the warm little house and I could see that after two glasses, the Poteen had already gone to Eileen's head. She looked at me with smoky eyes, her mouth slightly open and lips moist.

"You are an attractive man, Mr Tom Nelson. But you know that don't you?" she said softly, slurring her words. "You're not the nerdy computer freak everyone thinks you are." She laughed quietly. "I heard you met Sean Flynn today."

"You did, did you?"

"It's a small work force and anything that happens around 'The Lab' gets noticed."

"Ah. Gossip. That's why I stay away from hotels."

"Don't worry I won't tell, if you don't."

"That Sean guy seems a bit strange, scared the life out of me."

"Scares the life out of everyone. That's his job."

"Maybe he thought I was a spy or reporter looking for a story."

"Young Aidan got fired for taking a peek inside 'The Lab'. Nobody's seen him since."

"Better stick to my computer then."

She rose, picked up the glasses and bottle and left the room. I heard her wash the glasses, then make her way upstairs.

I got up, switched the light out and went up to my room, undressed, washed and climbed gratefully into bed. It had been a long day and an even longer night, and my leg was throbbing from the activity. I lay awake thinking about how to get into 'The Lab', but could not come to any conclusions until I had the plans from Oldfield. And as if to answer my plea, the burn phone buzzed softly in my jacket pocket. I slipped out of bed, slipped into a pair of tracksuit pants and retrieved the phone. It was the website and code from Oldfield. Taking the laptop I went downstairs to the kitchen and turned it on. While it booted up I helped myself to a glass of milk from the fridge to ease the acid in my stomach from the Poteen. I used the iPhone Danny had left for me to connect to the Internet, typed in the computer unlock code and went to the site Oldfield had given me. How he had managed to find the correct plans amongst what seemed to be a dizzying myriad of different editions, was beyond me, but then that was his skill, not mine.

From what I could see, the doorway leading from the main assembly floor to 'The Lab', was closed off by a thick wall. The plan was dated three weeks ago and I wondered if that coincided with young Aidan's adventure.

It was just the slightest sound of bare feet on the wooden floor that alerted me to Eileen's presence, so I quickly escaped the website, unplugged the iPhone and brought up the Venus GT system controller schematic.

"What are you doing?" she whispered accusingly. I jumped and turned quickly as if startled by her voice.

"Dear God, you nearly gave me a heart attack," I whispered hand over my heart. Eileen peered over my shoulder and stared at the schematic of which I knew she had no understanding. "I just had an idea and wanted to work on it. I didn't mean to wake you."

147

"It's nearly two o'clock in the morning."

"And I have a deadline to keep. If I don't get the system running properly, I'll lose my job."

"I just came down for a glass of milk," she said sleepily.

"Me too. That Poteen is pretty powerful. I'll get it, you sit down." I crossed to the cupboard and I fetched a glass from the cupboard, and then retrieved the milk from the fridge. Eileen yawned and rubbed her eyes.

"There you go," I said quietly, placing the glass in front of her. She drank half and then stood.

"Okay. I'm going back to bed. You better get some sleep too. The big boss is visiting tomorrow."

"Big Boss?"

"Mr De Costas. Flying in from San Francisco."

THIRTEEN

Over the past few days I had watched the security guard schedules, and plotted the locations of all the CCTV cameras. The fence at the far side of the test track had a small blind spot where one of the cameras did not quite rotate to cover the arc of the other camera fifty metres away. I discovered it when I had taken a walk around the track during my lunch break two days ago.

Earlier in the evening I had slipped sleeping powder into the cups of tea I made for Eileen and her mother, and waited until I knew they were asleep before I left the house and headed for the factory.

It had started to rain, again, and the anorak was no match for the cold wind that made me shiver as I slipped through the hole in the fence, and quickly ran to the test building where Billy and I had been working. From there it was a question of timing the camera rotations and slipping across the open space to the main manufacturing building. The unobtrusive back door, hidden behind a builder's dumpster left over from the construction opened easily, much to my surprise. But then the actual manufacturing facility wasn't in full production yet as the computer fuel metering glitch still had to be fixed, so there were still lapses in the security.

I closed my eyes and flipped through the office floor plan I had memorised, but it is one thing to have a map in front of you, it is quite another to go from memory. Dull security lights gave the robotic machines used for welding, lifting and turning, a strange haunting and decidedly creepy look, as if any moment they would leap into life, pluck me from the floor and weld me into one of the monocoque car chassis.

Eventually I found myself in the right section close to the manufacturing supervisor's office. I was just about to turn the handle of the door when the muffled sound of voices stopped me. I tried to pinpoint where the sound was coming from. It was difficult with the soundproofing. I opened the door and the voices became clearer. There were two men in the office I had to go through to get to what I thought might be a smaller office or store room in the rear where the blocked up doorway to 'The Lab' was located.

"So everything is set then? Are you sure the load is correctly marked?" It was a man's voice with a distinctly East European accent.

"Listen, I told you. It's all set. Everything's marked up just like the Boss wants." This man's accent was pure Brooklyn. There was silence for a moment or two except for the shuffling of papers. One of the men laughed, a short crude sound.

"Orange Moon. I ask you. What the hell kind of name is that?"

The other man grunted and mumbled a reply that I missed.

"OK. That seems to be it. Let's go." There was a scrape of chairs. I gently shut the door, and quickly slipped behind one of the part welded monocoque chassis. There was no shout. I hadn't been spotted. As I listened to the footsteps recede, I went over what I'd heard. They had obviously been talking about a shipment and, by the sounds of it, were probably filling in shipping manifests. But it was the use of the words *'Orange Moon'* that had caught my attention.

The words nagged at the back of my mind. I couldn't pin the memory down. What did *'Orange Moon'* mean? Where had I heard it before? There were still gaps in my memory from the crash, but I knew if I just kept at it, the memory that lurked so tantalisingly close would return.

Once I was sure that the two men had left the building, I slipped out from my hiding place and returned to the office door. A couple of seconds and the lock clicked open and I slid inside and relocked the door. I had come equipped with a small LED flashlight with red bulbs, which gave just enough light in the pitch-black office for me to find the storage room and begin my search for the doorway into 'The Lab'.

The office still seemed in the stages of construction, haphazardly arranged desks behind the main robot control panel, which was up and running waiting for a full manufacturing run. It was as if the manufacturing process was an after thought and I was even more curious to take a look inside 'The Lab'. Against the far wall were shelving units and two seven foot tall steel cabinets, right where I figured the doorway should be located.

'It can't be that easy,' I thought.

I picked the lock on the right hand cabinet and looked inside. It was stacked floor to ceiling with computer equipment, I guessed to run the manufacturing robots. The left hand cabinet was the same and yet something didn't quite seem right. Further investigation revealed a small, unnoticeable to a casual glance, biometric thumb pad right in the centre of the computer bank, disguised as a logo.

Now I needed Oldfield's help and hoped he wasn't going to be pissed and me waking him at this time in the morning.

"Yes Thomas," he said sleepily.

"Apologies for the hour but I need to get into a building that is secured by a biometrics pad."

"Have you been entered into the security system?"

"Yes, to open the Venus GT's doors."

"Was it coded in the central computer?"

"As far as I know. It was done on the office computer."

"Okay, stay on the line and give me a minute."

I could hear him moving about, the sound of the computer booting up, a bottle top being unscrewed, I guessed his favourite Talisker, and began to wonder if he was losing control and using the whisky as a prop. Perhaps the more involved he became in my mission, the better. But what did I know? I'm not a behavioural psychologist and if I were I'd be questioning my own sanity. He began typing rapidly and I pulled the phone away from my ear so I could hear if any security were prowling around. There wasn't a sound except for the low hum of a generator somewhere.

"Okay I found your print algorithm, now just need to find where the other biometrics pad files are stored." He was talking to himself, grunting on occasion. "Really?" he exclaimed suddenly.

"Really what?" I whispered.

"Very clever. Hiding in plain sight. I missed it the first time, and if I may say so, anyone other than me would never have found it."

"Okay. Now what?"

"I add your biometric print to the list and hide it so it won't show up on the lock access log."

"How long?" I was getting nervous about the time and wanted to be out of 'The Lab' before daylight.

"Done."

Taking a deep breath I pressed my finger to the pad and heard a soft click, then the cabinets slid apart to reveal a narrow entrance through a four-foot thick wall into what looked like some kind of airlock.

"Thanks Professor. Call you later."

"Anytime."

What on earth would De Costas want with an airlock in a car manufacturing plant? I stepped through and heard the cabinets slide shut behind me. After a momentary hiss of pressurised air the door in front of me slid open. I went through another four feet of concrete wall and stepped into 'The Lab'.

Compared to the outside dimensions, 'The Lab' was at least half the size, and I figured that each of the walls was at least ten feet thick. The ceiling was low and again I wondered what this was doing here. As I stepped through into 'The Lab' proper, lights snapped on, for a moment blinding me and I tugged the Glock from its holster and crouched, waiting for the first shot. But there was nobody in the room; a movement sensor activated the lights recessed into the ceiling.

The room was completely empty.

It was a 'clean room', but with no visible signs of any equipment anywhere. My thumbprint had allowed me entry, but nothing more, so there must be a secondary biometrics pad. I took out the phone and stared at the display. No signal. Of course not. With ten-foot thick walls there was no way.

I had no choice but to return the way I came and try again tomorrow night after a lengthy conversation with Oldfield. There was something we had both missed in the plans and in the central computer.

Once back in the office, I rummaged through the filing cabinets and drawers and located shipping manifests from the factory outside Mojave and from Suldiski in Estonia. Two manifests were for auto-parts and the third beauty products, which was so completely out-of-place. I photographed them with the iPhone and left the office, locking the door behind me.

Outside the rain had stopped, but it was still overcast, which was lucky as through the clouds I could see faint glimmers of light. Within two minutes I was back in the car and driving slowly back to the B&B. I knew Eileen would be asleep for another hour, and her mother would not be up for another forty minutes, so I slipped back into the house, undressed and crawled into bed. I don't remember falling asleep, just waking with a start.

'Orange Moon.'

I saw the words clearly written on the pot of face cream I'd found in my father's safe. I knew I'd seen the words and it still didn't make much sense. A pot of face cream and the words 'beauty products' on the manifests from Estonia were the only solid link to my father.

I got out of bed and walked over to the window. Outside it was raining again, hammering down onto the roof and sheeting down the window, but I hardly noticed.

What did it all mean? The simple explanation was that my father was heavily involved with this conspiracy or fraud or whatever it was, and perhaps been killed because of a feud with De Costas, but I didn't believe that. My father was a hard, tough businessman, but he wasn't a crook.

But just what was the link between the two?

Why was my family mixed up in this?

The questions kept coming. Spinning around in my head without answer. What was De Costas really up to?

A quick phone call to Oldfield got him re-investigating the building plans and construction materials orders for what used to be Rathborne Micro-Electronics. It would take some time and I was getting nowhere with my self-questioning, so I went back to bed.

By the time Eileen and I finished breakfast, with her complaining of a headache, and her mother blaming her for drinking the last of the Poteen, the rain had stopped.

I thought of Morgan and the ranch, the desert and the welcoming beach. Then thought of Julie as I entered the workshop. I was tired and the prospect of another long night after a full day's work didn't put me in a good frame of mind.

Eileen had told me that De Costas was expected in the afternoon. She couldn't be more specific about the time, which was a pity. I didn't want to end up face to face with him and run the risk of being recognised.

Billy wasn't at the office when we arrived, but had left a note saying he had a meeting in the morning and would be back mid afternoon and instructions for me to 'continue' with the diagnostic test, then maybe take the car for a test drive if I could get it working. Which meant that all I had to do was play act for a while and then start the car.

When I thought enough time had elapsed as I tinkered inside the car and in the engine bay, I shut the rear deck lid, climbed into the car and pressed my thumb on the starter button, after a couple of seconds, the display unit lit up and the engine jumped to life.

The semiautomatic transmission was a very sophisticated system, based on Formula One Racing technology, simplified for road use. Once the engine started the transmission remained in 'neutral' until the right hand paddle shifter was activated to select 1st gear, but without your foot on the brake, no gear could be selected. I let the car run for five minutes, supposedly checking the fuel system with the iPad Billy used to monitor the systems, then put my foot on the brake and flipped the paddle shifter. There was no noticeable engagement of first gear, but once my left foot came off the brake, a light touch on the accelerator had the car moving quickly out of the test building and onto the track. I knew that there would be quite a few workers taking time out to watch my run on the test track, so had be sure to put on a good show. Billy had posted an email to the effect that I had solved the fuel-metering problem, and the first test run would happen in the early afternoon.

"Ready to go are we? Track's dried out."

I looked up and saw Billy standing beside the car. I had been so engrossed in what I was doing I didn't see or hear him. And that worried me. I needed to be sharper than that.

"Yup. That okay?"

"Go for it," he smiled.

Turning onto the track, I settled back, tightened the seat belt and pressed the accelerator to the floor. I was surprised how quietly, smoothly and quickly the car hurtled down the straight to the first corner, easily reaching 290 kph (180 mph) before it was time to brake, downshift and turn in. There was no drama, just a little step out of the back-end that a touch on the steering wheel and feathered accelerator corrected, and then we were off to the next fast curving right-hander, taken just about flat out before braking again for the chicane.

It would have been easy to forget why I was here, except when I came down the main straight for the sixth time, I could see Samuel De Costas standing in the 'Pit' lane next to Billy. Just for the hell of it I put in another five laps until Billy finally waved me in.

"Well, Thomas, how did it go?"

"Fine Billy. No problems at all. She's a really beautiful machine," I said enthusiastically, trying to make my voice sound American and convincing, but any moment I was waiting for De Costas to recognise me. "I really gave the fuel system a work out and it's functioning perfectly."

"This is Mr De Costas, Tom, the owner of the factory. He's come over personally to supervise the delivery of the first car," Billy beamed with a pride I knew he only half felt.

I turned to De Costas. His cold eyes bored into me, for a moment they flickered with uncertainty, and then the veil closed again. Had he recognised me? I felt calm. It didn't matter. I was going to kill him and I wanted him to know that it was me, but not just yet.

"Hi. Great car you have sir," I said and extended my hand. He ignored it and turned his eyes to the car, walked around slowly scrutinising it from every angle.

"You say you fixed the fuel problem?" he said without looking at me.

"Yes sir. One of the algorithms that adjust the turbocharger backpressure was interfering with the fuel injection metering unit. I programmed a fail-safe so it never happens again."

De Costas looked at me blankly and then again there was a slight puzzlement in his eyes as he stared at me. I stared right back, trying to keep an excited expression on my face like a puppy that had just learned a new trick, and was waiting for a treat.

"You work for Orion?"

"Yes sir, we make the best on-board central...."

"Yeah right," he interrupted just as a black Range Rover braked to a halt. He looked annoyed and nervous as the rear passenger side window rolled down and a dark haired woman looked at De Costas imperiously. Sean Flynn stepped out of the driver's seat and stood between the woman and De Costas.

"Make sure all the other units are fixed," De Costas said between clenched teeth. "And make sure it gets cleaned up," he commanded and hurried away to the car, climbing into the front passenger seat. The woman stared at me for a long moment until the tinted window rolled up and blocked my view. I had a feeling I had seen her before, and cursed the head injury that was messing with my memory, but as the Range Rover drove away I knew where I had seen her. Once in De Costas' office in San Francisco and then again at the Mojave facility, but there was another memory nagging at the back of my mind. From her behaviour, it seemed that De Costas deferred to her, and if that was the case, then the mystery was deepening at every turn. And again I wondered if I had been recognised. Now it was even more imperative that I get back into 'The Lab' tonight. My time here was rapidly running out, and instinct told me I had less than twenty-four hours to get out of Ireland.

It was another late cold and rainy night, with Billy and I supposedly working on the other systems we had collected from the parts department. There was of course nothing wrong with them at all, and while we worked I filled Billy in with what I had found and what I was going to do.

"You shouldn't be here, so make some excuse and leave now," I told him quietly, my voice low so the microphone on the CCTV wouldn't pick it up. "Tell gate security I'll be at least another four to five hours, completing the fixes De Costas ordered."

"Okay."

Ten minutes later, Billy stood up and stretched.

"De Costas wants them all completed tonight, Tom. I told the wife I'd be back early. She's not feeling so well."

"No problem Billy, I've got it covered."

"I'll buy you a pint tomorrow."

"You're on, but it'll be two pints."

He laughed, winked at me and strolled away. I hoped our little play-acting convinced whoever was watching the CCTV that we were just a couple of workers under duress from the Boss to get everything done. For the past few hours, we had established a routine of stacking the units on the bench on the far wall, which was out-of-site of the CCTV camera, and talking to each other. I worked on the bench where I couldn't be seen and talked to Billy as he worked on the car.

When Billy left I turned on the car stereo and set the music to low as I whistled tunelessly and worked. Using the iPhone, I recorded my tuneless whistling, and every now and then, swore loudly and cursed De Costas time schedule. It was raining again outside and I knew none of the guards was going to check on me.

Another hour and I set the iPhone to play, made another trip to the car so the guard could see me, then slipped out of the testing bay into the night, dialling Oldfield as I went. I had one hour to see what I could find and get back to the testing bay before the iPhone stopped playing.

"I think I found what we missed last night," Oldfield said immediately, not wasting time with a perfunctory greeting. "There is a touch pad just inside the room to the right, about shoulder height. Don't know what it does, but try it anyway."

"I won't be able to tell you what's happening, the walls are too thick."

"Okay. Good luck."

The problem with rain is that the only way to avoid leaving a trail is to strip off shoes and any other wet clothing. The temperature had dropped considerably and it looked as if the rain may turn to snow, which would not be good. There was no heating inside the main manufacturing building and as I stripped off my shoes and outer clothing, I could feel the freezing temperature begin to bite into me. Cold is not a temperature I enjoy, and weeks of training days in the Brecon Beacons during winter when I was in the Army, always made me long for the Mediterranean sunshine. I must have been an interesting sight creeping between the robots in bare feet, underwear and a tee shirt, but at least I wasn't leaving a trail of footsteps behind.

Nobody was in the office and within thirty seconds I was in 'The Lab' and looking for the touch pad on the right hand wall. On the second attempt, I heard a whirring sound and turned to see the centre of the room start to rise revealing what I can only describe as a complicated pressure pump assembly, but with many more pipes, valves and what looked to be small round 'containment' vessels. But at the centre there were a series of long glass vacuum tubes, which looked to me like those used for lasers. At the far end was a foundry furnace with a metal tube leading to a metal stamping or moulding machine. Pulling out the burn phone I snapped as many photographs as I could. Already I had taken thirty minutes out of my self-imposed one-hour time limit and needed to get out of here. But curiosity took over, as I spotted what seemed to be another door on the other side of the machinery that hadn't been apparent before.

It took a minute to find the touch pad and, when triggered, the centre floor section lowered, concealing the 'machine', then a section of the wall slid upwards like a very sophisticated 'roll-up' garage door, and about the same size. It was a large air chamber and as I stepped inside, the door slid shut beside me, the air pressure changed and another door slid open revealing what could only be a loading bay. The big metal roll up on the far side of the loading bay being the one I had seen as Billy and I had walked around the factory. On the right-hand side were two metal cylinders about a foot in diameter and three feet long, and on the other side metal ammunition style boxes stacked to the ceiling. I took snapshots of the cylinders and ammunition boxes, especially the writing on the side, which looked East European. It was freezing cold and just when I thought I was done and could get the hell out, the outside door started to open.

The only place to hide was behind the cylinders, where I could just see what was going on. I could hear the sound of an engine and once the door was open, the Range Rover I had seen earlier drove into the loading bay. The door closed, lights came on and the woman with the expensive perfume stepped out of the rear passenger door. De Costas was nowhere to be seen but one of his henchmen accompanied the woman, opened the rear cargo door of the Range Rover and removed two long cylindrical cartons like those used to transport maps or drawings. These ones however seemed quite heavy. Raising the camera and ensuring that the flash was deactivated, I snapped a few shots. They entered the airlock and disappeared from view. I had no choice but to shiver in the cold dark and wait. The only way out for me without being seen was back the way I came.

When you're freezing cold, time drags by interminably. You invent all sorts of little games to keep your mind off the fact that your extremities might slowly be succumbing to frostbite and all the horrors that entailed. So you think up puzzles. Think of somewhere warm and sunny, and do as many exercises as you can to keep the circulation going. I had about fifteen minutes to get back to the testing bay before my time was up and the guards overcame their laziness and checked out the testing bay to see what I was doing.

Then 'The Lab' door slid open, and the woman and her bodyguard returned to the Range Rover and drove away. I waited another minute just in case they had forgotten something then ran to the door and pressed the touch pad.

Seven minutes later, I was back in the testing bay, whistling to myself and fiddling with one of the control boxes, when I heard the door opening.

"You not finished yet Mr Nelson," the security guard I knew as Martin smiled.

"Just two minutes, Martin," I said with what I hoped was a tired and somewhat pissed off tone. "If De Costas finds anything wrong with these I swear I'll.... Well... do something."

Martin laughed. "I heard a lot of swearing going on, that's for sure."

"Okay I'm done. Anymore and next time you come around I'll be hanging from the beams."

"That bad was it?"

"And more. Billy owes me big time," I said as I passed him, clapping him on the shoulder as I went. "Mind locking up Martin?"

"No problem. See you tomorrow, or would that be later today?" he said laughing, as he closed and locked the door.

As I approached the B&B, some instinct inside me that I never understood, made me stop. Instead of driving directly to the house, I parked the car a hundred metres away. Something just didn't seem right. Patrolling behind enemy lines in the dead of night sharpens your sense of survival. It can't be taught, it has to be experienced. Every part of my body tingled as if I'd been charged with static electricity.

I made my way down the pitch-dark street. A light snow had begun to fall, replacing the rain, but not settling yet. I had no idea whether De Costas recognised me, or maybe the woman. And I felt that if they had, they sure as hell wouldn't want me alive. As they say, 'dead men tell no tales'.

All my being was concentrated on the B&B up ahead. There were no lights on, except for the front porch, which Mrs Dillon left on when I worked late, but for an instant a shadow momentarily flickered across the window of my room. It was just a fleeting impression.

The house next door had a garage, the roof of which extended to just below the upstairs landing window. I slipped into the garden and quietly moved up to the garage. There was no sound from either house.

It took me three minutes to climb onto the roof, making sure that I didn't make a sound. The roof groaned softly as it took my weight, but hopefully the sound couldn't be heard over the wind. I was just about to grab hold of the window ledge when the sound of a car made me duck and lie flat. The headlights swept over me as the car turned around in the cul-de-sac and drove away. The landing window opened without a sound, and I waited, listening, to see if the intruder I thought I saw came to investigate as cold air started to flood into the house. I slipped inside and shut the window. Somehow I made it over to the door of my room without making so much as a squeak. It was time to do some thinking. The intruder inside the room would almost certainly have a weapon of some sort. If I were in his position, I would have a buddy downstairs, waiting for me to return. I moved away from the door to the head of the stairs. There, at the bottom of the stairs, outlined in the light from the porch flooding in through the hall window, lay Eileen. There was a dark patch on the carpet around her head, a sound of carefully placed footsteps, and a man moved into view. I knew I was dealing with professional killers. He moved over to Eileen's body and grabbing her under the arms started to pull her along the hall.

I was on top of him before he saw me, his cry dying in his throat as I chopped the edge of my hand hard and viciously into his Adam's apple. There was a satisfying crack and he slumped to the ground, clutching his throat and trying to shout. He died there on the floor with the blood that choked him bubbling out onto the carpet to mingle with Eileen's.

It had been quick and soundless.

There was no sign of movement from upstairs. I quickly searched the killer and found a MP-443 Grach 9mm automatic with a silencer attached. Useful piece of artillery, designed for the Russian military that had a seventeen round magazine and one 'up-the-spout'. The 9mm rounds were armour piercing and the gun only supplied to Russian Special Forces.

All the marks and maker's brand names had been removed from his clothing and there were no papers on him at all. I left him and went quietly back upstairs. Outside the door, I paused, took up position and coughed softly.

"Mikhail?" came a whispered voice from the room. I didn't reply and heard the sound of the man cautiously moving across the room to the door. I fired and kicked the door open. The round caught him in the side and torn out a great lump of muscle and flesh and threw him against the far wall. For a moment he stared down at the wound in disbelief, then fell to his knees, his gun falling from his hand. I kicked it away, grabbed a handful of hair, and wrenched his face up so he could see me.

"Right, now let's have some answers," I said. "Who sent you? Was it De Costas? Who?"

He looked at me without seeing. The shock of the 9mm steel core high powered round had stunned him, so I slapped his face hard. "I want some answers. Who was it? Answers." Another slap put some sparkle back into his eyes.

"Don't know. Maybe De Costas." His breathing was laboured. "Not.... our.... idea...." He coughed and a dribble of scarlet spit ran down his chin.

"Listen mate, you're dying, so you might as well tell me what I want to know."

He nodded his head weakly.

"Fine. So who the hell is hiring Russian Special Forces, or should I say ex-Russian Special Forces, if it isn't De Costas?"

He coughed again before replying. "We... have contact... London. Richard Stacy... he have insurance company." He coughed and retched, the effort making the hole in his side bleed more profusely. "Number twelve Cornfield R.... Road. Kensington."

"What's in the cylinders from Estonia," I asked.

He looked at me clearly for the first time. There was hate in his eyes.

"Go f.. f.. fuck yourself," he said. I hit him with the barrel of the gun, tearing the skin of his cheek to the bone.

"Where's Mrs Dillon?"

"Dead. B.... broke her n.. n.. neck. Kill me British pig." His eyes glazed and he started to laugh, a thin maniacal sound knowing he was going to die.

I took a picture of him, and then gave him his last wish.

The back of his head blew off and decorated the bedclothes and wall with crimson and grey. I looked down at the mess and felt no sorrow at all. He was just another dead reptile in the menagerie of violence that seemed to consume the world. Downstairs I wiped the Grach clean and put it in the Russian mercenary's hand, and took a photograph of him too. Oldfield was going to be busy.

From the time I fired the first round to the time I crawled back onto the garage roof, three minutes had elapsed. The silencer was very effective and nobody would have heard the shots. The street was empty and I looked back at the house where my presence had cost two innocent people their lives and wondered how many more were going to die because I wanted revenge.

Before driving off, I called Oldfield.

"I'm sending photos," I said quickly before he could say anything and hit the data send button.

"Got them."

"Don't call me, I'll be in touch in two days." Then I dismantled the phone, took out the SIM card, dropped the phone on the road and ground it into little pieces. The SIM card I would destroy later.

FOURTEEN

Below the black painted number twelve on the pillar beside the door, an ornate copper plate proclaimed *Richard Stacy - Insurance Broker.* Cornfield Road was in a fashionable part of Kensington. The freshly painted white exterior of the Georgian terrace and black wrought iron railings dripped with rain that made odd patterns on the impossibly clean windows, and pattered softly on the pavement. It seemed oddly fitting that this was where a Mercenary recruiter did business.

On the trip over from Ireland, I had put in a call to Danny, explained the situation very briefly and he gave me another alias and set up the appointment. I recognised the name as one of our team from way back, who had disappeared on a raid in Pakistan. After talking to Danny, I called Edwards at the Overseas League, who was not at all surprised to hear from me, and had him meet me in the back room of the Golden Lion Inn with a change of clothes I had delivered to the Club at what seemed a life-time ago.

I pressed the intercom button and looked up at the small unobtrusive CCTV camera.

"May I help you?" came a cultured woman's voice with the slightly bored tone used by rich girls we used to call *'Sloane Rangers'.*

"Bonhoeffer. Mr Stacy is expecting me," I said crisply.

The door opened and I walked into a brightly lit reception room, which oddly spanned the width of the building. Obviously Richard Stacy was careful with his own security, as was the Receptionist, who may have sounded bored, but kept her right hand below the desk. I guessed she had a rather large semi-automatic pointed right at my stomach. However when she saw me, she relaxed and even managed a smile, perhaps because I had cleaned up, was wearing one of my Kilgour suits and handmade shoes by Markus Scheer. The receptionist true to her *'Sloane Ranger'* ancestry recognised wealth and style when she saw it, and stood up from the desk.

"Mr Stacy is expecting you Mr Bonhoeffer. This way please." She led me through an open archway to the left of her desk, which I figured was probably a body scanner, to an imposing oak door and touched the frame. The door swung open and she stepped aside allowing me to enter.

Richard Stacy was tall, slim, just as elegantly dressed as I, and moved with an easy grace that comes from being physically fit. His gunmetal grey eyes matched his short almost US Marine Corps style hair.

He held out his hand and the warm smile on his soft lips did not touch his eyes that watched me carefully. "Mr Bonhoeffer, I'm delighted to meet you. Please sit, may I offer you tea or coffee?"

I shook his hand and was surprised to find it slightly clammy and not as firm as his manner suggested, then took a seat on the settee against the right hand wall. The office was just as I would have expected to find in a Victorian *'Gentleman's Club'*. Wood panelled walls, bookcases and photographs of Stacy in combat camouflage with groups of soldiers, and others in a dinner jacket at a black tie affair. I just glanced at them, not really interested, but taking them in none-the-less.

"Coffee. Yirgacheffe. Black, no sugar." I decided that my alter ego, Bonhoeffer, was a man of few words, and apart from the trappings of wealth, he like most mercenaries had little grace or manners. Killing for a living is not conducive to the finer points of social etiquette. I had asked for a particular Ethiopian coffee because I was pretty sure they did not have any in the office. And I was pretty sure the receptionist would have to leave to get it, as Stacy wouldn't want to piss off a client with millions to spend.

He pressed a button on his desk. "Camilla, do we have Yirgacheffe coffee for our guest?"

"Certainly sir."

Part of being a good assassin is not letting on that you just want to kill the person sitting opposite, or even looking as if you have any visible means by which to carry out the deed. Stacy would not have let me get this close if he thought I was going to kill him, but he would if he thought I was going to pay many millions for his services.

I pulled out my Jean Michel sterling silver pocket watch, a 21st birthday present from Mary, from my inside suit pocket and glanced at it quickly, making sure Stacy could see it. "I have little time and one of your competitors to see. I need the best, you understand."

"Certainly," he said quickly; a little too quickly as if eager to get my money as fast as possible. Most high-level mercenary recruiters have some background in Special Forces, but not Stacy. My guess is he was a 'wannabe' from one of the county Infantry Regiments that had been amalgamated into The Rifles, and that he'd had a less than stellar career. There were a lot of those kinds floating around the peripheries of private security firms. "I'm told that you are looking for a specialised unit for an operation in.... I'm sorry I have forgotten where exactly."

"That's because I do not divulge the details of my operations to anyone, only the team when I have approved the personnel."

"Oh. Of course. As I understand you are looking for former Spetsnaz soldiers."

"No. Spetsgruppa Alfa only." These were the cream of Russian anti-terrorist Special Forces who operated under direct control of the GRU.

Stacy's face betrayed fear for the first time, which he tried to cover with a smile, but his eyes told the tale. "I'm sorry but I don't know of any of those guys."

"Really," I said also smiling, "I was informed that you recently supplied a two man team for a job in Northern Ireland."

His face drained of blood and he seemed frozen to the chair. I stood, and looked down at him. "I'm sorry I wasted your time. Perhaps when I have a less important mission we'll be in touch again. I'm late for my other appointment," I said smoothly and turned to the door.

Stacy was on his feet and came around the desk quickly. "Perhaps I can sort something out for you," he said clutching at my sleeve. I knew I had about five minutes before Camilla came back with the coffee.

One thing you should never do is reach out and touch someone who has been trained in unarmed combat. There is a simple method of snapping the wrist that is excruciatingly painful and allows a quick chop to the throat with the other hand, which inevitably renders the person completely incapacitated. Stacy was on his knees before he knew what hit him, coughing and gasping for air, his wrist a limp rag with torn ligaments and broken scaphoid bone.

"Who hired you for the Northern Ireland job?" I said quietly, listening for any movement in the outer office indicating Camilla had returned.

"I don't know what you're talking about," Stacy wheezed. I hit him in the kidneys, a short sharp blow that was painful and marginally short of causing permanent damage.

"Not the right answer. Two innocent women I knew were killed. One of the Russians who murdered them gave up your name before I killed him. So once again, who hired you?"

"I don't know. I never met the woman. She was East European, I think. I got five hundred thousand cash delivered by courier."

"Are you the one supplying Mary Gunn with heroin? And what's Orange Moon got to do with it?"

Stacy looked shocked and stared at me, total consternation in his eyes. "It wasn't my idea. I just did as I was told. Who the hell are you?" he said with fear.

"Thomas Gunn."

"But that's impossible, De Costas said..." his voice trailed away as he realised he was talking too much.

"So there's you, De Costas and the woman De Costas takes his orders from. Who else is involved?"

I was almost too late, hearing the soft sound of the office door open, and seeing the fright in Stacy's eyes as I dove to one side. The bullets missed me and caught him in the right temple. He was dead before he hit the ground and I was rolling behind the desk as Camilla unloaded six more rounds into the desk. None penetrated and I knew she was out of ammunition as I'd caught a glimpse of the 9mm Beretta automatic with an eight round magazine. 'Lady's gun' Julie called it, but it certainly wasn't a lady using it.

By the time I rolled out from behind the desk and sprang to my feet, Camilla was running from the building. When I reached the front door, she had vanished into the traffic.

I returned to the office, quickly went through the filing cabinet and found nothing. There would be no point in checking the computer because it would be protected by a secure password, so I ripped the tower from under the reception desk, broke open the casing and unceremoniously removed the hard drive. In Stacy's office I found a new leather briefcase and slipped the hard drive into it. The CCTV camera would have recorded me entering the building and I didn't want the inconvenience of having the Metropolitan police trying to track me down. I'd pass the drive on to Oldfield.

Stacy had chosen the location of the office well, as there were no city surveillance cameras covering the building, so I took the first vacant taxi to Liverpool Street Station and bought a first class ticket to Diss, a small town about twenty miles south of Norwich. Once on the train I called Danny.

"I wondered when you'd show," he said conversationally.

"Can you get to Diss station in about an hour?"

"Just so happens my schedule is free this afternoon," he said sarcastically.

"There's a footpath that leads East from the Station to a small car park just off Nelson Road. I'll see you there," I said and hung up.

At this time in the afternoon, before the evening rush hour, the train was pretty much empty, so I had the carriage to myself as we sped through the dank British countryside, and assessed the situation.

There was a huge missing piece to this puzzle I had yet to uncover. I called Oldfield.

"Thomas, do you have any idea what I think you found?" he said excitedly.

"No I don't Professor."

"Rhetorical question. Firstly, as far as I can make out, the woman whose photograph you sent me, is Marika Keskküla. Quite an interesting background. Her father was a Russian submarine Captain name of Georgy Bondarev who ran the Suldiski Island Submarine Training Facility off the coast of Estonia. Marika was born there and sent to Russia for her education. She returned to Estonia after earning a degree in Physics at Moscow University and married Hannes Keskküla who made his billions mining oil shale, then bought the Suldiski Island complex for Marika. By all accounts he was an ugly bastard both physically and personally. He died suddenly several years ago, and his entire fortune along with control of his companies passed to Marika, who is also employed by the Estonian Government as an International Consul for Industry. She has an apartment in New York, a house in Beverly Hills, a one hundred and thirty metre mega yacht in Monaco, called *'Marika'*, and of course Suldiski Island."

"Curiouser and curiouser. What on earth is she doing with low-life's like De Costas?"

"This is where it gets more interesting. As far as I can make out, the 'machine' you photographed at Venus Automotive is some kind of a gas diffuser linked to a series laser array and a miniature industrial metal foundry. Just what it is for I have no idea. Yet."

"I have a funny feeling I think I do, but I'll tell you about that later when I've had the chance to think this through," I said the hairs on the back of my neck standing up. "Exactly what kind of physics degree did this Keskküla woman receive?"

"Non-specific, just general physics."

"And curiouser," I muttered, my mind racing.

"And just what does that mean, Thomas," Oldfield said irritably. He didn't like being in the dark about anything.

"Can you get to Diss station in about an hour?"

"Yes. I'm in Cambridge. Just finished a lecture on organic nano computer technology."

I gave him the same directions as I'd given Danny, told him to bring his laptop, and quickly disconnected before he could ask any questions.

Diss is a small market town in south Norfolk close to the Suffolk border, with a rich social and geological history, a *'Cittaslow'* project town with a small resident population of about seven thousand. I chose it because it was quiet, *'slow'* and peaceful. It was close to London, Cambridge and Norwich, so easy to get to for Danny and Oldfield. And because it was pretty and unassuming, a place I hoped nobody would even think of looking for me.

Oldfield would be here in about fifteen minutes.

I left the station and set off down the footpath, briefcase in hand, as if

I had lived here all my life. It was only about 200 metres to the small car park and it felt good to stretch my legs in the late afternoon. The rain had stopped sometime ago, and with no wind the evening was cool but bright in the weak sunshine, and the country air invigorating.

"You make me feel like a chauffeur dressed like that," Danny said as I slid into the passenger seat of his new BMW 6 series Gran Coupé.

"Looks like stunt work is paying well," I replied appreciating the car.

"It's a living, and I want one of those Venus GT's," he grinned. "What's the emergency?"

"Nuclear waste re-enrichment. I think."

"Okay," Danny said slowly. "Where?"

"Venus Automotive."

Danny turned to me with look of total incredulity. "We'd have spotted that a long time ago. The plant would be massive and use more energy than it takes to power Belfast."

"Whose we, Danny? The Government? You working for MI5?"

He shrugged and stared out of the window. "Something like that."

"I wondered why it was so easy for me to get in and out of Northern Ireland and all those aliases."

"We can talk about that later," he said gruffly and I could see his deception troubled him. "What makes you think it's a re-enrichment plant?"

"Not a plant, a laboratory. I think someone has discovered a way to combine old-fashioned diffuser technology with laser energy thus reducing the massive energy requirement for standard re-enrichment. It's almost like a portable lab with the ability to set up anywhere. Venus Automotive is a test and development centre."

"The proof?"

I watched as Professor Oldfield's car drove into the car park. "Just arrived," I said getting out of the BMW and catching the Professor's attention. He hurried over carrying his laptop and climbed into the back seat.

"Danny, meet Professor Oldfield."

They nodded to each other.

"What's this about?" Oldfield said bluntly.

"Fire up that thing and bring up the photographs I sent you, and tell Danny what you told me earlier. As the laptop booted up, Oldfield quickly ran through everything he had discovered about Marika Keskküla. The photographs I took of 'The Lab' and the loading bay popped up on the laptop screen and Oldfield turned it around for Danny to see.

I pointed to the cylinders. "These are in the loading bay. Remember the training we did for Iraq and that waste-of-time search for nuclear materials?"

Danny nodded ruefully.

"We were told to look for cylinders like this. Uranium Hexaflouride storage tanks, the by-product of uranium enrichment. Useless unless the price of natural uranium ore goes up, then re-enrichment becomes very viable, but still unbelievably expensive."

"Unless you can figure a way to re-enrich the Uranium Hexaflouride more cheaply, which means dramatically reducing energy costs," Oldfield said excitedly. "Anyone with a Physics degree would have studied Nuclear Physics as part of the syllabus in their last year."

I turned to Danny. "I need the travel log of Marika Keskküla's yacht for the past year."

"I'll see what I can do."

I reached down for the briefcase I had taken from Stacy's office and pulled out the hard drive. "You think you can get anything off this Professor?"

He took the hard drive, pulled some cables from his bag and plugged them into the drive and his laptop. "Quite cleverly encrypted. It'll take a minute."

While he worked I sat back and stared out at the darkening countryside. "When were you going to tell me?" I said quietly.

"When I'm allowed to." Danny looked everywhere but at me.

"I need to meet whoever is controlling you."

"Not when you're in this mood. Somebody's liable to get hurt," Danny said with a slight smile. "Besides, we need more proof from the Venus Automotive plant." Only then did he look at me.

"Your handlers want me to go back in?"

"You're expendable."

"They set it up that way."

"You know how they work. You fell into their lap, especially when you decided to 'do-your-own-thing'." He turned to me, his expression deadly serious. "I asked for this mission. You're my brother, different parents but you're my brother and we've been through a lot together. I told you I'd have your back."

"Okay. I'll go back."

"You'll need some equipment, I'll get it for you. Where will you be later tonight?"

"At the Hall. I have to check on Mary."

From the back seat, Oldfield swore softly. "I need more computing power to crack this," he said quietly, almost to himself.

"Will the computer at the Hall do?" I asked.

"Yes."

"Then you drive, I don't have a car," I said opening the door and hesitating a moment as pain shot down my leg. It had taken a crack as I dived for cover in Stacy's office.

"The leg?" Danny asked.

"Yep."

"You'll be okay?"

"No choice."

"See you later. I'll call." He tossed me a small highly sophisticated mobile sat-phone. "Compliments of your Government."

"I've got enough damn phones, I'll stick with what I've got."

"Not for this mission. If you need help fast, you'll need this."

Danny drove off and Oldfield and I headed for his car.

We parked the car in the barn with the Mini-Cooper that Oldfield took a few minutes admiring, which surprised me. I thought he only had eyes for computers and expensive single malt.

"Had one when I was an undergrad," he said nostalgically.

"We need to go," I said roughly and led the way across the fields to the Hall. After the debacle in Stacy's office, it was quite possible that somebody had put the pieces together and realised I was still alive. The

Government knew, but who else?

For an hour I scouted the perimeter after telling Oldfield to stay out of sight. I knew every part of the grounds and the approaches, and every conceivable hiding place, and having cleared them all, returned to Oldfield and together we crossed to the Folly. I could see he was quite excited about the secret passage to the Hall and giggled softly every now and then. At the door to the wine cellar, I waited, listening for even the slightest sound, but there was nothing. The door opened with a soft creak, just wide enough for Oldfield and I to slip through. I closed it and made sure it couldn't be seen behind the wine rack, then led the way into the kitchen and up the back stairs to the flat, avoiding the main living area.

It was just as Julie and I had left it. Her clothes in the closet, beauty items on the dressing table and the lingering smell of her in the air. Mary hadn't changed anything. It seemed a lifetime ago, a gentle warm memory mixed with inconsolable pain, and scrapbook images of us together, laughing, making love, her face as she slept, darted into my consciousness like pieces of old news film.

I shut the door to the wardrobe and the door to my memory with one movement. I was here for a purpose; there would be time enough when all this was over, to ponder on what might have been. Much to my surprise, Oldfield was already at the computer attaching the hard drive, seemingly oblivious to Julie's ghostly presence in the room.

"There's still some user encryption I can't fathom," Oldfield said quietly.

Staring down at the screen I had a thought. It was Stacy expression when I had mentioned Orange Moon that gave me an idea. "Type in *'Orange Moon'.*"

He did, the screen flashed then revealed Stacy's desktop. Oldfield quickly went through the folders and stopped at one entitled *'The Orange Moon Affair'*. It seemed to me that perhaps Stacy's flair for the dramatic made him name the folder like a book title. Oldfield clicked and was informed that access required a password. He ran his encryption code and came up with nothing.

"It's like a pretty standard zero knowledge cryptographic protocol, but with some very sophisticated extra layers. Normally I'd crack one of these in no time," Oldfield said obliquely after trying several algorithms. "I can verify who I am to the computer, but not get the information that's hidden on the drive. There's a key somewhere that's impossible to find."

"Orange Moon," I thought aloud, my mind racing. "Everything comes back to Orange Moon. In Northern Ireland the guys in the office at Venus Automotive talked about it."

"Well there's nothing I can do with this here. Maybe if I take it back to my office I can crack it."

"Did you get anything from the tracker Julie installed in the Coltrane Engineering server?"

"Actually come to think of it, I found a similar encryption. Again I'll have to get this back to my office."

Then the hairs on the back of my neck prickled as I thought I heard a sound downstairs. I thought it strange that Mary would be still up at this time.

"Pack up, I'll be back in a minute. I need to check on Mary." The upstairs landing was quiet. Mary was not in her room, so I went downstairs where I could see a light shining from beneath the door of the sitting room and the front door was open. In the distance I heard the sound of a car accelerating down the driveway. Whoever had broken into the hall probably had heard us moving around upstairs and had made a quick getaway. I opened the sitting room door slowly, Glock in hand. There inside, sitting in one of the high backed wing armchairs next to the fire was Mary, unconscious, the sleeve of her right arm rolled up and a tourniquet still wrapped above her elbow. On the floor next to the armchair were an empty syringe and a jar of Orange Moon Body Butter, but there was no body butter in it, just pure heroin. Whoever had administered the dose didn't have time to loosen the tourniquet, which was why she was still alive. I checked her pulse. It was low and slow. Then I called the emergency services telling them I was an employee and had found Mary who seemed to have overdosed, ringing off before the emergency operator could ask any questions. I looked towards the door and saw Milly the housekeeper's body crumpled in the corner.

I waited with her, long enough so that Oldfield came looking for me.

"Is she okay?" he said on entering the sitting room.

"She will be. But Milly isn't." I pointed over to the corner and thought for a moment Oldfield would throw-up, but he took a deep breath, and stepped out into the hallway. In the distance I could hear a siren wailing. It would be here in four minutes. "Let's go," I said, picking up the jar of Orange Moon and walking to the front door, leaving it open with the porch lights on, and ran with Oldfield quickly to the Folly. Whoever had done this to Mary probably figured that she wouldn't be found until morning.

Once Oldfield was safely on his way and I was sure nobody was following him, I returned to the Folly, called Ron who like everyone else thought I was dead, told him what had happened to Mary and asked him to get over to the Hall with the Mini-Cooper, I'd meet him later.

"Not a word to anyone that I'm still alive. Call Henderson and ask him to stay with Mary at the hospital."

"Mum's the word, Thomas. Don't worry I'll take care of everything. See you later," he said and I sat in the darkness waiting for Danny's call.

Returning to the Hall was a strange experience, especially with Julie's presence so strong in the flat. The smell of her shampoo lingered in my imagination and once again I heard her bright laugh and saw her perfect naked body diving into the clean blue waters of Gozo so long ago. My cheeks felt wet and I realised I was crying. Somewhere in my black soul she stirred the emotions I had driven so far down I didn't know if I would ever feel love and compassion again. Those were dangerous feelings I could not afford right now. Later maybe, when this was all over and I had reached the end of this deadly journey, but not now.

We left Capri in a blow; Julie giggling excitedly as the catamaran easily shook the waves aside and headed for our first destination, Cyprus.

" Enough adventure for you?"

"It beats the hell out of standing in front of a damn camera all day."

"I can imagine. Keep on this course and I'll rustle up some lunch for us. Any requests?"

"Surprise me."

I seemed to spend a lot of my time on that cruise making exotic meals. Julie surprised me more than I surprised her. She was smart, funny, self assured and down to earth, the antithesis of a typical super-model. Money hadn't spoiled her, simply given her the freedom to be independent and pursue her dreams. Quite what those dreams were I had yet to find out. We had a lot in common, not our backgrounds, but how we viewed the world. Hers was a simple philosophy of enjoying every moment of her life. She was not constrained by any religious dogma and yet was the most compassionate and unselfish person I had ever met. It was no wonder I fell in love with her.

And now she was gone, and all I felt was complete emptiness where my heart should be.

How long I sat in the dark I don't know, but finally my phone vibrated. It was Danny. I directed him to the Folly and waited until I saw two shadows. There was a low whistle I instantly recognised as Danny, and answered in kind. The shadows quickly ran to the Folly. I stayed in the darkness as Danny and the other man entered.

"Thomas?"

"Whose your friend," I answered.

"Paul," came the reply from the other man. "We met in Dundonald."

"Last time we met, you gave me the gypsy's warning," I said quietly, keeping my Glock aimed at his head. "What's changed?"

"Not much. I trust Danny. You, I don't know."

I lowered the gun. "Fair enough."

"You two done?" Danny asked. "What's with the ambulance?"

"Somebody tried to kill my stepmother with an overdose."

"Jesus Mother of Mary, these bastards don't give crap who they hurt, do they?"

"No they don't." I noticed that they were both carrying SAS bergens and were dressed in all black outfits, with the latest lightweight bulletproof vests, the same we used on special operations. "You going somewhere?" I asked.

"With you. Orders."

"Huh. So I work for you now?"

"No. I'm coming along to verify your findings, Paul's back-up."

"Your Bosses don't trust me?"

"They think you're a loose cannon."

"And what do you think?"

"That you're my friend and you need me, besides I've always been better at this shit than you." He grinned, white teeth flashing in the night. "Here." He tossed me my black outfit as Paul snapped open a small plastic Pelican storm case as I stripped off my suit and shoes and dressed quickly, and showed me the contents. Nestled in shaped foam were two instruments.

"The left hand one is a small Geiger counter for radioactive readings. The right hand one is a Uranium Hexafluoride sampler," Paul said crisply.

I looked at him, a glimmer of understanding flickering to light in my brain. "You're CBRN (Chemical, Biological Radiological and Nuclear Defence) aren't you?" I asked, to which he nodded. "You bastards know much more than you're letting on. What's in the bergens?"

"Plastique, and firepower. HK MP5SDs and Sig Sauer nine mils. "

"Planning on obliterating the place?"

"Maybe."

"I'm surprised your Bosses didn't want a full team on this."

"I convinced them that if we got bumped, it'd be really difficult explaining to the PSNI exactly what we are doing," Danny answered. "However they will be informed once we're on the ground and inside the building. We have about twenty minutes to get what we need and get out before they appear. We still don't know what the level of their internal security is and we've been pre-empted before."

"Good thinking. I wondered how you managed to have a team already in country."

"Had to pull them out, somebody in high places informed on us." He looked at me carefully. "Remember? That's how you got shot down in Nevada. Somebody talked."

The adrenaline started coursing as I realised I'd missed working with Danny. "Is this like old times, or am I just a spare part?"

"Like old times," he whispered.

The Ambulance left with siren blaring and within a few minutes, silence descended once more over Calder Hall.

"Let's get going then," I whispered and led the way to the back of the Hall and the Eurocopter hangar. While Danny and Paul pulled the helicopter onto the helipad, I went into the Hall to find Ron. He was in the kitchen making a cup of tea and nearly jumped out of his skin when he saw me, gun in hand, dressed in black.

"Dear God, I nearly had a heart attack. What's going on?"

"More than I can tell you, Ron. Just watch the Hall and give me updates on Mary's condition," I said tossing him a burn phone. "Use this, not the house phones or your own."

"Has all this got something to do with your father's murder?"

"Everything. I'll be back late tomorrow night. If you need any help...." I stopped as he held up his hand.

"I'll have some of my lads come over. Don't worry, we maybe local yokels but we know how to handle ourselves, besides I got the keys to the gun room," he grinned.

"Thanks Ron."

"Anytime," he said and I left him pouring a shot of brandy into his coffee. His hand shook a little, but I knew he would lay down his life before he let anything happen to Mary or the Hall.

FIFTEEN

My father had set up a non-profit mercy flight program for all the Gunn Group corporate aircraft ten years ago, collecting organs for transplant, and emergency airlifts of critically injured or ill patients. So it was no surprise to Norwich ATC (air traffic control) that I was requesting to file an emergency flight plan to Sheffield for a transplant organ pick-up.

Once en-route I was going to change the flight plan to Blackpool where I wanted to refuel for the flight to Dundonald. It was a simple way of disguising our true intentions. The weather was in our favour, with a tailwind all the way which would increase our 120 knot cruise by another ten knots and give us just under a two-hour flight time. Allowing thirty minutes to refuel, we could be on the ground in Dundonald by three o'clock in the morning.

As I finished with Norwich ATC and settled into the flight, Paul and Danny closed their eyes and were soon sleeping as if safely tucked up in bed at home, oblivious to the noise and the tension I felt as I flew on into the night. It was strangely comforting, just like Afghanistan when we would sleep as the Apache or Puma helicopters sped us on our way to an LZ in the mountains. Gradually I relaxed as the familiar feeling of flying came back to my mind and muscle memory, and once established at two thousand feet I switched on the autopilot that Scandinavian Avionics had installed along with the EFIS system, and relaxed, thinking about what we were heading into and listening to the en-route frequency.

If I had thought about everything clearly, rationally and logically when I first heard that my father had been killed, I would have figured out that the Government were going to use me for their own ends. But I was blinded by the desire for revenge and filled with my own sense of self-importance. Perhaps I should feel angry and betrayed by Danny, but I didn't. I felt that now I had a fighting chance to accomplish that which I had set out to do and there was time enough to settle accounts with whomever was pulling the strings. The puzzle wasn't going to be solved by me worrying at it, so I just concentrated on flying. As we approached Sheffield I called ATC and told them that I had been diverted to Blackpool, as the Sheffield transplant organ was not available.

Landing at Blackpool in the middle of the night, with a weather front moving in and visibility reducing by the minute was challenging. Danny and Paul were awake and watching without comment as I concentrated on the moving terrain display with obstacle warning indicators. ATC sounded a little bored as they guided me in and I requested fuel as we touched down.

"Piece of cake," Danny said cheerily. "Wonder if they have any sandwiches in the terminal?" He went off to look while I checked in with the tower, paid for the landing fees and fuel and waited for Danny to return.

Paul was watching me carefully.

"Nice landing," he said, I guess by way of being friendly. Nobody in our line of work trusted easily, especially as I was technically a civilian and no longer part of the *'inner circle'*.

"Thanks, but you might save the congratulations until we land in Dundonald. That's where this mess is coming from," I said looking at the sky. He nodded, and for the first time grinned.

"Wouldn't be normal if it wasn't raining," he said as Danny trotted back from the terminal with a fist full of freshly made sandwiches.

"Told the lady we were a mercy flight," he said cheerfully. "Well we are, officially, sort of."

Within minutes, ATC cleared us to Belfast and we lifted off into the dark night for the one hour fifteen minute flight. Rain sleeted off the canopy and wind buffeted us as we headed out across the Irish Sea toward the Isle of Man and then Northern Ireland. I'd been told by ATC that we would be out of the worst of it in ten minutes as the front moved through. Thankfully they were right and the small helicopter settled on course with Danny and Paul tucking into their sandwiches.

I'd wait until we were back safe and sound before I ate anything.

I contacted Aldergrove while we were still twenty minutes out and was relieved to hear them clear me straight into the Venus Automotive test track. Danny's contact had obviously been very convincing with the concocted story of a life saving blood delivery for a child with a rare blood type living in Dundonald. The people concerned would meet us and all the details had been arranged with Venus Automotive. Now as I listened to the controller I had to smile. He couldn't have been more helpful, giving me a detailed picture of the weather and wind speeds.

The cloud base was eight hundred feet as we crossed the coast and below me the darkened countryside of Northern Ireland spread out on either side, with glimmers of some house and car lights. I changed course over Strangford Lough and flew towards Dundonald. Landing in these blustery conditions with only the floodlights of the factory to guide me was going to be tricky, but better than nothing. A direct in approach from overhead Ards Airport would avoid power-lines and other obstacles.

"Five minutes to landing," I told Danny and Paul, who were checking their gear, loading the Heckler-Koch MP5SDs and slipping on ear buds and throat mikes. Danny prepared mine for me. It was the familiar routine that calmed the nerves and prepared the body for the fight ahead.

"Just get us down in one piece, Thomas," Danny grinned, enjoying the adventure.

Over Ards Airport, I turned onto a bearing of 295° and saw the lights of Venus Automotive factory right on the nose. There was a surreal quality to the approach to the darkened factory, the noise of the helicopter seeming to disappear as I concentrated on the landing.

That was when I started to sweat.

The memory of the flight from Mojave flooding back, and it took all my will power to calm down, steady my hands and feet on the controls and gently nurse the aircraft towards the ground. I felt Danny glance at me.

"Two minutes. And relax."

"I guess there'll be Venus Automotive security on the ground as a welcoming party," Paul asked.

"Sure to be. I'm hoping just the normal guards and not De Costas' men."

"We'll find out soon enough," Danny said quietly as I slowly dropped the collective and pulled back a little on the cyclic. The helicopter slowed and we headed down toward the test track close behind the testing bay where the helicopter would be shielded from view. I could see one of the security vehicles already driving toward our landing point from the main gate, stopping just as we touched down. Two men got out, one I recognised as Martin.

It was the best night landing I have ever done and Danny and Paul were out and running before Martin and his colleague knew what was happening. By the time I had shut down and joined them, Danny and Paul had them trussed up with zip ties and sitting with their backs to the testing bay wall.

Martin looked at me incredulously. "Tom Nelson? We were told you were dead."

"As you can see, not so, Martin. And the name's Thomas Gunn," I said gruffly. "Are any of De Costas' men here?"

"Been coming and going all night. The last van is due in twenty minutes. De Costas was in the main office block earlier, with a woman. That's all I know."

"What do they know about us flying in here?"

"Nothing. We only got the call a minute before you landed."

"Sorry mate, have to do this," Danny as he injected him in the neck with a sedative. Paul had already dealt with the other guard. Watching Martin and his friend slump over, I have to confess I felt nothing. We had a job to do and that was all that mattered.

"Looks like we have company, there's movement at the main gates." Paul said.

"Better get in there before they do," I said. Having checked my weapons, I slipped in the ear bud and strapped on the throat mike, then led the way quickly to the door behind the dumpster. It looked exactly as I had left it, and the door opened easily. We slipped through into the main assembly plant, which was lit with low-level security lights. Almost immediately alarm bells started clanging in my head and that gut instinct clawed away telling me something was not right.

"Boys, this is not good," I whispered. "The security lights were never on."

"You sure?" Paul said softly.

"I'm sure."

"Then we are going to have to do this the hard way," Danny said, covering me as I moved forward between the robots.

"This place is wired, Danny," I whispered looking straight at several pounds of Semtex strapped to one of the robot welders.

"Crap," he replied. "See anyone?"

"No."

"Keep moving, we'll deal with that on the way back."

What surprised me was that we made it to the control room office without mishap.

Slumped in the chair behind the desk lay Samuel De Costas, his chest a bloody mess and surprised look on his face. There was no time to get sentimental, but I felt angry that somebody had got to him before me. I crossed to the cabinets and within fifteen seconds we were through into 'The Lab'. The re-enrichment device was almost completely dismantled, but Paul set to work with his equipment as Danny and I walked to the far wall and opened the loading bay air lock.

The uranium hexafluoride tanks were gone as were most of the ammunition boxes. Just then, we heard the sound of vehicles pulling up outside the loading bay. Danny followed me quickly back to the airlock and into 'The Lab' where Paul was packing up his equipment.

"They've wired this lot too," he said as we headed for the air lock to the office.

Danny stopped. "If they are out there they know we only have this way out."

"Or do we?" Nobody's going to expect us to be coming out through the loading bay air lock. Besides if we kill the lights, nobody will see us."

"They'll hear us," Paul muttered, a touch scornfully I thought.

"Not through ten foot thick walls, using these." I held up the HK

MP5SD sub-machine gun, one of the few silenced sub-machine guns in the world.

"Good point."

"Just wait until I find the biometrics pad again before you put the lights out."

The sound inside 'The Lab' even with silenced weapons was deafening, and then it was silent. I pressed my thumb to where I hoped the biometrics pad was and sure enough the air lock door slid open.

The men, whoever they were, knew we were there. But that moment of time that it took for them to realise what was going on, was all we needed.

There's not much time to think when you're in a firefight, just do what you have to do. Sense where the enemy is, know where your own men are and go for it. It was over in moments, just the last body rolling across the floor and silence amid the smell of gunpowder and death. But we had no time to ponder on our work as there were sure to be others that would have heard the battle, so we retreated back into 'The Lab' and to the control office, but not before I photographed the side of the Transit van where the words *'Abby's Catering – Dublin'* was printed on the side. I was in no doubt that Abby's catering did not exist.

Sean Flynn and his men were waiting for us as I opened the office door to the main assembly area. They had been disciplined to stay where they were, but the sound of the fire fight had them jumpy and we spotted three of them as we slipped out of the darkened office into the eerie light and shadows cast by the robot welding machines.

Over confidence is a killer and one of the men, six foot four at least, thought that he was hidden from view because he was in shadow, but the small image intensifying sight on the MP5SD picked him out against the angular steel of the one of the welders.

The gun bucked in my hands, and through the sight I saw the big man's head snap forward from the impact and the blood and brain spatter the bench and boxes in behind him. His body thudded into the bench and he slid to the floor pumping crimson blood all over the concrete.

Danny fired and another of Flynn's men fell into view, clutching his throat and out of the corner of my eye I saw Flynn stand and aim directly at Paul's back. I fired quickly without aiming, but Flynn's reactions were fast. He dived behind a robot and slithered out of sight.

"Do you know who this is, Flynn?" I shouted. There was no reply. "It's Thomas Gunn." Still silence. "I'm going to kill you, you little bastard." My voice echoed in the budding.

There was a loud report from a pistol and the security lights went out plunging the assembly line into total darkness. I heard the sound of someone running and fired in that direction.

"For Christ's sake Thomas, what the hell are you doing?" Danny whispered urgently into my ear.

"I'm going to kill the bastard who murdered my father," I replied, feeling surprisingly calm.

"The PSNI will be here in under ten minutes and we need to be long gone."

"Secure the chopper, I'll be there in five," I told him, moving carefully down between the rows of partly finished body shells. "I've got you covered. Paul, follow Danny." I covered them as they sprinted for the door, bullets clanging off the machinery around them, then they made it to the door and where gone.

Suddenly the whole assembly line came to life in a cacophony of sound. I dived to the floor as an automatic welding arm swung across nearly separating my head from the rest of me. No sooner had I escaped that, than I had to roll out of the way to avoid being run over by one of the moving jigs carrying the body shells. The lights in the building were still turned off, but the flashes from the welders lit the whole area like a firework display.

Molten metal sprayed off the body shells and burned through my clothing, my hair singed and the smell of burning was everywhere. Flynn must have started the assembly line remotely. Somehow I had to get to him before I got mangled in all this machinery. There was a crack by my head and a riveter swung around out of control and started to punch the welding arm next to it. I looked up and saw Flynn on a steel walkway above; he was taking aim. The shot hit a welding arm and it spun around sparking and shorting off any metal close by.

I raised the MP5 and fired a loose shot before it was knocked aside by a passing jig, spoiling my aim, but it caused Flynn to duck and move back toward the shadows. Somehow I had to get up there and winkle him out. I looked around just in time to dive out of the way of another passing jig.

The metal above my head clanged and I felt a burning sensation on my left arm. I looked down saw a trickle of blood and thought *'not again'*. There was no pain. The third shot literally parted my hair. Flynn had moved out of hiding again and was standing on the steps leading down to the control room. I couldn't understand why he was coming down to me. His best advantage was up there. The rattle of rounds on the concrete by my feet answered my question. Somehow one of the men I saw hit by Paul had survived, but lucky for me his injuries meant he was slow from pain and blood loss. As I rolled I brought the MP5 and sprayed the area where he was standing. The majority of the rounds caught him in the stomach and threw him back against the wall, a surprised look on his face. His legs buckled and he slid down the wall leaving a red smear on the white paint. The flashes of the welding machines danced off his dead eyes.

Flynn stopped dead in his tracks, for the first time fear showed in his eyes as I turned the gun on him and pulled the trigger.

Nothing.

I was out of ammunition. That last burst had emptied the magazine. Flynn hesitated for a second, just long enough for me to scramble round the corner of one of the big machines. His shot bounced harmlessly off it and spun away.

With every shot a piece of the delicate automated system started to go crazy. Beside me a welder was trying to weld together a riveter and one of the car bodies. The heat had burned through one of the heavy electrical cables and turned the whole machine live. Sparks and molten metal flew everywhere. The whole system was breaking up and I was in the middle of it.

Flynn was a professional and knew my MP5 was out of ammunition, but he didn't know that I had the Glock. I pulled it out and checked the magazine.

He banged off another round that hit the concrete at my feet and ricocheted away, bouncing around the hardware.

"I got you now, Gunn. I'm gonna personally make sure you're dead this time." His voice was a high-pitched scream penetrating the cracks, crashes and ear-piercing sounds of the welders. "You can't get out Gunn. You're gonna die, just like your father, just like your girlfriend. You're gonna burn, Gunn." He started to cackle and I risked another glance from behind my cover. He was coming slowly toward me. I noticed that there was blood on the side of his jacket. I must have caught him with a lucky shot, which probably accounted for his mania. Shock and blood loss can do that. As he came down the steps, I raised myself onto one knee and fired. The round hit him in the thigh and he screamed. I leapt up from behind the machine to fire again but he had slipped into cover.

"Who pulls your strings Flynn? Marika Keskküla?" I shouted.

"Listen, I'll make you a deal. You let me go and that will be it. You'll never see me again." He yelled above the noise of machinery breaking apart.

"No deals."

He giggled. "Never know who your friends really are, do you Gunn? Try closer to home."

"Tell me who. And then maybe we'll talk." I shouted and moved out into more open space.

That was nearly my undoing.

Flynn had moved around and it was only his insane cackle before he fired that warned me. As I turned and ducked, I fired. The round hit him in the upper chest and he staggered backwards. A jig caught him behind the knees and threw him to one side against the 'live' machine. There was a series of flashes and the smell of burning.

"What's going on in there Thomas? Two minutes and we're bugging out," Danny's voice filtered through the chaos, calm and thoughtful.

Through the smoke and sparks I could see a welding arm descend and slice through Flynn's outstretched hand. He screamed and screamed until the combination of electricity and fire extinguished the life in him. His clothes were on fire and it rapidly spread to the cables and other inflammable items.

"Coming out."

I turned my attention to the rest of the production line. It had gone mad. The robot jigs were crashing into one another. Welders and riveters swinging round in wild circles cutting cables and shorting out. Very soon now the whole place would go up in flames and the explosives would blow.

Suddenly I felt tired, very tired. My arm started to ache where the round had sliced through the skin and muscle on my right upper arm.

It was time to go.

Danny and Paul were beside the helicopter. They had bundled Martin and the other security guard into the back seat. When they saw me, they climbed in. Martin and the other guard were just coming around from their sedative staring around in confusion. I quickly strapped myself into the pilot's seat and started the engine. In the distance we could hear sirens and the main building started to burn. There wasn't much time before the PSNI and fire brigade all appeared on the scene.

"Satisfied now?" Danny asked as I lifted the helicopter off the ground, hovered, turned a one eighty and took off low level toward Strangford Loch without turning on the navigation lights.

"No." I turned and nodded to the guards in the back. "Paul, give Martin a headset." I waited while Paul fitted Martin with the headset. "Martin where were the trucks headed?"

"Trucks?"

"The trucks at the factory. Where were they headed?"

There was an explosion behind us as the first of the charges detonated, the blast wave rocking the little helicopter.

"South."

"Danny, my burn phone. Right hand pocket. Dial star two."

He did as I asked. "I didn't think you are allowed to use mobile phones on an aircraft," he quipped.

"Ask him where that Keskküla woman's yacht is right now."

Danny talked quickly, waited watching me the whole time. "Last known GPS location is Carlingford Loch."

"Then that's where we're going."

"What about these guys," Paul asked.

"We'll drop them off in Strangford, let your bosses handle it."

"Oh they will love that," Danny chuckled.

"Ask me if I give a crap," I snapped, banking the helicopter along the shoreline of Strangford Lough as dawn broke on the horizon, thin clouds covering the sun, the gunmetal grey sky reflecting in the dark waters below the helicopter. My right arm hurt like hell. A little more than just a flesh wound but not as bad as the last time I flew. I could feel the blood seeping through my clothing.

As the sky lightened, I could make out the quay where I wanted to land. I pulled back on the cyclic as I pushed down on the collective, flaring the small helicopter very aggressively to slow down, and settled onto the concrete.

Paul and Danny climbed out and helped Martin and the other security guard leading them away from the helicopter, sat them down and cut off the zip ties.

Instead of climbing into the co-pilot's seat Danny came around to my door, opened it and looked at my arm, drew his knife and cut open my sleeve. Paul handed him a field dressing which he quickly wrapped around my wound, then shut the door and ran around to climb aboard.

"Duck next time," he said as we took off and headed east over Portaferry and the coast. "How're you feeling?"

"Pissed off that we didn't get there in time," I growled.

"And now we're chasing shadows."

"Maybe."

I glanced down at the engines gauges concerned that our fuel level wasn't going to be sufficient to get to Carlingford, do whatever we were going to do and then make it back to England.

"Can your boss arrange for us to refuel at RAF Valley in Anglesey?" I asked, quickly running some time, speed and distance calculations through my head with the remaining fuel load.

"I can try."

"And maybe a Navy vessel to meet us at Carlingford?"

"And create an international incident?"

"Just a thought."

Once over the coast, I banked south, dropped to wave top height, and followed the coast south to Carlingford, a ten-minute flight away.

Combat flying is very different from anything else, to start with, the mind-set. Any combat involves injury and death, so to be successful any combat soldier puts the thought of both out of his mind. Once that is accomplished, the rest is just a matter of concentration, a melding of mind and body so that both worked fluently together. Flying at ultra-low level requires an instinctive touch on the controls as waves rolled toward the aircraft. It's like a roller coaster without boundaries. Rising falling, banking, slithering sideways and all the time staying as low as possible so that coastal radar couldn't pick us up. The Irish Air Corps base was at Casement Aerodrome about twenty minute flight time from Carlingford, and they'd be airborne in five minutes from the moment we appeared on their radar. So we didn't have much time.

"Did you get anything Paul?" I asked, not wanting this trip to be a total waste of time.

"Enough to know it's not a nuclear enrichment plant, at least not as we would classify it."

"Then what the hell is it?"

"They were manufacturing DU ammunition, but with a difference. There are a higher concentration of radioactive isotopes in the metal, and the bullets are small enough for use in high velocity rifles and handguns."

"How do you know that?"

His gloved hand appeared between Danny and me and held up a dull sharply pointed bullet that I guessed was a .226 destined for an M16 military style assault rifle cartridge.

"What the hell were they up to?"

"Whatever it is just got a whole lot worse than we thought," Danny said quietly.

"Meaning," I asked rudely, tired of being kept in the dark.

He didn't answer immediately, just stared straight ahead and pointed at the tiny outline of a yacht heading out of Carlingford Loch into open water. "Looks like we're too late."

Instead of heading directly for the yacht, I swung the helicopter toward the mall town of Carlingford.

"What now," Danny asked testily.

"The vans. I want to know if they met the yacht here."

It only took two minutes to over fly the town and scan the roads. There was only one vehicle driving slowly away from the small loading dock with the name *'Abby's Catering – Dublin'* on the side. I flew inland and north, and then circled back but there were no other trucks on the road, so I banked and headed out to sea. The Irish Air Corps would have been alerted by now, and their EC135 scrambled to intercept us.

"Just one van. What does that tell you, Paul?" I asked.

"Just right for the Uranium Hexaflouride tanks. My guess is they've loaded them onto the yacht."

"And the DU bullets?"

"Could be anywhere."

"The Real IRA or one of those other splinter groups could have a lot of fun with those," Danny broke his silence.

"Paul, can you test that bullet if you had a cartridge?" I asked, ignoring Danny.

"In a Lab under strict conditions. I detected enough radioactive isotopes in this thing to really mess with the human body. Even touching it gives me the creeps."

"We need to get back to the mainland, Thomas," Danny urged.

"Not yet, I want to know what's on that boat."

When you're the one flying the aircraft, it's pretty easier to decide what happens and no amount of threats were going to change my mind. Danny knew that and heaved a big sigh, blowing his cheeks out and shaking his head.

"Too-ra-loo-ra-loo-ral," he sang softly.

"Too-ra-loo-ra-li," I countered and we both burst out laughing as the memory of driving through Eire in the middle of the night, singing *'An Irish Lullaby'* flooded back. It was an adventure before life became serious again.

"I've been stuck with a couple of idiots," Paul said ruefully. "This'll look good in my obituary."

"Lucky nobody's taping this isn't it?" Danny laughed.

Up ahead the motor yacht was making good headway, I estimated nearly twenty-five knots and surprisingly, headed out of the Republic's territorial waters into British. By the time the Irish Air Corps helicopter got to us, we'd be out of their waters.

Perhaps the idea that was forming in my mind was completely insane, but that wasn't going to stop me. I needed to see what was on the yacht and I certainly wasn't going to get permission from Danny's control. They thought I was a 'loose cannon'. So be it.

As we approached from the stern, I could see the name and hailing port *'Marika – Suldiski'* below the aft helipad, on which sat a Sikorsky S-76C with Gunn Group markings.

"That's embarrassing," Danny said sarcastically.

"And confusing," I replied.

"So where are you planning on landing?"

"Forward, on the bow," I said as if I knew what I was doing. "How about you two make up a couple of Plastique bombs, unless you brought grenades with you."

"For what purpose?" Paul asked.

"Those armed men won't want to risk shooting us if they see explosives in your hands."

We overflew the yacht as armed men spewed onto the deck.

At any other time, the stunt I was about to pull would not even have entered my mind. I had to land the helicopter on the small bow helipad while the yacht was doing over twenty knots and avoid the superstructure with the tail rotor. But this wasn't any other time and there was no doubt in my mind that I could do this.

Flying alongside the yacht I inched forward, then sideways until we were over the deck, then put it down as if this was something I did every day.

Before the rotors stopped turning, we were surrounded by Marika Keskküla's private security.

Danny opened the door and held his improvised grenade up for them to see. Confusion showed in their faces and they backed away as Marika Keskküla stepped from the bridge onto the bridge wing and looked down at us.

"Vähendada oma relvad," she commanded, and her men obeyed, lowering their weapons. "Perhaps, Mr Gunn you would be kind enough to dispose of those bombs and join me in the saloon," she said smiling slightly. "Näidata neile, et salongis," she said to one of the men, who inclined his head and extended his arm, pointing the way.

The yacht's saloon was more like the living room of a baronial hall. Tapestries and 17th century oil paintings hung on the walls, and sumptuous brown leather settees and armchairs were arranged around an exquisitely hand made mahogany coffee table, big enough to play pool on. But my eyes were not on the furnishings; they were on Adrian Newell, who sat nervously clutching a glass of red wine and smoking a cigar. To his left sat a blonde haired woman I thought I recognised from CEO magazine, as the new head of a major Investment Bank in the USA, and three other men whose faces were vaguely familiar.

Marika Keskküla walked slowly around the back of the saloon toward me, smiling like a leopard stalking. She was poised, confident and unafraid.

"You know you are trespassing on Estonian Sovereign territory, Mr Gunn," she said silkily, her voice low. "I could have you and your men shot."

"Then why don't you?"

"What would be the sense in that," she laughed. "We are law abiding citizens, unlike, it seems, you."

"I'm not sure Samuel De Costas would agree," I said watching the blood drain from Adrian Newell's face.

"Samuel? I hope he is in California making sure my shipments of high pressure pumps for my oil shale company will be delivered on time," she said smoothly, still smiling.

"Perhaps you should try calling him."

Her smile never left her lips, but her eyes grew dark with menace and the atmosphere in the saloon changed noticeably.

I turned to Adrian. "I'm surprised to find you here Adrian. What company business would you be conducting?"

"Mrs Keskküla has expressed an interest in our African coltan mining business, we were discussing a possible partnership," Adrian replied shakily.

"Without board approval?"

"You were reported dead, Thomas."

"As you can see. Not so."

Marika Keskküla stepped forward impatiently. "What can I do for you, Mr Gunn?"

"Tell me where the DU ammunition is and let me search this vessel for the Uranium Hexaflouride storage tanks."

"If I knew what you were talking about, I'd be happy to, but alas I have absolutely no idea." She had recovered her composure a little and I wondered how much time I had before she changed her mind and let the dogs loose. "You have outstayed your welcome, Mr Gunn." She looked past my shoulder and in the mirror behind her I saw the reflection of Hamish McDougall with a small automatic in his hand.

"There is a navy vessel on its way and if you listen, the Irish Air Corps have just arrived, Hamish. So I suggest you put that toy away." I said coldly as a helicopter flew low overhead, banked and steadied above the yacht. "So we'll be leaving now." I looked at Adrian. "Make sure the Sikorsky is returned, Adrian. And you're fired."

I turned and faced Hamish. "I had a feeling you were behind this."

"You never did listen, even when you were a boy, Thomas. I told you to leave it alone," he said reproachfully as if apologetic.

"You killed Mary," I lied, wondering if he knew she was still alive. "Why did you do that?"

He shrugged. "I thought with your father dead, then you, it would be tidier. It's for the greater good. If I thought you'd join us I would ask, but I think the time has passed for that. Don't you agree?" He held the gun higher.

"Not here," snapped Marika Keskküla. "Not now."

"That will be a mistake," Hamish said gritting his teeth.

"That is my problem, not yours. Put the gun down. He doesn't know anything."

"Next time take the shot Hamish, if you get the chance, because I won't miss," I said as I pushed past him out onto the deck. Danny and Paul were standing beside the helicopter, in a 'Mexican stand-off' with the Estonians. Overhead the Irish pilot stared down at us. I waved and climbed aboard, started the engine and waited.

"What are we waiting for, Thomas, let's get the hell out of here," Danny shouted.

"We'll be in British territorial waters in less than one minute," I replied, as I felt the yacht start to slow, hoping I was right. Feeling a sense of satisfaction as the Irish helicopter dropped back behind the yacht. We cleared the bow by a matter of inches and I dropped to sea level and sped away before the Estonians could bring their weapons to bear, not that they would risk a fire fight in full view of the Irish Air Corps.

As we flew away from the yacht, I knew two things for certain.

The first was that Adrian was a dead man. Marika Keskküla could not afford me getting hold of him. He was a liability.

And the second was that whatever she and Hamish McDougall were involved in went far beyond the shores of the UK, and into the highest levels of Government and International business.

The aerodrome at RAF Valley in Anglesey was the closest British military installation, a seventy-five minute flight, and by the time the Hawk T2 trainers from IV Squadron intercepted us, the EC120 was flying on fumes. Danny had been on the radio since we took off from the yacht and arranged the reception committee, for which the trainee Hawk pilots were more than willing to oblige. Not to mention the SARTU (Search And Rescue Training Unit) AW139 pilots who had been scrambled in case we had to ditch. Their briefing was that it was a training exercise in support of 22 SAS, and obviously excited them judging by the radio traffic.

"No way am I ditching," I said emphatically as Danny finished his last call. "This little baby is going on the ground in one piece."

"I'd like that," Paul quipped. "The Irish Sea is cold this time of year."

"Where's your sense of adventure," Danny chimed in and we laughed, releasing the tension of the last twenty four hours as I saw the airport ahead and the pair of hovering, and no doubt disappointed, AW139s.

Much to my chagrin, the landing was less than perfect, as we ran out of fuel just as I flared and we skidded across the tarmac before coming to a stop. At least that would give the trainee pilots something to talk about. We were whisked away to a drab building before anyone had the chance to shake our hands.

Danny wasn't saying anything, nor was Paul, just staring out of the window of the de-briefing room with a couple of armed RAF Regiment from No.2 Squadron judging by their Parachute wings. If ever I felt more like an outsider, it was now. My past service in 1PARA as part of SFSG didn't seem to count.

The door open, interrupting my melancholy reflections and Jonathan Radley strode into the room.

"I see you've managed to create quite a stir, Mr Gunn," he said as if addressing a local Woman's Institute meeting. "The Estonian Embassy have filed a formal complaint that you violated their sovereign territory by boarding their yacht, the *'Marika'*."

"Really. I was simply attending a meeting regarding a possible business partnership in Africa between the Gunn Group and Keskküla Mining," I replied evenly. I knew this was being recorded.

For the first time Radley's eyes showed a sense of humour and his lip twitched slightly. "Dressed like that?"

"Paintball practice. No time to change. The meeting was last minute."

This time he allowed a small cough that could have been mistaken for a suppressed laugh. "And my agents here?"

"Same thing. We get together now and again. For old time's sake."

"Come," he said turning and walking briskly from the room out into the cold Anglesey day. When we were far enough from the building and close to the runway where Hawk T1 pilots were practicing 'touch-and-go' landings, he stopped and turned to me. "You are a signatory to the Official Secrets Act, Mr Gunn," he said watching me carefully. "So whatever we discuss is between us. Do you understand?" I nodded. "Are you prepared to work with us, or are you simply on a vendetta to avenge your father's death?"

"Not only my father. Julie and Mary. You have a responsibility too?" I said angrily. I was not a puppet. I refused to be a puppet.

"Mary is alive and recovering," he said pausing, watching me carefully. "And so is Julie."

For a moment the world seemed to topple on its side. The horizon tilted and the grey sky flickered with multi-coloured lights.

"Julie's not dead?" I said meaninglessly. "She's alive? That's not possible, I saw her die."

"She's alive. We needed you to think she was dead," Radley said slowly, all the time watching my eyes carefully. "Hatred is a great motivator."

Danny moved alongside me, hand on my shoulder as I tensed, staring at Radley. "Easy mate. Easy."

"I always did hate you sons-of-bitches. Who are you? MI5. MI6?"

"Does it matter?"

"No it doesn't," I said, barely able to keep my voice and anger under control. "Where is she?"

"First we talk, then I tell you," Radley said sensing that my anger had subsided somewhat. "You always knew there was more to this than just a friend helping a friend, Mr Gunn. Danny and Paul have been your personal bodyguards. Their idea, not mine."

Danny stared down at the ground as a Hawk blasted overhead, and Paul watched the aircraft fly into the distance. Neither wanted to look at me, though I knew they were doing what they had to do. It was their job.

He was right. All the time, deep down I knew I wasn't on my own. I was being guided, allowed to flex my desire for vengeance. It had been so easy to slip in and out of Northern Ireland, get fake IDs, passports, and weapons. I just didn't want to think about it, just exact revenge for my father's death.

"Professionally," Radley continued. "I don't give a damn about your reasons for pursuing this vendetta, I need your expertise, recklessness and expendability. I didn't expect you to survive, and yet, here you are."

"And how do I know you're not in league with Hamish McDougall?"

"Because you would be dead, zipped in a body bag and consigned to the deep by now. As would your friends."

"What about the Increment? Where do they fit in?"

"McDougall's boys. They tried to enlist Danny and Paul here, along with a few others, but they failed as you can see."

"I don't trust you."

"The feeling is mutual, I can assure you." He held up his hand and I noticed he was wearing a wrist brace. "But I do take comfort from the fact that if you can do this to an ally, what will you do to an enemy," he said quietly, allowing himself another small smile.

"What do you want from me?"

"I want McDougall and his organisation. I want all the information you can possibly get on who they are and what they plan. And then I want them destroyed before they destroy us, and by us, I mean this country," Radley replied with venom.

"And what do I get?"

"Your life back, and the satisfaction of once again serving your country."

"You're all heart."

"I have no heart. I have a job to do and I'll use the best tools at my disposal to do that job," he said emphatically. "Are you with us?"

I looked at Paul and Danny, and then nodded. "I want to see Julie."

"You have twenty four hours, and then we meet again. Danny knows the location." He walked away toward the private jet I had spotted on our arrival, then turned and looked at me. "You're a natural warrior, Gunn, whether you like it or not. That's why I chose you." Then turned and continued toward the jet that was already winding up its engines.

"We're refuelled and ready to go," Danny said.

"Where?"

"Back to Calder Hall. Julie's waiting."

SIXTEEN

She was standing near the helipad with her father. As beautiful as ever, with her blonde hair blowing in the downdraft, smiling as we landed. And then she was in my arms and I never wanted to let her go ever again. Gently she pulled back and held my face in her soft hands. When she spoke it was not the soft lilting, laughing voice I knew, but strained as if the act of speaking was an effort.

"I'm so happy you're safe," she said haltingly, holding my face tightly, tears streaming down her cheeks.

"They didn't tell me you were alive," I said watching her eyes staring at my lips. "What happened?" Alarm coursed through every cell in my body.

"I'm deaf," she said. "Maybe just temporarily. The crash... I hit my head and dislocated the bones in my inner ear."

"She needs an operation to have the ossicular bones repaired." Oldfield said softly.

"I need an operation," Julie said not hearing that her father had already spoken.

"You've known all along?" I asked Oldfield. He nodded. I stared at him coldly. "I'm sorry Thomas. I had no choice but to lie to you."

Julie saw the exchange. "It's not his fault, Thomas. You didn't need the distraction." She looked away and then back at me. "I asked them not to tell you." She kissed me lingeringly, and then took my hand. "You need a shower and a change of clothes. You stink."

I'd forgotten just how desperate Danny, Paul and I looked. Covered in dust and dirt, still in our black combat outfit and flack jackets, and me with congealed blood from the bullet wound in my arm. For the first time since landing, I looked around and saw armed men at strategic points around the Hall. Radley was as good as his word. Julie and Mary would be safe here.

Henderson and Ron greeted us at the back door, and showed Danny and Paul to their rooms, while I let Julie lead me to the flat and slowly take off my clothes, tears springing to her eyes as she saw the wound.

"It's looks worse than it is," I said, almost forgetting to turn face her so she could lip-read.

"I'll be the judge of that."

"Does it hurt?" I asked.

"What?"

"Your head. Where you were injured," I said awkwardly.

She smiled and shook her head. "No. Just a ringing in my head that drives me crazy some times, but they tell me the surgery will fix that."

"I... missed you..." I started to say, but she pressed her fingers to my mouth.

"I know."

"I've never told you how much I love you, Julie," I said softly. It was hard to say the words, but I needed to tell her. "I do. More than anything else."

"That's why we couldn't tell you I was alive," she said, tears flowing down her cheeks. "This is bigger than us, Thomas. Remember that. I'll still be here when it's finished."

For the rest of the night we pretended we were back in Gozo on the yacht and that everything that had happened; hadn't happened. That lip reading was a game and security outside didn't exist. Oldfield, Danny and Paul left us alone knowing that tomorrow, reality would break with the dawning of the day, and we would once again be soldiers.

Oldfield typed the words *'Orange Moon'* into the user field and I then read off the reference number that was on the label of the pot I found beside Mary. As soon as the last figure was typed, the computer linked through to Stacy's files hidden in his cloud account. His insurance policy was there for us to see. Obviously he had been thinking like my father and didn't trust a soul, but his downfall was greed and not Patriotism.

We all sat in total disbelieving silence and read. There on the screen was a complete dossier on an organisation that none of us had ever heard of, called the International Security & Economic Council. However I did suspect that Radley probably knew. It had its base in big business and recruited from the top echelons of Parliament, the military and the civil service. There were lists of targeted possible donors in investment banks, venture capital companies, unions, universities and lobbying groups from around the world. It was a 'Who's-Who' of the wealth of the world. Then there were the lists of those actually on the Board of Trustees of the Council. Adrian Newell's name topped the list as chairman, which perhaps didn't surprise me, but what did surprise me was that neither Hamish McDougall nor Marika Keskküla's name were mentioned anywhere. Nor were Rathborne Micro-Electronics, Venus Automotive or Samuel De Costas. Unless you actually knew the connection between them, there would have been no way of knowing that the ISEC was anything but a group of high level businessmen and politicians whose concerns were the economic future of the Western World. There was nothing in the general description of the ISEC to distinguish themselves from other organisations such as the Bilderberg Group, whose members included Kings, European aristocracy, American politicians and corporate giants from Europe and America. The ISEC were less discerning, listing among their members Asian business tycoons and Dictators, Russian billionaires and African Warlords.

Stacy had kept meticulous records, but nothing that suggested any law breaking activities. Unless we could definitively link Marika Keskküla, the Gunn Group and Samuel De Costas, we had little to go on.

The only link was Hamish McDougall. Danny, Paul and I officially did not exist. Even the Gunn Group accounts had been 'cleansed' of the Government injection of capital for Rathborne Micro-Electronics, converted into the investment into Venus Automotive, which conveniently had been blown up and burned to the ground. Any evidence of DU ammunition manufacture, destroyed. The only notation were the letters 'CDS' in the Gunn Group's accounting of the Rathborne Micro-Electronics loan, next to the final figures, followed by more letters 'ABTC'.

The following morning, the Daily Telegraph carried a front-page story of a fire caused by an electrical fault that had decimated the Venus Automotive factory, causing the loss of valuable jobs in the province and a statement from the Prime Minister that the car plant would be rebuilt. De Costas' name was not mentioned in the column and other newspapers carried the story on page two with little interest. The only other piece of news that caught my attention was that the body of Adrian Newell was recovered after he was washed into the sea while fishing off rocks near Falmouth.

"They're circling the wagons," I said coldly, not caring a jot about Adrian, however it did mean that I would have to put in an appearance at the company and stop the Board appointing another Chairman.

"We don't have much time," Oldfield broke in. "Somebody is already accessing the cloud link."

"How is that possible?"

"Because they're are probably hooked into a super computer that can decrypt just about anything two hundred times faster than we can."

"Anyway to stop them?"

"Maybe if I can backtrack a trace." He typed furiously while Julie, Danny, Paul and myself paced the room. After a few minutes Oldfield looked up. "We have about a minute before they break through. I traced the code to a super computer operating out of Estonia."

"Now there's a surprise," Danny said sarcastically. "Who would have thought?"

"Can you download those files onto Stacy's hard drive? We can then disconnect it from the internet."

"Already did that," Oldfield snorted, as if I had insulted his expertise in the worst possible way. "And sent back a worm that'll take them some time to unblock."

"Could somebody tell me what's going on," Julie said quietly. We had been so absorbed that we had forgotten she could not hear. I took her on one side and explained what we had found and what was happening.

"Okay we're offline," Oldfield said, sitting back and taking a deep breath. "I've shut down all Internet access through this IP and closed your father and stepmother's accounts."

"Thank you."

"I also closed my University account, because no doubt they'll have accessed that too."

Danny laid his hand Oldfield's shoulder. "We'll fix you up with secure access. It'll take twenty-four hours. In the meantime we'll use this," he said holding up his mobile satellite phone.

For the next two hours we poured through the files Oldfield had downloaded, sifting through every single piece of information looking for any anomalies. The members of ISEC were an assorted lot, which included recently retired senior military figures from Britain and the USA, who were listed as security advisers. What caught my eye were two investment banks whose names I remember seeing on some Gunn Group company memos. The Griffin Trust of Atlanta and the Von Kurt Fund of Münster. At the time I paid little attention and Adrian Newell had brushed them off as hedge funds owned by the Gunn Group for utilising foreign investments.

But as I read the file it became clear that they were arbitrage banks engaged in the sale and acquisition of Government bonds in many countries, of which the members of ISEC were either senior government officials or the actual leaders of those countries. On their website the organisation touted itself as an International *'Think Tank'* with no political ties or agenda.

"This is interesting," Julie said breaking in my thoughts. She was lying back on the settee looking through a sheaf of papers. "It's a calendar which is completely blank except for a small notation on the 25th of each month *'ISEC-MT 8pm'.*" She looked up. "What on earth does that mean?"

"Every month ISEC have a meeting at the same time in the same place." Not a very useful thing for me to say, but I was tired and my arm and leg hurt like hell.

Danny was in the corner of the room deep in conversation on the sat phone and Paul was going through the computer records with Oldfield. I felt like a spare part, brain in neutral and my usefulness over at this point.

The telephone rang eight times before Morgan answered.

"Hello?" her voice was thick with sleep and annoyed at being woken at three o'clock in the morning.

"Morgan? It's Thomas. Thomas Gunn."

There was a long pause. "Thomas? Is that really you?" sounding a little more awake.

"Yes. I've got a couple of questions for you. Something I'd like you to do for me."

"I might have guessed," she said abruptly. "We read about the Venus Automotive factory getting burnt out. We thought you'd be one of the bodies." She paused again. "It's a shock to hear the voice of a dead man at three in the morning."

"I'm okay. Tell the doc he did a good job."

"I will. What did you ring for, Thomas? You said you wanted me to do something for you. What is it?"

"Have you heard of the Griffin Trust Company?"

"I have."

"Could you do a bit of digging for me? I want to know if there is a connection with any companies in Eastern Europe."

"Yeah, now you mention it, there is something that I came across a few months ago. The Federal Reserve Bank of Atlanta just appointed the former President of Griffin Trust, Ted Lieberman, to its board. Lieberman recently travelled to Estonia as part of a *fact-finding* mission set up by Senator Kyle Kingston-Smith, who was formally CEO of Shale Corp in Texas."

"Anything else you can find out would be great. There's one more thing. Why didn't you tell me Julie survived the crash?"

"You know why, Thomas," she said softly. "I'll find out what I can about Lieberman and the Griffin Trust."

"Thanks. Morgan. I'm going to be busy for a few days so here's a number you can call and leave the information." I gave her Edwards iPhone number.

"Okay. Just take care, you hear, I'll get back to you," she said and the phone went dead in my hands. I stared at the wall.

What had any of this to do with nuclear isotope enhanced Depleted

Uranium bullets and a car company in Northern Ireland? None of it seemed to make any sense at all. The ISEC was a *'Think Tank'*, albeit not of the calibre of the Bilderberg Group, but still involved in similar activities.

So we were looking at parallel issues.

Financial and Military.

I thought of the multinational companies over the years that had been responsible for the successful coups in Africa, South America and Middle Eastern countries. Coups in which the outcome not necessarily been beneficial to western governments as there had been no effective control over the new Government.

I let my mind wander, considering almost impossible scenarios and came back to the list of the members of the ISEC consisting of Government leaders, military chiefs and the heads of International banks and hedge funds. All the countries represented held valuable resources. The economic value of those resources, such as uranium, gold, columbite tantalite, iron ore, coal, platinum and much more were conservatively valued at over $50 trillion per year.

By laying waste to entire countries through revolution and violence, the way was paved to create a new society; a new industrial climate; a new wealth built upon the misery and deprivation that all forms of war bring. Was that the aim of the ISEC? Was it a global market place for international power brokers? And if so how on earth was I going to prove that.

Gradually it was beginning to become clear to me just why there had been so many attempts on my life, and why my father had been killed. There was nothing in the file to directly incriminate anyone of illegal activities, but once the knowledge of the real aims of the ISEC were known, that would spell disaster. All I had were some half baked ideas and disconnected activities, none of which would stand up to scrutiny.

"About a two years ago, about the time you were injured in Afghanistan, Sir Ivan was approached by an American from the ISEC, or should I say from a man from the Griffin Trust," Radley informed us, standing near the fireplace, warming himself. He had flown to the

Hall in the late afternoon. "With him was a German woman from the Von Kurt Fund. Your father wouldn't play ball until your stepmother had her accident and became an addict. They tried to blackmail him with Mary's drug addiction, but he wouldn't play their game, and contacted Danny who brought him to me. We asked him to play along, to work for them, to use the Gunn Group as the investment vehicle for the ISEC and operations like the one in Northern Ireland." Radley talked quietly and I looked across at Danny, who avoided my eyes. "Your father kept a secret file. De Costas' knew what he was doing, but didn't know where this information was kept. Neither did we. How we first came to hear of the organisation doesn't matter. Just know that information came our way concerning several ex-Army Generals trying to form their own private armies in the guise of security companies." He paused to pour himself a cup of coffee. "We started to track and log all the people we knew who might possibly have been connected. Your father didn't trust anyone and kept the information he had garnered secret. He called me from Belfast to arrange a meeting on his return, but as you know, that never happened."

"And that's where I came into the picture," I said slowly. "You knew that the only person he would trust was me."

"Correct."

"Then why all the deception? Why didn't you just tell me all this when I came back from Gozo?"

"If they thought you were in on it, then they would quite probably have regrouped in a different form. Hamish McDougall was there to keep an eye on you, and I was keeping an eye on him. For a while they were happy that you knew nothing. But you decided to investigate, and that's when, in their eyes, you became expendable, just like your father. The only thing we could do was keep an eye on you, trust you were as good as your training and service suggested, and then wait and see what happened."

There was a tide of anger beginning to rise inside me. "Your strange sense of security got two innocent women killed in Northern Ireland."

"Yes, it did. And that is something I have to live with." Radley looked me in the eye and I believed him, the anger dissipating slowly.

"Now that you've got your information, you don't need us anymore."

"That's up to you."

"Or is it?"

He didn't answer my question immediately, just watched me carefully.

"Thomas," Danny began, then bit his lip as I stared at him coldly. "Believe it or not we are on the same side. And we need you."

"Really," I said sarcastically. "And just what else are you keeping from me?"

"We need you to infiltrate ISEC headquarters here in the UK. Adrian Newell was to attend a seminar as the guest speaker at a location in Scotland, near Perth. We have the address and have added a Mr James Camden, newly appointed Chief Financial Officer of EuroTrend Mining, to the guest list."

Of course it was a company within Gunn Group Industries and naturally I was now James Camden. Radley was insistent on using me until I cracked or died.

"You'll have Danny, Paul and the tech team as back-up." Radley seemed to be enjoying himself.

"This is a nanotechnology transmitter. The effective range is about five hundred metres." The technician, who had been introduced to me as Bill, explained as I stared through the microscope at the device that looked like a bundle of globes stuck onto a tubular object. "It uses whatever transmitter or receiver is in the vicinity to boost its signal. We can then access either voice or video dependent upon the component it is piggybacking upon. Your body's own electrical circuit powers it."

"And this goes *in* my body?" It was a stupid question and I was wondering what the hell science was going to think up next, recalling an article I read some time ago about the potential toxicity of nanotechnology in the human body.

"We coated the molecular nanowire transistors with a non-leaching polymer and a built-in organic self-destruct," he explained patiently, as if that was supposed to placate me.

"Oh great. Now I'm an experiment in *'Mission Impossible'*."

"What?"

"A film. Tom Cruise. Action adventure."

"We deal in reality here Mr Gunn, not fiction."

"I hope so, Bill. I really hope so."

He looked at me with disgust. "I'll inject it into the base of your thumb. You have a nice scar there which will hide the pin prick." He need not have sounded so enthusiastic. I have to admit the needle was so tiny I didn't feel anything.

"And just when does this little beauty self-destruct?"

"Three days. It'll be absorbed into the blood stream and be ejected as waste."

"Wonderful," I muttered with as much lack of enthusiasm as I could. "And just how do I communicate?"

"Just talk."

"Into my hand?" I was feeling more like Maxwell Smart than Thomas Gunn.

He gave me a witheringly tired look. "Just talk, we'll pick it up."

"And what about you talking to me."

"One way only. We're working on the receiver side. Should be ready in six months. Quite an interesting nano ear implant actually."

Julie watched the whole procedure nervously. Something had changed over the past few days. She was withdrawn, quiet, and unresponsive to my attempts at lovemaking. The Hall had become the centre for the operation and we were no longer alone. Surrounded by technicians, secret service and MI5 officers our lives were not ours anymore and I knew Julie was feeling the strain. Over the past few weeks much had happened that changed us, and we were not able to focus on our relationship. And when we were alone in the quiet of the flat at the back of the Hall, it was with the knowledge that there were guards outside the door and in the grounds.

Mary returned to the Hall under cover of darkness, her place in the hospital filled by a brain dead car accident victim with no family. She was still seriously ill from the affects of the heroin and the prognosis wasn't looking too promising. Radley provided around the clock medical care.

'It's the least he can do,' I thought angrily, trying to purge all emotion from my mind and concentrate on the task at hand. Tomorrow night I was heading into the enemy's lair.

SEVENTEEN

The Gunn Group Gulfstream 550 drew up near the Perth airport hangers and lurched to a stop, the whine of the engines slowly disappearing as the pilot flipped off the switches. I went forward and opened the doors. There, pulling up beside the aircraft, was a black Mercedes saloon. The uniformed chauffeur got out and opened the rear passenger door. He took my bags and waited until I had made myself comfortable in the back seat, then shut the door without a word.

The drive out to the mansion was uneventful and I tried to relax and enjoy the rugged scenery. It was difficult, because there was a knot in my throat trying to throttle me. Disconcertingly, the chauffeur drove in silence without once glancing in the rear view mirror.

After what seemed an age of twisting roads and hills, we turned off the main road onto a private road that wound its way over a hill between open areas of heath land where sheep grazed lazily.

On the tops of the mountains in the distance there was snow, and the sheep's breath hung like a fine fog in the cold still air.

Beyond a formidable gatehouse and narrow bridge that crossed a fast flowing river, the driveway to the mansion must have been a good half-mile long. Eventually the brooding grey stone building appeared around a corner, tucked back into the side of yet another hill.

The chauffeur stopped the car, got out and opened the door for me. At the top of the stone steps, as if by magic, two people appeared. One I took to be a servant as he came down the steps and took my bags from the boot of the car. The other was obviously the welcoming committee. He came towards me with his hand outstretched. His grip was firm and dry.

"Welcome, Mr Camden. I'm glad you could make it. My name is Charles Lambert." The voice was cultured and sounded friendly enough. Only the eyes held a hint of danger. They were slate grey like the building and just as cold. The smile that played around the lips never touched his eyes. "I trust you had a pleasant journey. Come and meet some of the guests. They haven't all arrived yet, but we expect them soon." He led the way. "I was very sad to hear about the sudden death of Mr Newell." There was no sadness in his expression.

"Very sad indeed, and so unexpected. Please call me James." I was surprised at the ease with which I matched Lambert's detached tone.

"I'll show you to your room and then let you loose with the others. We don't expect to begin for a few hours yet, so feel free to explore the grounds if wish." The inside of the mansion was as forbidding as the outside. Dim corners and suits of armour, large oil paintings Highland Chieftains and heavy wood panelled walls. The bedroom that I was allocated wasn't any more cheerful, with a huge carved wooden four-poster bed and ancient drapes. Only the view of the window across the land and the mountains was worth looking at. Once I had dropped off my bags, which I was sure would be inspected as soon as I left the room, Charles Lambert led me downstairs, showed me the bar, games room, lounge and dining-room. There were a few other men in the lounge gathered in a small group. He introduced me and then left.

All the men were of my age and held senior executive positions in high technology computer and research companies, as well as the banking and investment companies that were already on the list of ISEC members. And all were ambitious, aggressive young financial executives. I doubted there would be anyone amongst them I could trust. The conversation was all shop, so I decided to do a little research into how I was going to get out of this place when the need arose.

I excused myself and went out into the cold late morning air, and walked down the main driveway that led down to the river and the guarded bridge we had crossed earlier. At the bridge I turned right and followed the curve of the river to the back of the mansion where desolate sparsely treed moorland stretched to dark forbidding mountains beyond. Any escape in that direction would be folly unless fully equipped to deal with the harsh reality of the rugged Scottish countryside in winter. The river was a different proposition. It was about twenty metres across, fairly shallow but fast flowing. The only way to the far bank was either by the bridge or an ice-cold swim. There were guards and barriers at either end of the bridge, so that wasn't a reasonable choice.

That left the river.

To swim across in this weather would mean that you would probably freeze before you got half way across. I felt sure that although the natural barriers were formidable enough, that they would have other methods of preventing people from getting in or out. I moved slowly along the bank trying to look deep in thought. Perhaps pondering on the enormity of my role in ISEC. But I was really putting myself in their place. I would have some form of booby trap, both in and out of the water, as a back-up to the CCTV cameras that covered almost every inch of the grounds and the inside of the mansion.

I picked up a piece of reed and walked along casually swinging it across my body through the gaps in the grass and reed beds that grew to waist height along the edge of the bank. After a few swings, I felt the slight resistance that told me there was a wire running at about calf height along the edge of the bank. The wire was almost invisible, very thin and a dark matt green colour. Unless you knew what to look for you wouldn't see it. I carried on walking and wondered what was at the end of it. I doubted that it would be an explosive device because of the noise, so it was probably linked to a *'silent'* trigger that sounded an alarm in the security room. So now I had a fair idea what was on the bank, but the question was, what was in the river? Perhaps I was over-thinking. The river itself was a barrier. Ice cold and fast flowing. Whilst I was mulling everything over in my mind, I figured I might as well tell the back-up team, wherever they were what I had found.

Walking along ostensibly blowing on my hands as if they were freezing cold, which they were without gloves, I described everything that I could see, and the things that I thought lay in store. When I'd finished, I went back to the mansion.

The black Mercedes passed me returning from having presumably collected the remaining guests.

"We have brought you here under a slight misconception, for which I apologise." There was no sense of apology in Lambert thin smile. "We are very sensitive of security. ISEC is a multi-national organisation but we are not non-political. We are a global political party that brings together like-minded people from business, the military and foreign governments. This particular cell is known as *'ISEC Europe'* and operates solely within the European Community. The object is to safeguard the role of the business in the free world. At the moment, we have two controlling companies of which you will all have heard. The Griffin Trust and the Von Kurt Foundation. You may well be asking yourselves why the entire charade? Well, over the next few days you will be shown exactly why this is necessary. I must assure you that in no way is the ISEC an illegal organisation. But we feel that the business communities of all nations have the right to be able to invest their hard won profits in areas of their choice that offer the most protection and the most rewards without government intervention. I ask you not to formulate a fixed opinion at this moment in time, but to let us show you over the next few days just how membership of our organisation, can help both you personally and your companies."

His introductory speech sounded so bland; so reasonable; so logical. But it wasn't the full story. No doubt Lambert and his cohorts would cull the doubters fairly quickly and they would more likely find themselves washed up on a lonely beach somewhere, just like Adrian Newell.

Once the introductory speech was over, we were split into two separate discussion groups and spent the rest of the day going over the details of ISEC's mission and goals. Needless to say it all differed very much from the information that I had. However, I managed to sound as interested as I knew how, and asked what I hoped were pertinent questions.

At last the day was over and I could escape to my room for a little think. There were parts of the mansion that had been made off limits to us, with the excuse that they were reconstructing those wings. I wanted to have a look there and see just what it did contain. Whilst I had been out walking earlier, I thought I saw what could only be described as the tip of a microwave antenna. Unfortunately, the light was bad now so any poking around outside wouldn't do any good.

That left an internal search.

At night, the grounds and walls of the mansion were lit by powerful spotlights, ostensibly to highlight its rugged beauty, but serving as an effective deterrent against breaking in or out. The lights were positioned in such a way that they shone only on certain parts of the upper part of the building. It would be the unlit parts that housed the closed circuit TV cameras.

The wing that housed the Administrative Offices was to the right of my room. It was impossible to get there from the ground floor, so I had scouted a route across the ledges and small roof area, to a point where I could enter through one of the top floor windows. I reckoned that the rooms on the top floor were the quarters of the 'staff', but there seemed to be a couple of rooms from which there was never a light showing at night and no movement during the day.

Patience has never been one of my strong points and it was with growing restlessness that I waited until everything was quiet.

Finally at two o'clock in the morning, I considered it safe enough to venture out, but not before sending a message to my back-up team.

"I need the CCTV cameras to go on the blink for about half an hour. Like a persistent short or something." And hoped they heard me. If they hadn't I'd be dead in five minutes.

It had become a lot colder, with a hint of snow in the air, as I slid the window open and gingerly climbed out onto the ledge that led to the sloping roof off to my right. There had been rain during the day that had turned to ice making the ledge very slippery. Once or twice I slipped and nearly fell, but somehow managed to make it to the roof.

By the time I reached the apex of the roof, my hands were raw from the rough stone and sharp spikes of ice. I lay for a minute just to catch my breath. It was only when I started to feel the cold biting into me that I moved on. Now it was a question of sliding down the roof and crawling along another ledge until I came to the window I had earmarked.

Perhaps the cold and the snow that had started to fall had numbed my brain because I let go of the apex of the roof and started to slide on the ice-covered tiles. Not just slide. I shot down the sharp slope and in panic dug my finger nails frantically into the ice and stone. I was about to shoot out into the void and thirty-foot drop when my hand caught one of the protrusions on the gable end and my legs swung out over the edge of the roof.

Desperately I launched for another handhold as I felt my grip loosening on the brick. Made it. Used all my strength to haul myself back onto the roof. Lay shaking on the cold surface trying to control the rising panic and terror, the cold creeping into my bones forcing me to move along the edge of the roof.

Fifteen minutes after starting this insane venture I was perched on the ledge outside the window. Naturally it was locked, but I had come prepared for that. At dinner I had slipped one of the steak knives into my pocket. The catches on the mansion windows were of the old-fashioned type, with enough room to slide the flexible blade between the two halves of the sash window and slide the catch. My fingers were numb with cold, and the falling snow that was settling all round me made the tricky process even more difficult. At last the catch slid across and very gently I eased up the bottom window.

Once inside with the window closed, I set about trying to warm myself up. The room was empty and had the musty smell of all places that have been unoccupied for some time. There were no curtains at the window, so I daren't use my small pocket torch.

Instead, I felt my way to the door in the darkness. No light showed under the door, so it seemed this part of the wing was unused, as I had hoped. The door opened without a sound and I slowly stepped out into the corridor. If it hadn't been for the light at the end of the landing where the other corridors joined this one, then I wouldn't have been able to see a thing. As it was I tripped over a chair and just caught it before it toppled over.

There was no sign that anyone had heard. Breathing a sigh of relief I carried on. This time more carefully. It was only on reaching the ground floor that there was there was the sound of muffled voices from behind one of the doors leading off the small passageway, a chair being pushed back and footsteps. The door behind me opened when I turned the handle and I slipped into the dark interior just as the opposite door opened. Footsteps retreated down the passageway and I risked a look. There was nobody in sight.

I shut the door again and turned to explore the room. The small torch made a thin beam that sliced through the black interior illuminating an office with large mahogany desk with a wireless keyboard and mouse and several filing cabinets. On the wall opposite the desk was a large computer monitor. I settled myself behind the desk and moved the mouse. The screen lit up.

"Okay guys. I'm in an office and just turned on the computer. There is a Google earth map of a place called the Dominion of Pakhia, a volcanic island in the South Pacific." It felt absurd talking to myself and I hoped they could hear me and locate the room and the computer through the nanotechnology transmitter. "The office is on the ground floor of the west wing." In a scene straight from an old spy film, I had been given a one hundred gigabyte flash drive, concealed in the heel of my shoe. The logic was that it was so ridiculous, nobody would even think of looking there. Once it was plugged in and the file downloaded, I keyed in a code Radley's tech guru had given me and uploaded the contents of the computer's storage into the cloud address. Then I sat back and looked at the map on the screen. There were several markings including the position of a factory complex labelled The Pakhia Research Foundation. Other marks on the map identified the main telecommunications centre, the Central Government buildings and the airport. The capital of the island, Pikua, and the port were ringed in red.

I turned to the filing cabinets. They were locked, resisting my efforts to open them. Defeated I went over to the desk. Perhaps I would have better luck there. The third drawer came open, and inside were several folders. Most of them were really of no consequence at all, but the last couple I came to spread a different light on the matter. They seemed to be draft computer printouts of what could be best described as a business proposal. The meat of the proposal was to encourage member companies of the Party to invest their resources in the Pakhia Research Foundation, who would in turn buy property and establish a tax-free operating base for these companies. It then went on to detail the areas that had been earmarked for development, they related to some of the markings on the wall map. I put the papers back and went over to the map again. The areas actually covered two of the islands. The capital Pikua, and one of the smaller islands to the north, called Sahito. The puzzle was most certainly getting more complex the further I dug into it.

Just what were they up to? There was only one real answer.

They were trying to stage manage a take-over of the whole Dominion. That would explain the marking of strategic points such as the telecommunications centre and the government buildings.

But how?

No government was going to stand by and let somebody buy the entire land from right under their feet.

There was only one way.

Finance a coup by interested local parties and then rule by proxy.

My knowledge of the Dominion of Pakhia was sadly lacking, so I had no idea just what the politics of the country were, but I guessed Radley would know. Now all I had to do was get the information to him.

I didn't fancy another trip across the rooftops. Still, it had to be done. Before that though, I wanted to have a look at a couple of the other rooms down here. The one opposite that the man had come out of, intrigued me.

I replaced the papers and made sure that there was nothing else that looked out of place, and then went back to the door. As I was about to open it, the sound of footsteps came down the passageway. The door opposite opened and I risked a quick look. I caught a fleeting glimpse of a control room with large wall monitors, computer terminals and a microwave satellite setup.

They obviously thought that nobody could get into this part of the house, except lunatics who risked life and limb climbing around rooftops and they weren't expecting any of those.

There was a layer of snow all over everything, and it was falling faster than ever. I climbed out onto the ledge and within a few seconds was covered from head to foot. If I didn't keep moving, my fingers would go numb and I wouldn't be able to grip anything.

The trip back to the apex of the roof went fine, mainly because I was so petrified of falling my grip couldn't have been broken with a crowbar. Instead of sliding down the tiles to the next ledge, I used the ornamental brickwork on the gable end and let myself down slowly and carefully. Once on the ledge, it was easy to crawl gingerly along to the window of my room.

"Well, well, Mr Camden, been practising for the next Everest expedition have you?" Lambert sat in the chair at the far end of the room, an automatic held loosely in his hand. There wasn't time to think, I just threw the jacket at him and leapt forward. He wasn't expecting it and I was onto him before he had time to react. There was a small table next to where he was standing and on it an ornamental vase. I picked it up and crashed it down on his head. He grunted and slid to the floor unconscious.

Then I broke his neck.

It was over in seconds.

Rifling quickly through his pockets I found a letter of invitation to a dinner at the Tower of London, and a Samsung smartphone. It was on but I couldn't access any information.

"Okay guys I need help unlocking a smartphone."

After an interminable ten seconds the phone came to life. I checked the calendar app and found a cryptic notation two days from now.

Keskküla. Suldiski. 236. Load.

Whatever ISEC was planning would be in Suldiski and I bet my life that Marika Keskküla was getting ready to move her supply of DU ammunition. I put the phone and the invitation in my pocket and cleaned up the room. After stuffing his body under the bed I straightened the covers and looked over the room. I wanted it to look as if nobody had slept there.

"Slight problem. Had to take out Lambert." The back-up team would have heard the noise and needed a quick explanation. "So I've just outstayed my welcome."

Yesterday I'd had time to look around to the east end of the estate along the river. There was a waterfall of about sixty feet in height at the bottom of which were some natural stepping-stones across the river. The only problem was a sheer drop of sixty feet and only a fly could have stuck on the face of that rock. But the nearest place that any of Radley's men could get was the bottom of the waterfall.

So here I was, back out on that damned roof again with the snow blowing all the harder and I was colder than I've ever been in my life.

There was no way I could take out both the guards on the bridge without creating too much noise. So the waterfall was the only solution.

I came to the fire escape ladder that served this wing of the house and was soon on the ground and wading through the already drifting snow. At the moment, I was in shadow and so, hopefully, out of sight of the all-seeing CCTV, but as soon as I ventured out into the lit area I was going to be picked up.

From then on, it would be a matter of luck. What I hoped was that the glare of the lights on the snow would effectively 'white-out' the TV screen. I would soon know anyway. Just in case, I headed in a northerly direction and as soon as I was out of the pool of light shed by the spotlights, I turned back towards the river. It wouldn't keep them off my tail for long because of the tracks in the snow, but it may just give me that little extra time I needed to find a way down the rock face if there was one. I could have sworn the snow was driving down harder now that I was out in the open with no shelter. As if someone had been watching and decided to make life even harder. Every now and then I had to keep rubbing my face to keep the circulation going and wiggling my toes in my already sodden shoes. A couple of hours out in this and I was going to be frozen meat, preserved until the thaw. Not a pleasant thought. I must keep moving above all else. To stop even for a few minutes would begin the process of hypothermia, or should I say, speed up the process.

Keep moving. Keep the brain active. Think, man, think.

I tripped over a mound and fell few feet from the riverbank. A couple more and I would have stumbled right into the trip wire.

Come on Gunn, use your brain. You're no use dead.

The cold scored deep into me and my teeth were chattering

uncontrollably. I had to move faster and harder. But if I did, when I stopped, I would cool down too rapidly with the sweat caused by the exertion. Take off the coat. Maintain a rhythm, do just enough to keep warm and keep that brain working, but above all keep moving. Survival was what it was all about.

I worked my way along the edge of the river towards the waterfall. It was a good six hundred metres from the bridge so there was no danger of being seen by the sentries and it was too late to worry about surveillance devices.

It took the best part of ten minutes to reach the waterfall.

A searchlight snapped on from the mansion and swept the grounds.

Either they had discovered I was missing, or found Lambert's body. Either way I was dead meat unless I got out of here.

The ground was cold and wet and as I waited for the beam to pass, I could feel my body cooling rapidly without the coat on. It reminded me of a film I'd seen as a boy. *The Great Escape*. The only problem was most of the escapees got caught.

There were shouts from the sentries on the bridge and the sound of an engine. The beam passed and I rolled over, struggled back into the coat and looked back toward the mansion. A strange looking vehicle had just pulled up by the front door. It jogged a memory. I couldn't quite make out the details from this distance. It was the way it moved and the shape of it.

Then I remembered. It was one of those 'go anywhere' machines with a two-stroke engine and eight wheels. It was as long as a Mini and mostly used by farmers. This one had a searchlight mounted in the back and no doubt the men that were climbing into it were armed. I didn't wait to see what they going to do next, but scrambled to the edge of the rock face. The water gurgled and crashed the sixty feet to the pool below and a fine icy cold mist sprayed over me. Within minutes I was soaked. I thought I saw some movement at the bottom, but it was difficult to tell because of the darkness.

The choice wasn't very great. If there was somebody down there it would be either Danny or the opposition. Either way, I had to know.

"Hello, is anyone down there?" The only sound was the water

cascading over the edge and the distant noise of the buggy-type vehicle. "Danny?"

This time a light flashed up in my direction. I ducked instinctively. Then thought that was pretty stupid if it was Danny. The light fell on me and I closed my eyes to save my night vision.

"Thomas?"

"Take the damn light off my face." The light snapped off. "I don't know how the hell I'm going to get down from here."

"Jump. This is the only way out. Paul checked the perimeter and this is the only way that is not covered by guards, mines, booby traps and the like."

"Hold on a minute. I have to think." I turned to see what was happening. The vehicle had taken off in the direction I had hoped they would, due north. As I watched, the vehicle came to a halt and the searchlight swept the immediate area. Then my heart turned cold as I saw the buggy swing round and follow the tracks I'd made down to the river. All the while I watched, I had ignored the cold and wet. Now, when I moved the fine mist of spray that had fallen on me from the waterfall cracked as it turned to ice. My face felt numb and I set to work rubbing the skin to get the circulation going again.

"There's only one way. Jump."

"You come up here and do it."

"Mother of Mary, just jump and stop whining."

"Whose side are you on?"

"Listen to me. It's deep where the water crashes into the pool. If you can jump clear then you'll hit the pool just right. It's either that or be caught, because no way can you get down that rock face."

What a choice. Kill myself in the fall or be shot by the guys who were now fast on my trail. I looked back again. The buggy had reached the river's edge and was less than two hundred metres away.

Still, I hesitated.

My mind was made up for me as a searchlight beam swept over me. The first round cracked past my ear as I launched myself into space.

The drop sent my guts up into my mouth as I tumbled in the air for an eternity, then hit the water with a stunning impact that knocked the breath out of me.

Somewhere a part of my brain was functioning as a rational logical machine. It took over and told my frozen aching body that I had to swim away from the fall of water before I could surface. I was only under for about twenty seconds, but to me it seemed like an eternity before I felt someone grab my arms.

Everything went black as I passed out.

When I came to, I was lying on the bank wrapped in an emergency space blanket and Danny had his hand over my mouth. I could see a shaft of light playing on the surface of the pool from above and caught the intermittent sound of voices through the crash of the waterfall.

".... gone over..... didn't kill him the fall would have.... an anorak...... else.... let's go."

The light went out and we were left with the sound of the roaring water. Danny let go of my mouth and I coughed, spluttered and retched.

"Jesus, I thought you weren't going to make it. You missed the edge of those rocks by a fraction."

The only thing I could do was stare at him, unable to talk because my teeth were chattering too much.

"Let's go we've got a Range Rover just round the bend." Danny started running along a narrow path, with me stumbling behind.

The run did me good, the blood sluggishly flowing to my extremities and with it the pain as my fingers and toes warmed up. Within a few minutes we reached the Range Rover with Paul waiting impatiently in the driver's seat. He handed me a flask.

"Get that down you."

With hot strong sweet tea inside me, and the heater full on, I gradually thawed out as we drove to Perth. I started to tell Danny what I found but could still barely talk.

"Save it for Radley, Thomas. I can hear it then. You just rest yourself. I'm still trying to figure out how you survived that drop."

"It w.... was you're s.... suggestion." My mouth felt like it had a mind of it's own.

"Well we couldn't have you falling into their hands could we?"

"N.... next time y.... you go in. I'll s.... stay on the outside."

We drove on in silence. I sat back wondering if I'd ever get warm again.

Radley was waiting in the jet. I recounted all the details to him about the Dominion of Pakhia. When I had finished he sat for a time deep in thought. It wasn't until the aircraft was off the ground and climbing to cruise altitude that he spoke.

"It does tie in with reports we have been getting about an under current of unrest that has been rippling through the Islands for the past six months. Nothing specific."

"I think ISEC is planning a coup in Pakhia."

"What makes you think so?" His eyes already told me he was thinking along the same lines. I took Lambert's phone out of my pocket. It was soaked through but that wouldn't be a problem for Radley's *'tame techies'*.

"On there is a calendar note on the 28th. It reads *Keskküla. Suldiski. 236. Load.*"

"What does that mean?"

"That this Keskküla woman is selling DU for the coup in Pakhia. Then they'll turn the country into a tax haven for ISEC members and manufacture and sell the ammunition to the rest of the world from there. Probably to Governments who want to keep their neighbours in check, or rebels who want a *'game changer'*."

Radley leaned forward. He had listened intently to everything I had to say. "We tested the bullet Paul recovered. It does indeed have a higher radioactive signature. So we loaded it into an AR15 cartridge and fired it. It will take out any known armoured vehicle. The bullet also heats up to a far higher temperature than normal DU ammunition, creating a fire blast ahead of the bullet in flight that'll slice through any flesh it passes close to. It doesn't have to hit a body to cause lethal damage. Not to mention the local area toxicity once the round hits something."

"We need to stop whatever's happening in Suldiski and we've only twenty fours to do it."

Radley unbuckled his seat belt and stood. "Thanks for all you're doing. It's much appreciated." I looked into his eyes and for the first time since thought I detected a spark of humanity. "Rest. I'll arrange everything." I made a feeble gesture with my hands and watched him walk down the aircraft.

Rest, the man said. I needed no more prompting. The events had caught up with me. I felt very tired, stiff and sore. Sleep didn't take long in coming.

EIGHTEEN

A special forces Hercules MC-130 is not the most comfortable aircraft in which to travel any great distance; especially when you're loaded down with equipment, such as a self-contained oxygen breathing apparatus, two parachutes and a bergen carrying weapons, ammunition, explosives, medical supplies, and water. But it was strangely comforting to be sitting on the webbing seat barely able to talk above the roar of the four Allison Turbo-props.

This aircraft was fitted with satellite surveillance ground imaging, communications, and eavesdropping equipment, which filled most of the cargo bay leaving little space for the team, composed of two four man units. I was tasked with leading one and Danny the other. The other six men were Paul, Bob another member of CBRN, and four former SAS troopers, Bill, Al, Gerry and Pete. Because I knew them from Iraq and Afghanistan days I didn't feel quite so uneasy and out-of-practice, even though it had been a while since I made a HALO jump from over nine thousand metres, nearly thirty thousand feet in old money.

"Satellite infra-red imagery discovered that the old submarine pen in Suldiski has been excavated and rebuilt with a blockhouse between the former Russian defence systems. Those consist of watchtowers and missile launch tower, which look like they have been rebuilt. Now the facility is being used by Marika Keskküla as the base for her yacht and most probably a DU manufacturing facility." Radley pointed out the area on the blown-up photograph on the large TV. "What were the old barracks here we believe have been rebuilt as the factory." He pointed to the dome shaped structure beyond the newly constructed dock. "The mission is simple. Take out the facility, secure the ammunition and destroy everything. My guess is that the headquarters are below the blockhouse, underground, using the old tunnels that lead to the submarine pen." The photograph was replaced by an old Russian building plan of the underground tunnel complex. The briefing continued until we were completely familiar with the complex. "We can jam their radar just before you exit the aircraft for a few minutes. That'll give you enough time to descend to opening height. Unit one lands on the blockhouse, there's a ventilation shaft we believe leads down into the underground bunker. Unit two beside the dome structure."

I was exhausted and could barely stay awake. Last night I catnapped on the flight to RAF Marham near Norwich where Radley the rest of the team and the Hercules MC-130 were waiting. I was still frozen from my midnight swim, and the thought of jumping from a sub zero thirty thousand feet into a winter night over the Baltic, did nothing to warm me up.

When Radley finished talking, I felt a nudge on my elbow and turned to see a big mug of hot Stones Ginger Wine stuck in front of my face.

"Get that down you boss. It'll put you straight." Alan, one of my section, grinned and winked. "My old granny put me up to this. Works a treat."

"Thanks." I sipped the scalding liquor and immediately felt it warm through my entire body. Of course you have to like ginger, but I wasn't complaining.

We had spent all day going through the drills time and time again until we had it right. There would be no room for mistakes. Radley had taken over one of the hangers at the far end of the airfield and created mock-ups of the submarine pen and the dome ammunition factory. We had no idea of the interior except fuzzy details the infrared had managed to collect. It wasn't much but there was no time for a boots on the ground reconnaissance before we went in, just intelligence reports from sources within the Estonian government.

After we had brushed up on the use of oxygen, Danny went through the formation we were to drop in and the different opening heights. Glen would lead out as the heaviest, followed by the rest of us according to our all-up weight. I was to be fifth out. We each had ballistic helmets, oxygen mask, tactical goggles, O2 regulator, Twin 53 bailout bottle assemblies, MC-4 Halo parachute rig, high altitude altimeters and a tiny high altitude GPS navigation module and thermal insulated jumpsuit. Additional equipment consisted of AN/PVS-15 night vision binoculars and miniature video cameras attached to our helmets.

The day went past in a flash of rehearsing, memorising signals, details of the Suldiski complex, the PUP (pick-up-point) after the mission was over, and all the aircraft procedures.

The smell of aviation turbine fuel penetrated into the interior of the Hercules as the pilot ran up the engines prior to take-off. Most of the team spent the time reading or playing cards, but I was too restless to concentrate on anything, so to hear the engines winding up to full power and feel the rumbling vibration as the aircraft began its take-off roll was a relief. Nobody felt like shouting above the noise, so busied themselves making last minute adjustments to their kit.

Once airborne and climbing steadily to our cruise altitude of thirty thousand feet, Danny got up and beckoned me to follow. We went up into the cockpit and sat on the bench seat behind the pilots and drank coffee. Outside it was a perfect night, with the stars bright in the sky and the lights on the coast of East Anglia sliding by beneath us. It seemed so peaceful and the thought that we were going into battle didn't seem real. The pilots quietly and confidently monitored the controls and instruments, with the navigator making odd comments every now and then.

The first hour passed quickly enough and then Peter gave me a nudge and I saw the pilots plugging in their oxygen masks, preparing for the last part of the flight. We returned to the rear of the aircraft and saw that most of the team already had their kit on and were sorting out their masks.

I was quite familiar with the MC-4 HALO rig and slipped it over my shoulders. It fitted perfectly and just required a last minute adjustment to make sure it was good and tight. Next oxygen tank, weapon, bergen, helmet and mask. For the next twenty minutes we'd be breathing from the main O2 apparatus in the centre of the cargo hold, aft of the satellite and communications equipment, as the aircraft slowly depressurised.

I looked at the strange sight around me through my goggles. We were now each in our own little world until we reached the ground, as the tiny radios had not yet been switched on.

We were like alien beings, sinister, dangerous, and inhuman.

The main lights in the aircraft went out, replaced by a dull glow from half a dozen red night vision lights that was enough to see by but not enough to damage our night vision; somewhat like being in a photographer's darkroom. Then, catching me totally unprepared, came the signal from the Jumpmaster to unhook from the central breathing system and go onto our own personal bottles. From now on it was all activity. The rear doors slowly opened and the noise became even louder. We stood, checked our equipment one final time and shuffled along the ramp.

Outside, all I could see was the light from a million stars shining off the surface of the Baltic Sea thirty thousand feet below. No sign of land anywhere.

I looked at the others standing there on the ramp, silhouetted against the starry sky. The Jumpmaster held up his hand, showing three fingers.

The red light blinked on, then switched to green and I followed the others over the end of the ramp and into the dark hostile night. At first I sensed panic as I somersaulted, then snapped into a fast 180-degree turn, before steadying into a stable position. I looked down and didn't see anybody so I slowly initiated a turn to the right. There, just below me and to the right were the other four. Somewhere above were the rest. The tiny red lights on the top of the helmets showed clearly and beyond them, tens of thousands of feet below, the small islands off the coast of Estonia. What Peter had said was absolutely right. It was incredible what you could see at night from this altitude. The promontory on the North Western most island, was quite brightly lit and easily seen. The Keskküla Company had turned the secret abandoned nuclear submarine base into a modern factory complex but there was no sign of Marika Keskküla's personal yacht.

I was so absorbed in the fantastic sight that I almost forgot to monitor my altimeter. I glanced at the luminous dial on my wrist. We were just passing through fifteen thousand feet. I brought my arms in and quickly found the radio switch and flicked it on, then settled back into a stable position again. There was no need to talk at this stage; everyone knew what they were doing.

We were now passing through eight thousand feet and getting close to our opening heights. The submarine base and arms manufacturing facility clearly visible close to the other buildings, and I could see where we were going to land.

Seven thousand feet.

Every now and then I risked a glance at the four below.

Six thousand.

At five thousand feet we split into our sections, speeding away from each other before reaching for the ripcord drogue. There was a momentary rustling and then a crack and a jerk and I was swinging beneath the canopy. I unclipped the oxygen mask, reached up took a hold of the toggles and steered the canopy round until I could see the one below blossoming out. Although they were black, they were easy to see because each canopy had a luminous panel stitched onto the top. The ground was starting to get closer and my altimeter was running out of steam. One thousand feet to go and then serious business would begin.

Five hundred feet and I started my final turn to follow the others onto the landing point on top of the blockhouse we thought was the roof of the underground complex next to the submarine pen entrance. To my left Danny's unit headed for the barracks.

There were either no guards in the watchtowers, or they were fast asleep as we glided between them and onto the blockhouse roof.

With barely a sound all four of us landed, rolled up our parachutes and lowered them down the side of the blockhouse to the ground, where we would later collect them before going to the pick-up-point. Then we headed for the ventilation shaft, our rubber soled boots barely making a sound. I looked across at the barracks through my night vision binoculars and saw that Danny's boys had landed and were preparing a mouse-hole charge to blast an entry into the dome. As soon as that went off all hell would break loose. Until then we were on radio silence.

Alan prised open the large metal cover and we looked down the narrow shaft; far too narrow for us to enter. Alan shook his head and I headed to the south side of the blockhouse. I remembered seeing a door in the wall on that side and figured we'd have to blow an entrance just like Danny. A glance at my watch showed that Danny would blow his charge in two minutes. There wasn't much time.

Alan dropped the rope down the side of the building as Gerry made it secure, and we quickly scaled down to the ground. Just as we approached the door, it opened and a young dishevelled guard stepped out, yawning, his weapon slung over his shoulder. Obviously Marika Keskküla had no idea we were coming, or even suspected that we would launch an attack. That bothered me.

The guard never knew what killed him as Gerry snapped his neck efficiently from behind. We slipped silently around the body into the blockhouse.

There were three small rooms. The guard in the first room looked up in surprise as we entered, and I shot him with my silenced HK before he had a chance to raise the alarm. The security monitor on the desk in front of the dead guard seemed to be on a loop and my instincts leaped into high sensory mode. The guards had no chance. They never saw us coming even when we were right outside the door, and the area where our parachutes had been left was empty ground. Behind the desk set into the far wall was a steel security door. To the right was a narrow corridor leading to the other rooms.

There was no time to think this through completely as Bill and Gerry cleared the second room, where two more guards lay sleeping. There was a small bathroom off the room and a door leading to a kitchen. We returned to the main room and Al felt around the door then placed charges against the hinges. We retired outside. Al looked at his watch and blew the door just as Danny blew the mouse-hole charge.

The steel door hung drunkenly on its hinges, beyond were stairs leading down to the next level.

Cautiously I led the way down, hugging the wall. The stairs turned to the left and I peered around the corner and stared into a empty hall size bunker that had been stripped clean of whatever had been in there. I pulled a grenade from my belt and tossed it into the hall. There was a brilliant flash and a deafening explosion followed by a cloud of smoke. Al and Bill rushed past me and down into the hall. The next minute was total confusion with shouts, screams and the sound of small arms fire.

It was all over in seconds, and Al's voice came through the earpiece.

"Clear," he said calmly.

The smoke hung in the hall like a sea fog and there were a couple of very bloody looking bodies on the floor, looking like discarded rag dolls. Bill was at the far end of the hall kneeling down beside an injured man. I went over.

It was one of the guards I had seen up at the house in Scotland.

He stared blankly at the hole in his stomach, pulling gently at the edges of the wound with blood soaked fingers.

"How do we get down into the bunker?"

The injured man looked up into my face uncomprehendingly. A bubble of blood at the corner of his mouth inflated and deflated with his breathing. The bubble burst as he opened his mouth but made no sound. The man's eyes cleared for an instant and he pointed down the hall.

"Lift shaft.... over there." He paused and sighed, then shook his head wearily. "Only way in."

"How many people down there?"

"Don't know." He looked up again quite sharply and his eyes showed panic. So far the shock of the wound had insulated him against the pain, now he realised he was dying and the pain was beginning to seep through the jangled nerves. He coughed and a dribble of blood ran down his chin, and I watched as the eyes glazed over and the life slowly went out of him.

Gradually the sound of voices drifted into my consciousness and I turned to see Al over by the lift door. He had already prised it open and was staring down the shaft.

"I'll sever the cables, we don't want the car coming up when we're going down."

I followed Bill through the hall moving from doorway to doorway, stopping at each one and throwing it open. Most of the rooms had been offices at one stage, some in the process of being rebuilt but not yet finished. We cleared them all and found nothing. Al's voice crackled through the radio again.

"OK, I'm just going to blow the cables."

There was a soft explosion and Bill and I ran to where Al was already dropping a rope into the elevator shaft.

The cable was neatly severed. Al tested that the rope was secure and then swung over the edge and disappeared down into the black depths. Bill and I waited. We didn't have to wait too long.

"I'm at the bottom, on top of the lift itself. It has an inspection hatch, so I can get through."

Danny's voice crackled through the earpiece. "Unit one this is two. Going in."

"Unit one. Blockhouse is clear. Seems like there's only a skeleton crew. They're busy packing up. Now descending to lower level."

"Roger that. Entering the DU facility now. Minimal resistance."

Once we were underground our communications would be cut off from the other unit.

"Gerry stay up here so we can communicate with Danny."

I followed Bill down the rope and landed on top of the elevator.

"Hold it. There's movement down here." Al whispered his voice low and urgent.

I heard it too, just a faint sound that didn't seem as if it came directly from below us but a bit further away, which meant the elevator door was open. We had no choice but to take a peek.

I slowly lifted the maintenance hatch and looked inside. It was empty, but the door was open and I could the sound of distant voices down a corridor.

Bill swung down inside the elevator just as Al slid down the rope. I swung myself down and together Bill and I cautiously peered into the corridor. I could see a couple of Marika Keskküla's personal guards waiting for us and tossed a grenade into the corridor. The explosion was incredibly loud in the confined space. Dust and debris swirled around and the lights flickered.

I could hear a low moaning and cry of pain. I followed Al and Bill out of the elevator into the corridor. The bodies of the two bodyguards lay on the floor five metres down the corridor that led to a door that was hanging off its hinges. Beyond I could see a short corridor with two doors leading off and one at the far end. Bill and Al were already halfway down. Working together they fired through the first door and then burst in. They were out within a few seconds and dealt with the other door the same way. That left the one at the end.

I followed behind as they carefully approached the door. It was rather like the twin doors of a lift shaft and Al extended his hand toward the button on the right hand side. I was still down by the carnage caused by the grenade and was just about to join them when the doors at the end sprang open with a swiftness that surprised us.

Al didn't stand a chance and was cut to pieces by the fusillade that issued from the barrel of the sub-machine gun held by a man in the room. Bill was just too late diving for cover and was hit in the upper chest. I felt a bang on the side of my head and everything went black for a moment or two. I fell forward, crashing against the already shredded door and rolled onto the floor to come up against the body of one of the guards.

The rattle of machine guns died away, to be replaced by the insistent voice of Gerry in my ear.

"What's going on down there?"

I collected my senses and glanced up the corridor. Al was a crumpled heap on the floor,

Bill had pulled himself back into one of the doorways. He was injured but moving.

"Gerry, get down here, but be careful. Al's dead and Bill's hurt. Relay the information to Danny."

"Roger. Just watch yourself."

I was partly hidden by the door that had fallen off the top hinge and lay in front of me. Now that I was the only one able to do anything about the guy in the room up ahead, I felt suddenly calm and in control. There must be a CCTV camera in the wall somewhere for the bodyguard to know exactly when we would be in front of the door, but where I had no idea. The wall opposite was a blank apart from those sliding doors and there was nothing on this side. Bill lay half in and half out of the door on the left-hand side.

"Bill, can you hear me?" There was no reaction. "Gerry, I think Bill's radio must have been hit. I can see him moving but he can't hear anything. Wait a minute he's trying to signal."

Bill was making a gesture of some sort. He was pointing.

"Gerry, you can come on down. I know where the camera is."

Moments later, Gerry appeared in the lift car. He joined me and was about to go forward to look at Peter when I stopped him.

"No. The camera is above this door looking down the corridor." I moved forward and peered up at the wall above the door. There it was. I took my balaclava off with my other hand and put it over the lens, then went up to check on Bill. As I did so, Gerry ran forward and flattened himself against the wall at the far end beside the door.

"I'm OK. One round clipped my shoulder the other hit the radio. Just get in there and get the bastard," he said, gritting his teeth against the pain.

I joined Gerry and he pressed the button. The door shot open and a hail of bullets poured from the submachine gun of the guard inside the room. Bob rolled in a grenade and we flattened ourselves against the wall as the explosion ripped through the room. We both rolled into the room as dust boiled from the door, going on opposite sides. The guard was dead, thrown against the wall by the blast, beyond him another door badly damaged and hanging from its hinges.

In the second office, Marika Keskküla stood beside an incongruously large mahogany 'Partner's' desk smiling from behind armoured glass, now pockmarked from bullet strikes and shrapnel. She looked as calm and beautiful as if she was ready to attend a formal cocktail party, dressed in her familiar black suit with string of black pearls at her throat.

"Mr Gunn. We meet again."

I knew that firing at the glass would be futile so lowered my gun and walked slowly forward.

I didn't take my eyes off her. "Gerry, secure the building, and get Danny down here." He ran off down the dust filled corridor. "There is no way out, Mrs Keskküla."

She smiled even more, her eyes sparkling with mischief. "Do not be too sure about that. And please, call me Marika." She walked around from behind the desk and approached the glass that separated us, placing her index finger on it, tracing the outline of my face, now just inches away.

"I could use someone like you in my organisation. Someone with your skills, to share my, how shall I say, assets." She looked me up and down somewhat coyly. Teasing. Appraising.

"I don't need the money."

"Who's talking about money?"

"Power?"

"It certainly has its attractions. But no, I like adventure. Life can be so boring, don't you think?"

Marika Keskküla's eyes narrowed at a sound behind me and I saw Danny's reflection in the glass.

"What's going on Thomas?"

"All clear at the facility?"

"Secure and ready for detonation."

I smiled at Marika. "Your finished here Mrs Keskküla. Your enterprise is over."

Rage flooded across her face, directed mostly at Danny, then she turned her glittering eyes on me. "You cannot take away what is in my head." She smiled brittlely. "And there is always a price to pay, Thomas." She turned and walked back to the desk, reached down and picked up a small remote device, turned and raised it. "Such a pity."

Danny grabbed me and bundled me out of the room ahead of him just as the explosion ripped through the room from the small mine. It threw us against the far wall of the corridor. I lay stunned, shrapnel wounds to my left arm and cuts on my face and left leg. Danny lay beside me moaning softly. I reached across and rolled him over.

It was bad. He had taken most of the blast saving my life.

"That wasn't such a good idea was it mate," he murmured softly.

"Gerry," I shouted. "Danny's been hit." I looked back into Marika Keskküla's office but there was sign of her. "Tell Paul to check out the submarine pen, the Keskküla woman may have an escape boat or something."

"Well this is fucked-up isn't it mate?" Danny muttered, his eyes trying to focus on my face.

"It's not the movies, Danny. That's for sure."

"That's a fact," he said softly. "God it's cold in here."

It wasn't.

The air conditioning in the bunker kept the temperature at a steady 72°F, but Danny was bleeding out and I knew the feeling as the cold overwhelmed your body, and that almost peaceful strange sense of everything slipping slowly away crept across your mind.

Except for the pain.

He groaned and I pulled out a morphine ampoule stuck the needle in his leg. After a moment he calmed down and smiled.

"Stay with me Thomas."

"Never going to leave you Danny. And shut the fuck up, save your strength."

He giggled and closed his eyes. "Whatever you say, Boss."

Gerry helped me carry Danny along the corridor that led to a second elevator he had discovered. Once we had loaded Danny in, we went back for Al. It took less than fifteen seconds to reach ground level.

"Nothing in the sub pen, Thomas," Paul's voice crackled over the radio.

"Meet us at the blockhouse door."

"Roger."

The helicopter arrived on time, landing on the roof of the submarine pen. I climbed in and helped as Gerry and Paul passed up Al's body and then gently loaded Danny on board. The rest of team followed, and within moments we were airborne. Dawn crept slowly across the sky as flames and small explosions destroyed what was left of Marika Keskküla's arms facility.

Danny lay in my arms, pale, shivering with cold even though we had wrapped him in survival blankets. He looked at me, urgency in his eyes.

"Watch your back, Thomas. Radley's not your friend. He runs the Increment." The rest of the Team looked at each other as if they had suspected all along.

"Are you sure?"

"Of course I'm bloody sure, these men here are the only friends you've got," he shouted, the effort making him cough up more blood. "Don't forget your promise," he said fiercely grasping my arm. "The kids. My sister."

"I promise."

He relaxed, smiled and closed his eyes for a moment. "We had good times, Thomas. Good times."

"Yes we did."

He opened his eyes and I knew he was slipping away. Then he started to sing, staring at me intently, gripping my arm.

"Over in Killarney, many years ago
My mother sang a song to me
In tones so sweet and low."

He sang softly, slowly and I joined in as the helicopter clattered through the lightning sky, and death slowly crept over him.

"Just a simple little ditty
In her good old Irish way
And I'd give the world if she could sing
That song to me this day."

The rest of the team joined in on the chorus as Danny died in my arms, the words drifting from his lips in that last gasp breath.

"Too-ra-loo-ra-loo-ral, Too-ra-loo-ra-li,
Too-ra-loo-ra-loo-ral, hush now, don't you cry!
Too-ra-loo-ra-loo-ral, Too-ra-loo-ra-li,
Too-ra-loo-ra-loo-ral, that's an Irish lullaby."

I held him as tears coursed down my face, and we continued to sing, softly, a gentle anthem to our fallen brothers.

NINETEEN

Radley's men were dismantling their equipment when we arrived back at the Hall. The bodies of Danny and Al were taken off the helicopter and driven away, and I knew that their families would be notified that they had been killed in an *'accident'*. Nobody would ever know the real circumstances of their courageous deaths. It is the nature of Special Forces in peacetime. To the rest of the world, we were non-existent.

Ron and George were busy helping the technicians load the vans in the driveway.

The coup in Pakhia had been averted. Marika Keskküla's DU ammunition enterprise destroyed, the ISEC headquarters in Scotland euphemistically *'under investigation'* and Hamish McDougall had apparently tended his resignation to the Prime Minister.

But, in spite of this I knew that for me, this was not over. Mary had been admitted to a private psychiatric hospital as she had descended into a catatonic state. The prognosis was not encouraging. My family and my life had been destroyed and I still had a score to settle.

Julie was sombre, uncommunicative, which was understandable under the circumstances. She had grown fond of Danny. I was in pain, tired, hungry and needed a plan.

"Some of the information we pulled off the ISEC systems server was quite interesting, including names of some people I know. Particularly General the Lord Dalton Percy, who has been in my cross hairs for quite some time," Radley was saying, standing at the end of the kitchen watching as Paul, myself and the remainder of the team ate ravenously, polishing off plates full of filet mignon with asparagus and croquet potatoes, washing it down with several bottles of 1986 Chateau Pétrus from Calder Hall's cellar.

Wealth has some advantages and I am a pretty good cook given a decent kitchen and access to the best ingredients. I wondered how much longer this would last. I was a ticking bomb to Radley, with almost unlimited funds, and he wouldn't want me shadowing his every move.

Julie sat watching us, observing, assessing, distant.

"He has been known to lobby for military contracts for certain less than savoury dealers representing dubious Governments, and on several occasions had meetings in Rome with Marika Keskküla."

"Supplementing his meagre pension no doubt," Paul commented dryly.

"Interesting family background. His grandfather was originally from County Donegal. Owned a property that was once a Knights Templar castle."

"I smell conspiracy theory."

"Maybe," Radley carried on ignoring the comments. "But when you put together young Mrs Keskküla, certain Generals with access to Government Ministers, such as Hamish McDougall, with a factory in Belfast making DU ammunition and a coup attempt in a foreign country, then we certainly have cause to suspect an international conspiracy of some sort. The Belfast facility was to provide DU ammunition to an ultra right wing Protestant group, with the aim of wiping out all the opposition. The idea being to create instability and force the Government to increase security measures within the UK."

"Just what the British National Independent Party wants."

"Precisely. And now we can thwart their plans."

"Status quo."

"There are worse things."

"And me?" I asked pointedly.

"Her Majesty's Government thanks you for your duty."

"And now you'd like me to gracefully disappear."

"It would be best. The people responsible for your father's death are dead, or at the very least incapacitated...."

"I'm not finished yet."

"Yes you are. This was never your own personal revenge mission, Mr Gunn."

"Thomas," Julie's voice cut through the charged atmosphere. "It's over. You've done all you can. It's over."

She was wrong it wasn't over, but I needed Radley to think that for me it was over. Danny confirmed in his dying breath what I already knew. Radley could not be trusted. The Team we had put together for this last mission were expendable to Radley. But I did have one piece of information I had been keeping to myself. The dinner invitation I found in Lambert's pocket, to which was attached a list of eleven other dinner guests. And the reason I hadn't told Radley about it was that his name was on that list.

"You need a rest Thomas. We all do. We've done our job, now it's time to bury our dead. Listen to the man," Paul said quietly and held my eyes a moment longer than usual, then his eyes flickered sideways toward Radley.

I dropped my shoulders and heaved a sigh, hoping that my acting was good enough, and nodded. "Okay. You're both right. It's not my fight anymore." From the corner of my eye I saw Radley visibly relax and a slight smile twitch his thin lips.

"Take a holiday. Go back to Gozo for a few weeks, get well and soak up the sun, you deserve it." Radley crossed the kitchen and held out his hand. "Thank you for everything you've done." There was no warmth in his voice, and after a brief nod to Julie and me, he left.

Paul and the other four finished their meal and sat back.

"Best thing mate," Paul said loudly, standing, crossing to the window and watching as Radley's entourage climbed aboard his helicopter. "Wouldn't mind joining you in Gozo. Could do with a spot of sailing." He looked back as the helicopter took off and put a finger to his lips. "But I guess I'll just settle for the farm in Wales."

The others fanned out through the house and I knew they were looking for bugs. Radley wanted to keep tabs on us. To him we were all mercenaries, former soldiers who had been let go, until the next time. We had lost two friends and to Radley that was acceptable. Not to us.

It took thirty minutes to clear the house of the bugs, but we still had to be careful and Paul turned on the TV, choosing an action adventure film and turning up the volume.

"Danny was right. We can't trust Radley, we suspected all along he was the man behind the Increment."

I looked at each man. Gerry, Bob, Paul, Bill and Pete. Good men, every one, and every one a friend. Sometimes that made things difficult. To be perfectly callous, you can get over acquaintances being killed, but with friends it was different. It was personal. It scored deep into your psyche.

"What now?" Julie looked at us and I could see the fear in her eyes. Now she knew this wasn't over.

"We'll have to convince Radley we're going our separate ways."

"How?"

For an answer I picked up the house phone and called the Gunn Group Industries maintenance crew at Norwich airport, asked them to prepare the Mustang for a flight to Malta. Radley's men would intercept the call and relay the information to him.

"There was something I didn't tell Radley that you should all know." They stared at me. "While I was in Perth at the ISEC seminar, I found an invitation to a very select dinner party at the Tower of London tomorrow night. Radley and Hamish McDougall are both on the guest list."

"I knew the bastard was fucking us over," Gerry exploded. "Excuse me Miss, but he's a fucking bastard."

I pulled the still damp invitation from my pocket and spread it and the guest list on the table for them all to see.

"What Radley didn't tell us was that General the Lord Dalton-Percy is the Constable of the Tower of London and he's running this little dinner shindig. Along with ISEC's own man, Sir Jason Lancaster, formerly Director General, Humanitarian, Security, Conflict and International Finance at the Department of International Development. Sir Jason's last big job before he 'retired', was providing British Government funding for infrastructure development in the Dominion of Pakhia. He'll not be too pleased that the coup has been averted."

Also on the list was Nicholas Hansard of the British National Independent Party; Ted Lieberman of the Griffin Trust and now a Board member of the US Federal Reserve Bank; Karl Von Schoenberg of the Von Kurt Foundation; Lauren Tanner, formerly a Director of

Gunn Group Industries and newly appointed CEO; Carly Swann, CEO of Caymans Venture Capital Investment Group; Andries Artman, Chairman of Artman Banking Group and Sir John Manx, recently retired British Ambassador to South Africa.

"What about Marika Keskküla?"

"Assuming she's still alive and even if we could find her we couldn't touch her. Diplomatic immunity."

"Looks like a who's-who of global fascist extremists," Paul echoing what everyone was thinking.

"And just *what* is the plan?" Julie the voice of reason wanting details we didn't have.

"We stop them."

"Great plan." She turned away in disgust and busied herself clearing the table. "When you cowboys get your heads together, then maybe you can think this through."

Paul looked at me sharply and I knew what he was thinking. She was the weak link in the chain. He walked over to Julie and turned her to face him so she could read his lips. "I have a friend at the Tower. He'll get us inside. We can set up a listening device and find out what they are up to."

"And what do you do with the information then? Go to someone like Radley with it?"

"Actually I was thinking more along the lines of publishing it on YouTube." He meant it as a joke, but to the rest of us it suddenly became a real option. Even the threat would be enough to change the dynamic.

Julie dropped her head. "I apologise. It's just...."

Paul wrapped his arms around and held her close for a moment. She rested her head on his chest. "We'll take care of Thomas and bring him back to you. I promise."

She looked up at him angrily brushing tears away. "I'll make sure you do. I know how to use a gun. Ask Thomas."

Paul smiled as the others gathered their gear together. "I'll remember that. Tomorrow morning 0500hrs, Danny's house, Muswell Hill."

"Hold on just a minute." I left the kitchen ran upstairs to the bedroom and retrieved the last spare burn phone and took it down to Paul.

"Burn phone. I have one as well, this is the number. Just in case." I handed him the phone and a card with my number.

Paul nodded and then they left through the front door. No doubt Radley would have some of his men, probably Increment, watching the Hall to make sure they were on their way. They climbed into a white Range Rover and drove away down the drive, the taillights disappearing behind the trees.

"I'm coming with you." Julie facing me, face set and determined. The tears were gone and there was a resolve in her expression. "Your family is my family. What happens to you happens to me."

"The Professor may not see it that way."

"My father has no say in my decisions." She was obviously not to be dissuaded. "These people nearly killed me as well and I may never hear properly again. Because of that I have learned to pay attention to everything around me and read lips. I'm an asset not a liability." She stepped toward me her eyes softening, and her coldness of the last week evaporating in the warm kitchen. "My life is with you, wherever that may be."

We made love slowly, as if for the first time. Enjoying each other as we had in Gozo, in a time that seemed so long ago now. The difference was that we now understood each other more deeply. Knew we could not demand more than there was to give, and realised the fragility of our lives, determining to enjoy whatever time we had together.

"We need to get moving." I was already dressed and repacking the bergen Paul had left with extra ammunition for my Glock and the night vision binoculars.

Julie stretched catlike across the bed. "How do we get past Radley's men? They are sure to be out there."

"A little deception they know nothing about."

She dressed quickly in a black exercise outfit, black sneakers and black sheepskin jacket, topped with a black ski hat that hid her blond hair.

"Just an outfit I picked up online while you were away playing soldiers in Estonia." Answering my surprised expression. "I knew you wouldn't let this go. Not now." She grinned. "And I'm a better actor than you. Radley needed convincing."

"Predictable, eh?"

"Sometimes."

"Did Danny tell you about Radley?"

"No. My instincts. Radley's a sociopath. No emotion. He'll use anyone to get what he wants."

She followed me downstairs, through the kitchen and into the wine cellar, shaking her head in disbelief at the hidden tunnel that led to the Folly. Earlier in the evening I had a short whispered conversation with Ron and George, who would keep up the pretence that Julie and I were still at the Hall, and told them to keep the outside floodlights on throughout the night. Then I called Vincenzo in Gozo and arranged for him to organise a private jet to fly to Blackbushe airport to pick us up in two days. Ron told me the Mini-Cooper was in the barn, fuelled and ready.

I was gambling that the Increment unit Radley had left behind would be small and concentrating their focus on the normal exits from the Hall. Any night vision binoculars would be useless to them in the glare of the floodlights, but I would be able to use mine to pick out their positions because I would be focused away from the Hall.

Silently opening the door into the Folly, I checked that no one was using it as an observation platform before taking up position on the landing at the top of the stairs where I could view the immediate area.

Within moments I had picked two of them out. No doubt two more would be staked out at the back of the Hall. And as I thought they were watching the Hall, unable to use their night vision binoculars because of the floodlights.

It took and hour to reach the barn, taking a circuitous route. Stopping every few minutes to make sure we were not followed and upon reaching the barn, ten minutes to check the immediate area. Radley's men had not found the Mini-Cooper.

Julie climbed into the passenger seat grinning from ear-to-ear. "It's like being in a time-warp. Inside an old newsreel film from the sixties."

"These are expensive cars now. Collector's pieces."

"Well let's go."

Just being in the little car was an escape from reality. There was something about it that wiped away the horrors we had been through and for two hours we chatted and laughed behaving like a young couple on honeymoon. But this was no honeymoon and ahead of us the dark cloud of reality awaited.

Danny's house was a dark, lonely brooding monolith, as if it felt the loss of its owner more than we did. At this time in the morning before dawn, most of the residents of Muswell Hill were fast asleep. Julie and I slipped silently through the back garden and into the kitchen where Paul and the others were gathered. Gerry pulled heavy drapes across the windows and switched on the table lamp in the small sitting room off the kitchen where Danny and I had spent nights listening to Caruso and Gigli and drinking Jameson. But now was not the time for reminiscing.

Paul rolled out a plan of the Tower of London on the large coffee table. "The dinner is held in the Martin Tower over on the north east corner, here." He pointed to the tower that was previously known as the Jewel House. "Access is not too much of a problem as the Government in its infinite wisdom has decided to employ an outside security firm to patrol the outer walls. The Yeoman Warders are responsible only for the inner walls and the main White Tower complex, barracks and administration buildings."

"Surely Radley will have infiltrated the contractors and have a few of his own men stationed at the Martin Tower." Bill interrupted. "I would if I was him."

"Two to be precise."

"How do you know?" Gerry asked.

"My contact, one of the Yeoman Warders."

"Figuring that's what you'll do when you retire Paul?" Gerry laughed.

"We're muckers from way back, he was my first CSM and really put me through it." He smiled and then turned to me. "Thomas is going in through the front door, with the lovely Julie. That'll be a surprise for them and get their attention while the rest us take out the contractors on the outer perimeter and the two at the Martin Tower." He paused looking at me carefully. "We can't help you once you're inside. Not until we've secured the area, so you two are on your own."

"Not ideal, but we do have the advantage of surprise. Presumably you can get a bug into the dining room?"

"My man has it in place and will activate it once Radley's men have swept the room. We'll record everything."

"Straight to YouTube, right," Julie said dryly. "If only we had a camera."

Gerry grinned and reaching down to his bergen produced a small box containing a beautiful opal ring and handed it to her. "Milady. There's a micro camera lens in the centre of the leopard opal and a nano transmitter similar to the one Thomas had inserted into his hand, hidden in the setting."

"Never thought I'd be an American spying on the British."

"Never thought I'd be British spying on the British." Gerry echoed her sentiment. "Life gets weird sometimes."

We spent the rest of the day planning our evening's work. Julie and I changed into our evening clothes. Me into a dinner jacket and black tie, Julie in stunning black evening gown that covered her black cat suit and we were set. I just had two phone calls to make. One to Edwards to meet us in the Golden Lion at ten o'clock tomorrow night, and the other to Professor Oldfield to also meet us there. If we didn't make it then Edwards was to give the letter to Professor Oldfield.

The Tower of London is one of Britain's oldest surviving Royal Palaces; home to the Yeoman Warders who guard the Tower complex, the Crown Jewels and give tours and lectures to milling tourists, wearing their traditional dress. All are retired Warrant Officers.

The chauffeur dropped us off near Saint Katherine's dock and we walked to the entrance by the Cradle Tower as instructed, where a Yeoman Warder in full uniform waited patiently with two of the security contractors. I hadn't worn a dinner jacket and black tie for a while and felt somewhat overdressed, but that was overridden by the thrill of anticipation that always comes with the beginning of a mission.

"Good evening sir, this way please." He didn't use my name and the contractors looked a little unsure, but stood aside, appreciating Julie's beauty and not investigating me much at all. As Julie said, she was an asset and surprise was on our side.

I smiled courteously to the stocky bearded Yeoman Warder who stood before us, his eyes direct. He gave me a slight nod, turned and led the way into the Tower complex. The last time I visited the Tower of London had been as a ten year old on a prep school outing. All we wanted to see was the Bloody Tower, Traitors Gate and the site of the executions. At night the Tower exuded more menace than during the day when tourists milled around its walls and towers. But perhaps that was because I knew the true nature of that which lay within the small Martin Tower, where a game of wealth and death would be played out.

"Robert Wrightwood," the Yeoman Warder said quietly, barely moving his lips. "Paul's friend. There are two contractors at the entrance to the Martin Tower, which Paul assures me he will take care of, then you're on your own. All the guests have arrived and the listening device activated."

"Thank you Robert."

"Any friend of Paul's..." he let the sentence hang as he led us up the stone stairs to the battlements that led to the entrance of the Martin Tower. Robert stopped in the shadows and pointed along the battlements to the Martin Tower, where two men blended as well as they could into darkness lit only by a small light. We waited for a moment and I hoped Paul's timing was right, and then heard a soft 'plopping' sound from silenced handguns and the two men slumped to the stone battlement.

Julie and I slipped off our evening wear and I noticed she had a thigh holster.

"That come with the outfit?"

She grinned, and while Robert returned to his other duties, we ran quickly along the battlement and slipped inside the Martin Tower. Immediately we could hear voices and the clink of glasses from the small dining room as the ISEC group tucked into their gastronomic feast.

I looked at Julie, gauging whether she was up to this. She stared back at me coolly. Detached. I looked past her and saw a sign pointing to the dining room with the graphic of an Orange Moon over a darkened landscape and beneath the letters I.S.E.C.

Radley stared at us in shock as we entered the small dining room, guns drawn. His expression turned to one of intense anger. Of all those gathered for dinner, Hamish McDougall seemed the least surprised. The General the Lord Dalton-Percy turned a deathly pale, and I wondered how he had been awarded a Military Cross if the sight of a gun in my hand made him pee himself with fright. I wasn't feeling very charitable.

"Well, Thomas, you seem to have stumbled upon our little organisation. That's a pity, a great pity. You've caused us a great deal of grief over the last few months, but I must admit I thought you were dead for sure when they reported that you had gone over the waterfall." He stood up smiling. "As you can see there is not enough room for you to join us for dinner."

"Dinner is the last thing on our minds, Hamish."

"What do you think you are doing, Gunn," Radley shouted, attempting to stand, sinking back into his seat as Julie pointed her gun in his direction. He was sensible enough to realise the weapon was cocked and her grip steady, aim unerring. "None of this is your concern." He added much like a petulant child.

"All of it is my concern, and the concern of this country which you seem to think is up for sale to the highest bidder."

"Not exactly true, Thomas." Hamish stood back a step, appraising us and wondering where his security team were. "We are in fact the saviours of this country. Of Europe and the Western hemisphere. We are all represented here, as you must now understand."

"Rather delusional of you, don't you think Hamish?" He smiled even more, an almost maniacal glint in his eye. I looked down the table to a thirty-five year brunette, all uplift bra and carefully applied executive style make-up. "And Miss Tanner, you're fired from the Gunn Group."

She looked down at the tablecloth, her hands shaking in her lap.

"*I* have been the real father to you for more years than you perhaps care to remember, Thomas. Not Ivan. Who was it you turned to after you quarrelled with him? Me. Who took you in when your world fell apart? Me." He paused and snorted contemptuously. "Put the gun down. You won't kill me because you can't. It would be like killing what's left of your family. And besides, you want to know why, don't you? Why I formed this coalition of like minds. Why I created The Order of the Orange Moon? You want to know what it's about, don't you?" He was right, of course. One side of me was pulling the trigger; the other side was putting the gun down.

So far, it was a stalemate. He turned and pressed a button on the sideboard and a large flat screen plasma TV slid up into view, automatically turning on as it did so.

"I was going to keep this for the cigars and port, but now seems to be as good a time as any for everyone to see the full proposal." The picture cleared and I could see it was the start of a promotional film, the first frames of which were a map of the world. Over it were dotted many digital flags, all with the symbol of the Orange Moon I had seen on the pot of body butter. The film ran silently showing mineral resources in different countries. Radical Islamic organisations in the Middle East. Zionist activities around the world. Christian evangelicals protesting abortions. Bombings. Riots. Chaos. Then images of a peaceful world. Wealthy. Healthy. Secure and totally unreal. "This is what it is all about. Power. The power to destroy and rebuild. The power to create, to form, to weld together a mass of people. To control the destinies of millions without them ever knowing they are being controlled for the greater good. That's what it's all about, Thomas. Power."

"And I thought you were an intelligent man, Hamish. You stand there like every other madman from Genghis Khan to Hitler, spouting about world domination."

"Power is the key," Hamish continued as if he hadn't heard a word I said. "People want stability. They want safety. They want security. They want to live their lives as they've always lived their lives. They need people like us to retain the values that made us great nations, to retain our true identity as Britons, or Americans or Germans, or Dutch. People do not want their country given away piecemeal to any culture that decides to take it." He paused to catch his breath and looked around the table. "These people here want what I can give them. People like your father thought he could control us with his billions, but it is us who controlled him."

"You mean killed him."

"I asked him to join us but he was too arrogant. Too full of himself and he threatened to destroy me, so I destroyed him instead, just like I will destroy anyone who opposes me."

I turned to Radley. "And you're going along with all this are you? Or was it your idea to kill my father?"

"There are matters beyond your comprehension, Gunn."

"I understand that I am in a room full of lying, murdering, greedy megalomaniacal bastards, which this country would be better off without."

"Join me Thomas," Hamish tried to smile but it was a grimace. "Join me. I could use someone like you."

"That's what Marika Keskküla said just before she tried to blow me into little pieces."

"An inconsequential woman with little sophistication."

"Who stopped you from shooting me on the yacht."

"I was angry."

"You're probably insane."

"I just hoped that you might see that what I'm doing is not evil. We can control industries and resources throughout the globe. Have them working in harmony and reach that Eden that we all want." Hamish's eyes had a far away look and I could the see the others in the room were becoming more agitated as our tête-a-tête continued.

"It's over, Hamish. We recorded everything on audio tape and video."

"Nobody stops me, Thomas. What we are doing is not murder. It is surgery. How can the cancer be eradicated without cutting it out at the root, by cleansing the whole diseased body? People get hurt, that is a fact of life, but out of the ashes a new, cleaner system will be born."

"That's the only thing you've said that makes any sense." Julie stepped forward, staring with hatred and contempt at Hamish McDougall. "You're the cancer that has killed too many people and destroyed lives, so consider yourself cleansed," she said quietly, and shot him between the eyes.

Everyone in the room froze as Hamish slid to the floor leaving a smear of blood against the ancient stone wall of the Martin Tower dining room. For a moment I was stunned as Julie had fired close to my left ear, but gradually the hearing returned as she lowered her gun and turned to Radley who stood with his back against the wall.

"I suggest you have someone take these people out of here, Mr Radley," she said evenly as we heard the sound of running on the battlement. Three Yeomen Warders, led by Robert Wrightwood, burst into the room.

"Mr Wrightwood please escort these people out," Radley said stiffly, his eyes never leaving mine.

Robert looked at Hamish McDougall's body, then at me. "It seems that the Tower is a fitting place for traitors to meet their end, Robert," I said and turned to Radley. "Wouldn't you agree Mr Radley?"

"So it would seem."

"I take it this was a Secret Service operation sir," Robert asked Radley.

"It was, Mr Wrightwood. It was."

Robert smiled slightly and followed the line of dinner guests out of the dining room. We waited until they were all gone, leaving just the three of us, and Hamish's stiffening corpse.

"That was unnecessary."

"Was it? Try looking at it as rodent extermination."

"You are both still liable under the Official Secrets Act. One mention of this business and I'll have you arrested faster than you can spit."

"What are you afraid of, Radley? That someone might get to know that the British Government almost let an insane organisation stage a coup in a foreign country in order to protect them from so-called insurgents. After all, we can't allow all that mineral wealth that has been newly discovered fall into enemy hands, can we?"

His face turned pale as I talked, and I knew I had it right. Hamish had been fed and nurtured, just as I had, and when the time was right we were thrown in and given enough information to keep us going, like salmon swimming up river. The stronger the current, the faster they swim.

"That is rubbish. You come out with a story like that and the British Government will tear you into little pieces. Besides, who would believe you?"

"We have audio and video tape, Mr Radley. We've done your dirty work for you, but just remember this, one threat against my family, or myself and I spread this story around. Some of the muck will stick and I'm betting that you won't last long if it does. I should have realised in the beginning that you were the one controlling everything. The members of ISEC were like schoolchildren playing a naive game compared to you. Well, for me it's over."

"Whatever you may think of me, or as you say 'people like me', I have only the best interests of this country at heart. My methods may seem immoral to you, but it is the best way I know of getting the job done. Neither you, your family, friends or the others who helped you tonight will be harassed. You have my word. Just one last thing. Would you have done what you did, if I had told you what was going on?"

There was silence between us whilst I considered the question.

"Probably not. "

"I didn't think so. Neither would I, if I had been in your place."

I raised my gun and shot off the lobe of his left ear. He reeled away clutching the wound in shock. "That's to remind you of what you did to my family, Mr Radley."

"You know you can never come back to this country, Mr Gunn," he gasped.

"That's not for you to decide. And if I do decide to come back, it will be to finish what I started here tonight. We have the audio and video, and you figure prominently. So I suggest you keep your word."

"I would have taken McDougall down. Now that I know the full extent of his operation."

"Maybe you would. Maybe you wouldn't. Maybe you would just use him and these others for whatever nefarious little game of international intrigue you like to play."

I took Julie's arm and we walked from the room.

Our escape from the Tower was more of a casual stroll to the waiting car than a frantic getaway.

Gerry and the team ran interference on our journey, cutting off the 'tail' Radley had put on us and allowing us to disappear into the late evening London traffic. Even the helicopter circling overhead could not pick out our vehicle because it was a 'blind car', especially equipped with laminar paint that changed the shape and GPS signature, so that it could not be seen by the city's CCTV cameras or the helicopter's surveillance devices. The nano transmitter the technician had injected into me had self-destructed late that afternoon. Paul checked his receiver to make sure.

Radley should have known that we still had access to special forces assets, but he had been too comfortable in his game. Too confident in thinking for us the mission was over, believing that like good soldiers we would just hand in our weapons and say goodbye. Until the next time we were needed.

Edwards and Professor Oldfield were waiting for Julie, Paul and myself in the Golden Lion. Edwards led the way into the basement room beneath the auction house across the street. Oldfield booted up the computer while I opened the letter Edwards had kept for me.

"Do you want to tell us what this is all about?" Paul stared around the room looking for hidden cameras.

"Money. Gunn Group money." That caught their attention. "This whole Orange Moon scheme has been about syphoning liquid assets to Banks, Trust funds, and offshore venture capital investment companies. It's been about acquiring mineral resources in foreign countries in order to control the world price. The more ISEC and the members of the Order of the Orange Moon have, the more they can dominate Governments around the globe. My father knew this. When Edwards handed me the letter a few months ago I knew what was going on but not exactly who the players were."

"So what does it say?" Julie leaned over trying to read the letter upside down.

"It's a list of money transfers. Gunn Group companies that Adrian embezzled from on behalf of ISEC, and a bank account that was set aside for me." I looked at Edwards. "You are the trustee Mr Edwards, but you knew that didn't you."

"Indeed sir. Nobody looks at a little old man working as a porter in a gentleman's club." He smiled as if remembering an old joke. "Your father thought it quite amusing." He looked up at me and I saw tears in his eyes. "I loved Sir Ivan, Mr Thomas. Loved him like a brother. He told me to look out for you. That you were a contrary man, but he loved you very much and knew you would get to the bottom of this. The trust account is your legacy, because he also knew that you could never inherit the Gunn Group. They wouldn't allow it."

"Did you receive a call from Morgan Alvarez, Edwards?" I asked.

He looked puzzled. "No sir. I've never heard of her."

"When she calls, let me know."

"Of course."

Paul frowned. "It's not finished?"

"I'm not sure. Maybe not. I have a friend checking some finance companies in the US."

"Just let us know."

"You know I will."

Julie crossed to Edwards and put her arms around his thin shoulders, held him for a moment and then kissed him on each cheek, then kissed each of the team.

I turned to Oldfield and handed him the letter. "I need you to empty the accounts of these companies. Wipe them out."

"But that will bankrupt them and Gunn Group Industries."

"Indeed it will, but would you rather Radley and the remnants of ISEC and the Order of the Orange Moon line their pockets instead."

He nodded. "I see your point."

"And I would like a payment made every month from my trust account to Saint Theresa's House in Shannon of £30,000 in perpetuity." I glanced at Edwards. "If that is okay with Mr Edwards."

"Of course sir. Mr Danny would want it so," he said with a twinkle in his eye. I looked at him a little more carefully. "Sir Ivan watched over

254

you very carefully Mr Thomas."

"One more thing." I turned to Paul. "You and the rest of the boys will be out of a job now. The trust will put you all on a retainer. Give Edwards your account details; the Professor will encrypt them so that not even Radley will ever find out. Right Professor?"

"Whatever you say?" There was a lingering question in his reply.

"And I believe you have been looking for a research grant."

"You have a plane to catch," he said dryly, with a broad grin.

Available in paperback soon
The second book in the Thomas Gunn Thriller series

AFN CLARKE

THE JONAS TRUST DECEPTION

A Thomas Gunn Series Thriller

Other books by the Author

autobiography
CONTACT

literary fiction
COLLISIONS
AN UNQUIET AMERICAN
DRY TORTUGAS

humour & satire
THE BOOK OF BAKER: *Part One - Dreams from the Death Age*
THE BOOK OF BAKER: *Part Two - Armageddon*

thrillers
THE JONAS TRUST DECEPTION (a Thomas Gunn thriller)

I hope you enjoyed this book and would very much appreciate if you would post a review on my amazon page. To learn about new releases, special offers and free books please leave your email address on my secure website.

www.afnclarke.com

www.ingramcontent.com/pod-product-compliance
Lightning Source LLC
Chambersburg PA
CBHW050728180626
46814CB00002B/655